W9-AVN-884

Critical acclaim for Peter Robinson and the Inspector Banks series

GALLOWS VIEW

'Peter Robinson is an expert plotter with an eye for telling detail' – *New York Times*

'An impressive debut' – *Publishers Weekly*

'Fans of P. D. James and Ruth Rendell who crave more contemporary themes should look no further than Peter Robinson' – *Washington Post*

A DEDICATED MAN

'Robinson's profound sense of place and reflective study of human nature give fine depth to his mystery' – *New York Times*

'A deftly constructed plot . . . Robinson's skill with the British police procedural has been burnished to a high gloss' – *Chicago Tribune*

WEDNESDAY'S CHILD

'A dark, unsettling story . . . Impressive' – *New York Times*

DRY BONES THAT DREAM

'Highly entertaining' – *Scotland on Sunday*

'High-quality crime from one of Canada's top crime-writers' – *Toronto Star*

INNOCENT GRAVES

'Atmospheric' – *Time Out*

DEAD RIGHT

'Every page here is readable and compelling'
– *Washington Times*

'This book has everything that makes a Peter Robinson
book good . . . He writes absolutely perfect dialogue.
And the plot keeps the reader guessing until
the end' – *Mystery Scene*

IN A DRY SEASON

'A powerfully moving work' – Ian Rankin

'A wonderful novel. From Robinson's deft hand comes
a multi-layered mystery woven around the carefully
detailed portraits of characters all held tightly in the
grip of the past' – Michael Connelly

'This unsettling story, haunting and subtle in its blending
of past and present, is the most powerful novel by the
star of the middle-generation of British crime writers'
– Robert Barnard

COLD IS THE GRAVE

'Absorbing' – *Scotsman*

'Full of twists and surprises' – *Chicago Tribune*

'Exhilarating' – *Toronto Star*

A DEDICATED MAN

Peter Robinson grew up in Yorkshire, but now lives in Canada.

His Inspector Banks series has won numerous awards in Britain, Europe, the United States and Canada. There are now fifteen novels published by Pan Macmillan in the series, of which *A Dedicated Man* is the second. *Aftermath*, the twelfth, was a *Sunday Times* bestseller.

The Inspector Banks series

GALLOWS VIEW

A DEDICATED MAN

A NECESSARY END

THE HANGING VALLEY

PAST REASON HATED

WEDNESDAY'S CHILD

DRY BONES THAT DREAM

INNOCENT GRAVES

DEAD RIGHT

IN A DRY SEASON

COLD IS THE GRAVE

AFTERMATH

THE SUMMER THAT NEVER WAS

PLAYING WITH FIRE

STRANGE AFFAIR

Also by Peter Robinson

CAEDMON'S SONG

NOT SAFE AFTER DARK AND OTHER WORKS

PETER
ROBINSON

A DEDICATED MAN

AN INSPECTOR BANKS MYSTERY

PAN BOOKS

First published 1988 by Viking (Canada), Toronto

First published by Pan Books 2002

This edition published 2012 by Pan Books
an imprint of Pan Macmillan, a division of Macmillan Publishers Limited
Pan Macmillan, 20 New Wharf Road, London N1 9RR
Basingstoke and Oxford
Associated companies throughout the world
www.panmacmillan.com

ISBN 978-1-4472-2638-3

Copyright © Peter Robinson 1988

The right of Peter Robinson to be identified as the
author of this work has been asserted by him in accordance
with the Copyright, Designs and Patents Act 1988.

All rights reserved. No part of this publication may be
reproduced, stored in or introduced into a retrieval system, or
transmitted, in any form or by any means (electronic, mechanical,
photocopying, recording or otherwise), without the prior written
permission of the publisher. Any person who does any unauthorized
act in relation to this publication may be liable to criminal
prosecution and civil claims for damages.

1 3 5 7 9 8 6 4 2

A CIP catalogue record for this book is available from
the British Library.

Typeset by SX Composing DTP, Rayleigh, Essex
Printed and bound by CPI Group (UK) Ltd, Croydon, CR0 4YY

This book is sold subject to the condition that it shall not,
by way of trade or otherwise, be lent, resold, hired out,
or otherwise circulated without the publisher's prior consent
in any form of binding or cover other than that in which
it is published and without a similar condition including this
condition being imposed on the subsequent purchaser.

Visit **www.panmacmillan.com** to read more about all our books and to buy
them. You will also find features, author interviews and news of any author
events, and you can sign up for e-newsletters so that you're always first to hear
about our new releases.

For Jan

They were right, my dear, all those voices were right
And still are; this land is not the sweet home that it
looks,
  Nor its peace the historical calm of a site
Where something was settled once and for all . . .

W. H. AUDEN
'In Praise of Limestone'

1

ONE

When the sun rose high enough to clear the slate roofs on the other side of the street, it crept through a chink in Sally Lumb's curtain and lit on a strand of gold blonde hair that curled over her cheek. She was dreaming. Minotaurs, bank clerks, gazelles and trolls cavorted through the barns, maisonettes and Gothic palaces of her sleep. But when she awoke a few hours later, all she was left with was the disturbing image of a cat picking its way along a high wall topped with broken glass. Dreams. Most of them she ignored. They had nothing to do with the other kind of dreams, the most important ones that she didn't have to fall asleep to find. In these dreams, she passed her exams and was accepted into the Marion Boyars Academy of Theatre Arts. There she studied acting, modelling and cosmetic technique, for Sally was realistic enough to know that if she lacked the dramatic talent of a Kate Winslet or a Gwyneth Paltrow, she could at least belong to the fringes of the world of glamour.

When Sally finally stirred, the bar of sunlight had shifted to the floor beside her bed, striping the untidy pile of clothes she had dropped there the night before. She could hear plates and cutlery in the kitchen downstairs, and the rich smell of roast beef wafted up to her room. She got up. It was good policy, she thought, to get downstairs as soon as possible and help with the vegetables before her mother's call – 'It's on the table!' – came grating up to her. At least by showing a willingness to help, she could probably avoid too probing an investigation into her lateness last night.

Sally stared at herself in the full-length mirror of her old oak wardrobe. Even if there was still a little puppy fat around her hips and thighs, it would soon go away. On the whole, she decided, she had a good body. Her breasts were perfect. Most people, of course, complimented her on her long silky hair, but they hadn't seen her breasts. Kevin had. Just last night he had caressed them and told her they were perfect. Last night they had gone almost all the way, and Sally knew that the next time, soon, they would. She looked forward to it with a mixture of fear and desire that, according to what she had read in magazines and books, would soon fuse into ecstasy in the heat of passion and longing.

Sally touched her nipple with the tip of her forefinger and felt a tingle in her loins. The nipple hardened and she moved away from the mirror to get dressed, her face burning.

Kevin was good. He knew how to excite her; ever since summer began he had played carefully with the boundaries of her desire. He had pushed them back a little further each time, and soon the whole country would be his. He was young, like Sally, but still he seemed to know instinctively how to please her, just as she imagined an experienced older man would know. She even thought she loved Kevin a bit. But if someone else came along – somebody more mature, more wealthy, more sophisticated, someone who was at home in the exciting, fast-paced cities of the world, well, after all, Kevin was only a farm boy at heart.

Dressed in designer jeans and a plain white T-shirt, Sally drew back the curtains. When her eyes had adjusted to the glare, she looked out on a perfect Swainsdale morning. A few fluffy little clouds – one like a teddy bear, another like a crab – scudded across the piercing blue sky on a light breeze. She looked north up the broad slope of the valley side, its rich greens interrupted here and there by dark patches of heather and outcrops of limestone, to the long sheer wall of Crow Scar, and noticed something very odd. At first she couldn't make it out at all. Then she squinted, refocused and saw, spreading out along the slope just above the old road, five or six blue dots which seemed to be moving in some kind of pattern. She put her finger to her lips, thought for a moment, then frowned.

TWO

Fifteen miles away in Eastvale, the dale's largest town, somebody else was anticipating a Sunday dinner of succulent roast beef and Yorkshire pudding. Detective Chief Inspector Alan Banks lay flat on his stomach in Brian's room watching an electric train whizz around bends, over bridges, through signals and under papier mâché mountains. Brian himself was out riding his bike in the local park, but Banks had long since given up the pretence that he only played with the trains for his son's sake and finally admitted that he found the pastime even more relaxing than a hot bath.

He heard the phone ring out in the hall, and a few seconds later his daughter, Tracy, shouted through, 'It's for you, Dad!'

As Banks rushed downstairs, the aroma from the

kitchen made his mouth water. He thanked Tracy and picked up the receiver. It was Sergeant Rowe, desk officer at Eastvale Regional Headquarters.

'Sorry to bother you, sir,' Rowe began, 'but we've just had a call from Constable Weaver over in Helmthorpe. Seems a local farmer's found a body in one of his fields this morning.'

'Go on,' Banks urged, snapping into professional gear.

'Chap said he was looking for a stray sheep, sir, when he found this body buried by a wall. Weaver says he shifted one or two stones and it's a dead 'un all right. Looks like someone bashed 'is 'ead in.'

Banks felt the tightening in his stomach that always accompanied news of murder. He had transferred from London a year ago, sickened by the spiralling of senseless violence there, only to find in the Gallows View case that things could be just as bad, if not worse, up north. The business had left both him and Sandra emotionally exhausted, but since then things had settled down. There'd been nothing but a few burglaries and one case of fraud to occupy his attention, and he had really begun to believe that murders, peeping Toms and vicious teenagers were the exception rather than the rule in Eastvale.

'Tell Constable Weaver to get back up there with as many local men as he can muster and rope off the area. I want them to start a systematic search, but I don't want anyone else closer to the body than ten yards. Got that?' The last thing he needed was half a dozen flatfoots trampling down the few square feet where clues were most likely to be found.

'Tell them to put everything they find into marked envelopes,' he went on. 'They should know the procedure, but it won't do any harm to remind them. And I mean everything. Used rubbers, the lot. Get in touch with Detective Sergeant Hatchley and Dr Glendenning. Tell them to get out there immediately. I'll want the photographer and the forensic team too. Okay?'

'Yes, sir,' Sergeant Rowe replied. He knew that Jim Hatchley would be enjoying his usual Sunday lunchtime pint in the Oak and that it would give Banks a great deal of satisfaction to interrupt his pleasure.

'I suppose the super's been informed?'

'Yes, sir. It was him as said to tell you.'

'It would be,' Banks complained. 'I don't suppose he wanted to miss *his* Sunday dinner.' But he spoke with humour and affection. Superintendent Gristhorpe, of all his new colleagues, was the one who had given him the most support and encouragement during the difficult transition from city to country.

Banks hung up and slipped on his worn brown jacket with the elbow patches. He was a small, dark man, in appearance rather like the old Celtic strain of Welshman, and his physique certainly didn't give away his profession.

Sandra, Banks's wife, emerged from the kitchen as he was preparing to leave. 'What is it?' she asked.

'Looks like a murder.'

She wiped her hands on her blue checked pinafore. 'So you won't be in for dinner?'

'Sorry, love. Doesn't look like it.'

'And I don't suppose there's any point in keeping it warm?'

'Shouldn't think so. I'll grab a sandwich somewhere.' He kissed her quickly on the lips. 'Don't worry. I'll give you a call as soon as I know what's happening.'

Banks drove his white Cortina west along the valley

bottom by the riverside. He was entitled to a police car and driver, but he actually enjoyed driving and preferred his own company when travelling to and from a case. A generous mileage allowance more than compensated for the cost.

With one eye on the road and one hand on the wheel, he flipped through an untidy pile of cassette tapes on the passenger seat, selected one and slipped it into the deck.

Though he swore that his passion for opera had not waned over the winter, he had to admit that he had been sidetracked into the world of English vocal and choral music. It was a change Sandra heartily approved of; she had never liked opera much in the first place, and Wagner had been the last straw for her. After she had finally gone so far as to attack one of his tapes with a magnet – the one with 'Siegfried's Funeral March' on it, Banks remembered sadly – he had got the message. With Ian Partridge singing Dowland's 'I Saw My Lady Weepe', he drove on.

Like the larger and more famous Yorkshire Dales, Swainsdale runs more or less from west to east, with a slight list towards the south, until the humble river loses itself in the Ouse. At its source near Swainshead, high in the Pennine fells, the River Swain is nothing more than a trickle of sparkling clear water, but in carving its way down towards the North Sea it has formed, with the help of glaciers and geological faults, a long and beautiful dale which broadens out as it approaches the Vale of York. The main town, Eastvale, dominated by its Norman castle, sits at the extreme eastern edge of the dale and looks out over the rich, fertile plain. On a clear day, the Hambleton Hills and the North York Moors are visible in the distance.

He saw Lyndgarth on the valley side to the north, near the dark ruins of Devraulx Abbey, and passed through peaceful Fortford, where the remains of a Roman fort were still under excavation on a hillock opposite the village green. Ahead, he could see the bright limestone curve of Crow Scar high up on his right, and, as he drew closer, he noticed the local police searching a field marked off by irregular drystone walls. The limestone shone bright in the sun, and the walls stood out against the grass like pearl necklaces on an emerald velvet cushion.

To get to the scene, Banks had to drive through Helmthorpe, the dale's central market village, turn right at the bridge on to Hill Road, and then turn right again on to a narrow road that meandered north-eastwards about halfway up the valley side. It was a miracle that the track had ever been tarmacked – probably a gesture towards increasing tourism, Banks guessed. No good for tyre tracks, though, he thought gloomily.

Being more used to getting around in the city than in the countryside, he scraped his knee climbing the low wall and stumbled over the lumpy sods of grass in the field. Finally, out of breath, he got to where a uniformed man, presumably Constable Weaver, stood talking to a gnarled old farmer about fifty yards up the slope.

By the side of the north–south wall, loosely covered with earth and stones, lay the body. Enough of its covering had been removed to make it recognizable as a man. The head lay to one side, and, kneeling beside it, Banks could see that the hair at the back was matted with blood. A jolt of nausea shot through his stomach, but he quickly controlled it as he began to make mental notes about the scene. Standing up, he was struck by the contrast between the beautiful, serene day and the corpse at his feet.

'Anything been disturbed?' he asked Weaver, stepping carefully back over the rope.

'Not much, sir,' the young constable replied. His face was white and the sour smell on his breath indicated that he had probably been sick over the wall. Natural enough, Banks thought. Probably the lad's first corpse.

'Mr Tavistock here' – he gestured towards the whiskered farmer – 'says he just moved those stones around the head to see what his dog was scratting at.'

Banks looked at Tavistock, whose grim expression betrayed a man used to death. Ex-army, most likely, and old enough to have seen action in two world wars.

'I were lookin' fer one 'o my sheep,' Tavistock began in a slow, thick Yorkshire accent, 'and I saw that there damage to t' wall. I thought there'd bin a c'lapse.' He paused and rubbed his grizzly chin. 'There shouldn't a bin no c'lapse in a Bessthwaite wall. Bin there sin' eighteen thirty, that 'as. Any road, old Ben started scratting. At first I thought nowt on it, then . . .' He shrugged as if there was nothing more to be said.

'What did you do when you realized what it was?' Banks asked.

Tavistock scratched his turkey neck and spat on the grass. 'Just 'ad a look, that's all. I thought it might a bin a sheep somebody'd killed. That 'appens sometimes. Then I ran 'ome' – he pointed to a farmhouse about half a mile away – 'and I called young Weaver 'ere.'

Banks was dubious about the 'ran' but he was glad that Tavistock had acted quickly. He turned away and gave instructions to the photographer and the forensic team, then took off his jacket and leaned against the warm stone wall while the boffins did their work.

THREE

Sally slammed down her knife and fork and yelled at her father: 'Just because I go for a walk with a boy it doesn't mean I'm a tramp or a trollop or any of those things!'

'Sally!' Mrs Lumb butted in. 'Stop shouting at your father. That wasn't what he meant and you know it.'

Sally continued to glare. 'Well that's what it sounded like to me.'

'He was only trying to warn you,' her mother went on. 'You have to be careful. Boys try to take advantage of you sometimes. Especially a good-looking girl like you.' She said it with a mixture of pride and fear.

'You don't have to treat me like I'm a baby, you know,' Sally said. 'I'm sixteen now.' She gave her mother a pitying glance, cast another baleful look at her father, and went back to her roast beef.

'Aye,' said Mr Lumb, 'and you'll do as you're told till you're eighteen. That's the law.'

To Sally, the man sitting opposite her was at the root of all her problems, and, of course, Charles Lumb fitted easily into the role his daughter had assigned him: that of an old-fashioned, narrow-minded yokel whose chief argument against anything new and interesting was, 'What was good enough for my father and his father before him is good enough for you too, young lady.' There was a strong conservative streak in him, only to be expected of someone whose family had lived in the area for more generations than could be remembered. A traditionalist, Charles Lumb often said that the dale as he had loved it was dying. He knew that the only chance for the young was to get away, and that saddened him. Quite soon, he was certain, even the inhabitants of the dales villages would belong to the National Trust, English Heritage or the Open Spaces Society. Like creatures in a zoo, they would be paid to act out their quaint old ways in a kind of living museum. The grandson of a cabinetmaker, Lumb, who worked at the local dairy factory, found it hard to see things otherwise. The old crafts were dying out because they were uneconomic, and only tourists kept one cooper, one blacksmith and one wheelwright in business.

But because Lumb was a Yorkshireman through and through, he tended to bait and tease in a manner that could easily be taken too seriously by an ambitious young girl like Sally. He delivered the most outrageous statements and opinions about her interests and dreams in such a deliberately deadpan voice that anyone could be excused for not catching the gentle, mocking humour behind them. If he had been less sarcastic and his daughter less self-centred, they might have realized that they loved each other very much.

The thing was, though, Charles Lumb would have liked to see more evidence of common sense in his daughter. She was certainly a bright girl, and it would be easy for her to get into university and become a doctor or a lawyer. A damn sight easier, he reflected, than it was in his day. But no, it had to be this bloody academy, and for all he tried, he could see no value in learning how to paint faces and show off swimsuits. If he had thought she had it in her to become a great actress, then he might have been more supportive. But he didn't. Maybe time would prove him wrong. He hoped so. At least seeing her on the telly would be something.

Sally, after a few minutes' sulking, decided to change the topic of conversation. 'Have you seen those men on the hill?' she asked. 'I wonder what they're doing?'

'Looking for something, I shouldn't wonder,' her father replied dryly, still not recovered from the argument.

Sally ignored him. 'They look like policemen to me. You can see the buttons of their uniforms shining. I'm going up there to have a look after dinner. There's already quite a crowd along the road.'

'Well, make sure you're back before midnight,' her mother said. It cleared the air a bit, and they enjoyed the rest of their meal in peace.

Sally walked up the hill road and turned right past the cottages. As she hurried on she danced and grabbed fistfuls of dry grass, which she flung up high in the air.

Several cars blocked the road by the field, and what had looked from a distance like a large crowd turned out to be nothing more than a dozen or so curious tourists with their cameras, rucksacks and hiking boots. It was open country, almost moorland despite the drystone walls that criss-crossed the landscape and gave it some semblance of order. They were old and only the farmers remembered who had built them.

There was more activity in the field than she could recollect ever seeing in such an isolated place. Uniformed men crawled on all fours in the wild grass, and the area by the wall had been cordoned off with stakes and rope. Inside the charmed circle stood a man with a camera, another with a black bag and, seemingly presiding over the whole affair, a small wiry man with a brown jacket slung over his shoulder. Sally's eyesight was so keen that she could even see the small patches of sweat under his arms.

She asked the middle-aged walker standing next to her what was going on, and the man told her he thought there'd been a murder. Of course. It had to be. She'd seen similar things on the telly.

FOUR

Banks glanced back towards the road. He'd noticed a flashing movement, but it was only a girl's blonde hair catching the sun. Dr Glendenning, the tall, white-haired pathologist, had finished shaking limbs and inserting his thermometer in orifices; now he stood, cigarette dangling from the corner of his mouth, muttering about what a warm night it had been as he made calculations in his little red notebook.

It was just as well, Banks thought as he looked over at the spectators, that two of the forensic team had first examined the roadside. They had found nothing – no skid marks or tyre tracks on the tarmac, no clear footprints on the grassy verge – but it looked as if someone or something had been dragged up the field from the road.

Glendenning confirmed that the victim had been killed elsewhere and merely dumped in this isolated spot. That would cause problems. If they had no idea where the man had been killed, they wouldn't know where to start looking for the killer.

The doctor rambled on, adjusting his column of figures, and Banks sniffed the air, feeling again that it was too fine a day and too beautiful a spot for such unpleasant business. Even the young photographer, Peter Darby, as he snapped the body from every conceivable angle, said that normally on such a day he would be out photographing Rawley Force at a slow shutter speed, or zooming in on petals with his macro lens, praying that a bee or a butterfly would remain still for as long as it took to focus and shoot. He had photographed corpses before, Banks knew, so he was used to the unpleasantness. All the same, it was worlds away from butterflies and waterfalls.

Glendenning looked up from his notebook and screwed up his eyes in the sunlight. A half-inch of ash floated to the ground, and Banks found himself wondering whether the doctor performed surgery with a cigarette in his mouth, letting ash fall around the incision. Smoking was strictly prohibited at the scene of a crime, of course, but nobody dared mention this to Glendenning.

'It was a warm night,' he explained to Banks, with a Scottish lilt to his nicotine-ravaged voice. 'I can't give an accurate estimate of time of death. Most likely, though, it was after dark last night and before sunrise this morning.'

Bloody wonderful! Banks thought. We don't know where he was killed but we know it was sometime during the night.

'Sorry,' Glendenning added, catching Bank's expression.

'Not your fault. Anything else?'

'Blow to the back of the head, if I may translate the cumbersome medical jargon into layman's terms. Pretty powerful, too. Skull cracked like an egg.'

'Any idea what weapon was used?'

'Proverbial blunt instrument. Sharp-edged, like a wrench or a hammer. I can't be more specific at this point but I'd rule out a brick or a rock. It's too neat and I can't find any trace of particles. Full report after the autopsy, of course.'

'Is that all?'

'Yes. You can have him taken to the mortuary now if you've finished with the pictures.'

Banks nodded. He asked a uniformed constable to send

for an ambulance, and Glendenning packed his bag.

'Weaver! Sergeant Hatchley! Come over here a minute,' Banks called, and watched the two men walk over. 'Any idea who the dead man was?' he asked Weaver.

'Yes, sir,' the pale constable answered. 'His name's Harry Steadman. Lives in the village.'

'Married?'

'Yes, sir.'

'Then we'd better get in touch with his wife. Sergeant, would you go over to Mr Tavistock's house and take an official statement?'

Hatchley nodded slowly.

'Is there a decent pub in Helmthorpe?' Banks asked Weaver.

'I usually drink at the Bridge, sir.'

'Food?'

'Not bad.'

'Right.' Banks turned to Hatchley. 'We'll go and see Mrs Steadman while you attend to Tavistock. Let's meet up in the Bridge for a bite to eat when we've done. All right?'

Hatchley agreed and lumbered off with Tavistock.

There was no chance of a roast beef dinner at home now. In fact, there would be few meals at home until the crime was solved. Banks knew from experience that once a murder investigation begins there is no stopping and little slowing down, even for family life. The crime invades meal times, ablutions and sleep; it dominates conversation and puts up an invisible barrier between the investigator and his family.

He looked down at the village spread out crookedly by a bend in the river, its grey slate roofs gleaming in the sun. The clock on the square church tower said twelve thirty.

Sighing, he nodded to Weaver, and the two of them set off towards the car.

They passed through the small crowd, ignoring the local reporter's tentative questions, and got into the Cortina. Banks cleared the cassettes from the passenger seat so that Weaver could sit beside him.

'Tell me what you know about Steadman,' Banks said as he reversed into a gateway and turned around.

'Lived here about eighteen months,' Weaver began. 'Used to come regular for holidays and sort of fell in love with the place. He inherited a fortune from his father and set himself up here. Used to be a university professor in Leeds. Educated chap, but not stuck-up. Early forties, bit over six-foot tall, sandy hair. Still quite young-looking. They live in Gratly.'

'I thought you said they lived in the village.'

'Same thing really, sir,' Weaver explained. 'You see, Gratly's just a little hamlet, a few old houses off the road. Doesn't even have a pub. But now the newer houses have spread up the hill, the two are as near as makes no difference. The locals like to keep the name, though. Sense of independence, I suppose.'

Banks drove down the hill towards the bridge. Weaver pointed ahead over the river and up the opposite valley side: 'That's Gratly, sir.'

Banks saw the row of new houses, some still under construction; then there was a space of about a hundred yards before the crossroads lined with older cottages.

'I see what you mean,' Banks said. At least the builders were doing a tasteful job, following the design of the originals and using the same local stone.

Weaver went on making conversation no doubt intended to help him forget the sight of his first corpse.

'Just about all the new houses in Helmthorpe are at this side of the village. You'll get nothing new on the east side. Some bright sparks say it's because it was settled from the east. Vikings, Saxons, Romans and whatnot. Course, you don't find many traces of them now, but the place stills seems to spread westwards.' He thought about what he'd said for a moment and added with a smile, 'Spreads slowly, that is, sir.'

Much as Banks was interested in snippets of local history, he lost track of Weaver's words as he drove over the low stone bridge and crossed Helmthorpe High Street. He cursed to himself. It was early Sunday afternoon and, from what he could see around him, that meant car-washing time in the village. Men stood in driveways in front of garages with their sleeves rolled up and buckets of soapy water by their sides. Shiny car roofs gleamed and water dripped from doors and bumpers. Polished chrome shone. If Harry Steadman had been dumped from a local car, all traces of that grisly journey would have been obliterated by now in the most natural way: soaped and waxed over, vacuumed and swept out.

Steadman's house, last in a short block running left from the road, was larger than Banks had imagined. It was solidly built and looked weather-beaten enough to pass for a historic building. That meant it would sell for a historic price, too, he noted. A double garage had been built on the eastern side, and the large garden, bordered by a low wall, consisted of a well-kept lawn with a colourful flower bed at its centre and rose bushes against the house front and the neighbour's fence. Leaving Weaver in the car, Banks walked down the crazy paving and rang the doorbell.

The woman who answered, holding a cup of tea in her

hand, looked puzzled to find a stranger standing before her. She was plain-looking, with stringy, lifeless brown hair, and wore a pair of overlarge, unbecoming spectacles. She was dressed in a shapeless beige cardigan and baggy checked slacks. Banks thought she might be the cleaning lady, so he phrased his greeting as a question: 'Mrs Steadman?'

'Yes,' the woman answered hesitantly, peering at him through her glasses. He introduced himself and felt the familiar tightening in his stomach as he was ushered into the living room. It was always like that. No amount of experience purged that gut-wrenching feeling of sympathy that accompanied the soothing, useless words, the empty gestures. For Banks there was always a shadow: it could be *my* wife, it could be someone telling me about *my* daughter. It was the same as that first glimpse of the murder victim. Death and its long aftermath had never become a matter of routine for him but remained always an abomination, a reminder one hardly needed of man's cruelty to his fellow man, his fallen nature.

Although the room was messy – a low table littered with magazines, knitting spread out on a chair, records out of their sleeves by the music centre – it was clean, and sunlight poured over the red and yellow roses through spotless mullioned windows. Above the large stone fireplace hung a romantic painting of what Swainsdale must have looked like over a hundred years ago. It hadn't changed all that much, but somehow the colours seemed brighter and bolder in the picture, the contours more definite.

'What is it?' Mrs Steadman asked, pulling a chair forward for Banks. 'Has there been an accident? Is something wrong?'

As he broke the news, Banks watched Mrs Steadman's

expression change from disbelief to shock. Finally, she began to weep silently. There was no sobbing; the tears simply ran down her pale cheeks and dripped on to the wrinkled cardigan as she stared blankly ahead. They could have been caused by an onion, Banks found himself thinking, disturbed by her absolute silence.

'Mrs Steadman?' he said gently, touching her sleeve. 'I'm afraid there are a few questions I have to ask you right away.'

She looked at him, nodded and dried her eyes with a screwed-up Kleenex. 'Of course.'

'Why didn't you report your husband missing, Mrs Steadman?'

'Missing?' She frowned at him. 'Why should I?'

Banks was taken aback, but he pressed on gently. 'I'm afraid you'll have to tell me that. He can't have come home last night. Weren't you worried? Didn't you wonder where he was?'

'Oh, I see what you mean,' she said, dabbing at her damp, reddened cheeks with the crumpled tissue. 'You weren't to know, were you? You see, I wasn't expecting him home last night. He went out just after seven o'clock. He said he was calling for a pint at the Bridge – he often went there – and then driving on to York. He had work to do there and he wanted to make an early start.'

'Did he often do that?'

'Yes, quite often. Sometimes I went with him, but I was feeling a bit under the weather last night – summer cold, I think – and besides, I know they get much more done without me. Anyway, I watched television with Mrs Stanton next door and let him go. Harry stayed with his publisher. Well, more of a family friend really. Michael Ramsden.'

'What kind of work did they do on a Sunday?'

'Oh, it wasn't what you or I would understand by work. They were writing a book. Harry mostly, but Michael was interested and helped him. A local history book. That was Harry's field. They'd go off exploring ruins – Roman forts, old lead mines, anything.'

'I see. And it was normal for him to go the night before and stay with Mr Ramsden?'

'Yes. As I've said, they were more like friends than anything else. We've known the family for a long time. Harry was terrible at getting up in the morning, so if they wanted a full day, he'd go over the night before and Michael would be sure to get him up on time. They'd spend the evening going over notes and making plans. I'd no reason to report him missing. I thought he was in York.' Her voice faltered and she started to cry again.

Banks waited and let her dry her eyes before asking his next question. 'Wouldn't Mr Ramsden be worried if he didn't arrive? Didn't he call you to find out what had happened?'

'No.' She paused, blew her nose and went on. 'I told you, it wasn't that kind of work. More like a hobby, really. Anyway, Michael doesn't have a telephone. He'd just assume that something had come up and Harry couldn't make it.'

'Just one more thing, Mrs Steadman, then I won't bother you any further today. Could you tell me where your husband might have left his car?'

'In the big car park by the river,' she replied. 'The Bridge hasn't got a car park of its own so the customers use that one. You can't really leave cars in the street here; there's not room enough.'

'Do you have a spare key?'

'I think he kept one around. I don't use it myself. I have an old Fiesta. Just a moment.' Mrs Steadman disappeared into the kitchen and returned a few moments later with the key. She also gave Banks the number of Steadman's beige Sierra.

'Could you tell me where Mr Ramsden lives, too? I'd like to let him know what's happened as soon as possible.'

Mrs Steadman seemed a bit surprised, but she gave the information without questions. 'It's not so hard to find,' she added. 'There are no other houses within half a mile yet. Do you need me to . . . er . . .'

'To identify the body?'

Mrs Steadman nodded.

'Yes, I'm afraid we do. Tomorrow will do, though. Is there anyone you can get to stay with you for a while?'

She stared at him, her features ugly and swollen with crying; her eyes looked fishy behind the harsh magnification of the glasses. 'Mrs Stanton, next door . . . if you would.'

'Of course.'

Banks went next door. Mrs Stanton, a long-nosed, alert-looking little woman, immediately grasped the situation. Banks sympathized with her shock. 'I know,' he said. 'It must seem so abrupt. To think that you saw him only last night.'

She nodded. 'Aye. And to think what was happening while me and Emma were watching that silly old film. Still,' she ended stoically, 'who are we to question the ways of the good Lord?' She told her husband, who sat slouched in an armchair reading his *News of the World*, to keep an eye on the roast, then went over to comfort her neighbour. Sure that he was leaving the widow in capable hands, Banks returned to his car and got in next to Weaver, who had regained his pinkish colour.

'I'm sorry, sir,' he mumbled. 'About being sick. I've—'

'Never seen a corpse before? I know. Never mind, Constable, there's a first time for everyone, more's the pity. Shall we go to the Bridge for a bite to eat?' Weaver nodded. 'I'm starving, myself,' Banks went on, starting the car, 'and you look like you could do with a drop of brandy.'

As he drove the short distance down to the Bridge on Helmthorpe High Street, Banks thought about his interview with Mrs Steadman. It had made him feel edgy and uneasy. At times, after the initial shock, her reaction had seemed more like relief than grief. Perhaps the marriage had been shaky, Banks found himself thinking, and Mrs Steadman had suddenly found herself both wealthy and free. Surely that would explain it?

2

ONE

Weaver pulled a face. 'I don't like brandy, sir,' he admitted sheepishly. 'My mum always used to give me a drop for medicinal purposes whenever I got a cold as a lad. Never could stomach the stuff.'

The two of them sat in a corner of the Bridge's quiet lounge. Banks nursed a pint of hand-drawn Theakston's bitter, and Weaver complained about his brandy.

'Did it do you any good?' Banks asked.

'I suppose so, sir. But it always reminds me of medicine, of being poorly, if you follow my drift.'

Banks laughed and went to buy Weaver a pint to chase away the bad taste. They were waiting for Detective Sergeant Hatchley, who was still with Tavistock, no doubt enjoying a good cup of tea or something stronger and, perhaps, a plateful of roast beef.

'Tell me,' Banks asked, 'why is this place so empty? It's Sunday dinner time and the village is crawling with tourists.'

'That's right, sir,' Weaver said. His boyish face had fully regained its natural pink flush. 'But look around you.'

Banks looked. They were in a small lounge with faded wallpaper and a cracked brown ceiling. A few water-colours of local scenes, reminiscent of the ones in old railway carriages, covered the most obvious damp spots on the walls. The tables were worn and scored from years of dominoes and shove-ha'penny, and ringed by generations of overflowing beer glasses; around the edges were charred semicircles where cigarettes had been left to burn out. A rack holding tongs and a bent poker stood by the small tiled fireplace. True, it didn't look much.

'There are three pubs in Helmthorpe, sir,' Weaver began, counting them off on his chubby red fingers. 'That's if you don't count the country club, for the nobs. There's the Dog and Gun, and the Hare and Hounds; they're for the tourists mostly. Real olde worlde country inns, if you get my meaning, sir – horse brasses, copper bedwarmers, antique tables with kneecapper wrought-iron legs, you name it. They have big old fireplaces too, all done up with black lead. Now that every pub in Christendom seems to offer real ale, it's got trendy to advertise a real fire.

'The Dog and Gun's a kind of family place with tables out back by the river and a little enclosed area for the kiddies to play in, and the Hare and Hounds is more for the younger set. They have a disco there every Friday and Saturday in season and you get a lot of the campers going along. That's when we get most of our bother here – the odd fight, that kind of thing. Some nights during the week they have folk music, too. A bit more civilized, if you ask me.'

Weaver sniffed and nodded towards the wall. 'And then there's this place. It's fairly new by village standards – Victorian, I'd say at a pinch. And it's all that's left for the serious drinkers. The only people who drink here are the locals and a few visitors who know about the beer. It's a pretty well-guarded secret. Course, on weekends you do get a few hikers and whatnot in the public bar. They've all read their good beer guides these days, it seems. But they never cause much trouble; they're a quiet lot, really.'

'Why did Steadman drink here, do you think?'

'Steadman?' Weaver seemed surprised to be so quickly jolted back to business. 'Liked the beer, I suppose. And he was pally with a few of the regulars.'

'But he had money, didn't he? A lot of money. He certainly didn't get that house on the cheap.'

'Oh yes, he had money. Rumour has it he inherited over a quarter of a million from his father. His pals have money too, but they're not nobs. Much more down-to-earth.'

Banks was still puzzled why someone so well off would drink in such a dump, good beer or not. By rights, Steadman ought to have been chugging champagne by the magnum to wash down his caviar. Those were London terms, though, he reminded himself: ostentatious display of wealth. Maybe people with over a quarter of a million who lived in Helmthorpe by choice were different. He doubted it. But Steadman certainly sounded unusual.

'Liked his drink, did he?'

'Never known him drink too much, sir. I think he just enjoyed the company here.'

'Glad to get away from the wife?'

Weaver reddened. 'I wouldn't know about that, sir. Never heard anything. But he was a funny sort of chap.'

'In what way?'

'Well, sir, like I said, he used to be a professor at Leeds University. When he inherited the money, he just packed in his job, bought the old Ramsden house and moved up here.'

'Ramsden house?' Banks cut in. 'That wouldn't have

anything to do with Michael Ramsden, would it?'

Weaver raised an eyebrow. 'As a matter of fact, sir, yes,' he answered. 'It was his parents' house. Used to be a bed-and-breakfast place when Steadman and his wife started coming up here for their holidays ten years ago or more. Young Michael went to university and landed a good job with a publishing firm in London. Then, when old Mr Ramsden died, the mother couldn't afford to keep on the house, so she went off to live with her sister in Torquay. It all happened at just the right time for Steadman.'

Banks looked at Weaver in astonished admiration. 'How old are you?' he asked.

'Twenty-one, sir.'

'How do you manage to know so much about things that happened before your time?'

'Family, sir. I was born and raised in the area. And Sergeant Mullins. He runs the show around here usually, but he's on holiday right now. There's not much escapes Sergeant Mullins.'

Banks sat in silence for a moment and enjoyed his beer as he sifted the information.

'What about Steadman's drinking companions?' he asked finally. 'What kind of people are they?'

'He brought them all together, sir,' Weaver answered. 'Oh, they all knew each other well enough before he moved up here, like, but Steadman was a friendly sort, interested in everything and everyone. When he wasn't busying himself with his books or poking around ruins and abandoned mines he was quite a socializer. There's Jack Barker, for one – you might have heard of him?'

Banks shook his head.

'Writer. Mystery stories.' Weaver smiled. 'Quite good

really. Plenty of sex and violence.' He blushed. 'Nothing like the real thing, of course.'

'Oh, I don't know,' Banks said, smiling. 'Go on.'

'Well, sir, he's been here three or four years. Don't know where he started from. Then there's Doc Barnes, born and raised hereabouts, and Teddy Hackett, local entrepreneur. He owns the garage over there, and a couple of gift shops. That's all, really. They're all fortyish. Well, Doc Barnes is a bit older and Barker's in his late thirties. An odd group, when you think about it. I've been in here a few times when they were together and from what I could hear they'd take the mickey out of Steadman a bit, him being an academic and all that. But not nasty like. All in good fun.'

'No animosity? You're certain?'

'No, sir. Not as far as I could tell. I don't get in here as often as I'd like. Wife and kid, you see.' He beamed.

'Work, too.'

'Aye, that keeps me busy as well. But I seem to spend more time giving directions to bloody tourists and telling the time than dealing with local affairs. Whoever said "If you want to know the way, ask a policeman" ought to be shot.'

Banks laughed. 'The locals are a fairly law-abiding lot, then?'

'On the whole, yes. We get a few drunks now and then. Especially at the Hare and Hounds disco, as I said. But that's mostly visitors. Then there's the odd domestic dispute. But most of our troubles come from tourists leaving their cars all over the place and making too much noise. It's a peaceful place, really, though there's some as would say it's boring.'

At this point, Sergeant Hatchley walked in and joined

them. He was a bulky, fair-haired and freckle-faced man in his early thirties, and he and Banks had developed a tolerable working relationship despite some early hostilities – partly due to north–south rivalry and partly to Hatchley's having hoped for the job Banks got.

Hatchley bought a round of drinks and they all ordered steak and kidney pies, which turned out to be very tasty. Not too much kidney, as Weaver remarked. Banks complimented the landlord and was rewarded with an ambiguous 'Aye.'

'Anything new?' Banks asked the sergeant.

Hatchley lit a cigarette, lounged back in his chair, rubbed a hand like a hairy ham across his stubbly cheek, and cleared his throat.

'Nowt much, by the look of things. Old Tavistock went looking for a stray sheep and dug up a fresh corpse. That's about the strength of it.'

'Was it unusual for him to go poking around by that wall? Would other people be likely to go there?'

'If you're thinking that anyone could expect to dump a body there and leave it undiscovered for weeks, then you're barking up the wrong tree. Even if old Tavistock hadn't gone out looking for his bloody sheep, someone would've come along soon enough – hikers, courting couples.'

Banks sipped some more beer. 'So he wasn't dumped there for concealment, then?'

'Shouldn't think so, no. Probably put there just so we'd have to leg it halfway up to Crow bloody Scar.'

Banks laughed. 'More likely so we wouldn't know where he was killed.'

'Aye.'

'Why wasn't Steadman reported missing, sir?' Weaver

cut in. He seemed anxious to restore to the chief inspector the respect that Hatchley appeared to be denying him.

Banks told him. Then he told Hatchley to get back to the Eastvale station, find out as much as he could about Steadman's background and collate any reports that came in.

'What about the press?' Hatchley asked. 'They're all over the place now.'

'You can tell them we've found a body.'

'Shall I tell them who it is?'

Banks sighed and gave Hatchley a long-suffering look. 'Don't be so bloody silly. Not until we've got a formal identification you can't, no.'

'And what will you be doing, sir?'

'My job.' Banks turned to Weaver. 'You'd better get back to the station, lad. Who's in charge?'

Weaver blushed again, his pinkness deepening to crimson. 'I am, sir. At least, I am at the moment. Sergeant Mullins is away for two weeks. Remember I told you about him, sir?'

'Yes, of course. How many men have you got?'

'There's only two of us, sir. It's a quiet place. I called some of the lads in from Lyndgarth and Fortford to help with the search. There's not more than half a dozen of us altogether.'

'All right, then,' Banks said, 'it looks like you're in charge. Get a request for information printed up and distributed – shops, pubs, church notice board. Then start a house-to-house enquiry up Hill Road. That body wasn't carried all the way up there, and somebody might just have seen or heard a car. At least it'll help us narrow down the time of death. All right?'

'Yes, sir.'

'And don't worry. If you need any more men, let Eastvale station know and they'll see what they can do. I'm going to pay Michael Ramsden a visit myself, but if you ask for Sergeant Rowe, I'll make sure he has full instructions.'

He turned to Hatchley again. 'Before you go back, go and tell the men up in the field that they're temporarily transferred to Helmthorpe and they're to take their orders from Constable Weaver here. They'll probably understand the situation already, but make it official. And check the car park for a beige Sierra.' He gave Hatchley the number of the car and handed him the keys. 'It's Steadman's car,' he added, 'and while it doesn't look as if he got to use it last night, you never know. It might tell us something. Get forensic on to it right away.'

'Yes, sir,' Hatchley said through clenched teeth as he left. Banks could almost hear the 'three bags full, sir' that the sergeant probably added when he got outside.

He grinned broadly at the nonplussed young constable and said, 'Don't mind him; he's probably just got a hangover. Now, off you go, Weaver. Time to get to work.'

Alone, he slipped his new pipe from his jacket pocket and stuffed it with shag. Drawing in the harsh tobacco, he coughed and shook his head. He still couldn't get used to the damn thing; maybe mild cigarettes would be better, after all.

TWO

Excited, Sally had watched Banks drive off towards the village and followed in the same direction. She stopped to pick a campion by the hedgerow and casually admired its pinkish-purple colour, the petals like a baby's splayed fingers. Then, thinking about what she had to tell her friends, she let it drop and hurried on her way.

She had actually seen the man, the policeman in charge, close up, and had had to stifle a giggle as he lost his footing climbing the low wall. It was obvious he wasn't used to bounding about the northern countryside; perhaps he'd been sent up by Scotland Yard. She found his gaunt angled face under the short neat black hair attractive, despite a nose that had clearly been broken and imperfectly reset. The sharp restless eyes expressed energy and power, and the little white scar beside his right eye seemed, to Sally, a mark of exotic experience. She imagined he'd got into a fight to the death with a blood-crazed murderer. Even though he seemed too short for a policeman, his wiry body looked nimble and strong.

At the western edge of the village, near the Bridge, was a coffee bar where Sally and her friends hung out. The coffee was weak, the Coke warm and the Greek owner surly, but the place boasted two video games, an up-to-date jukebox and an ancient pinball machine. Of course, Sally would rather have expertly applied a little make-up and passed for eighteen in one of the pubs – especially the Hare and Hounds on disco night – but in such a small community everyone seemed to know a little about everyone else's business, and she was worried in case word got back to her father. She had been in pubs in Eastvale with Kevin, though even that was risky with the school so close by, and in Leeds and York, which were safer, and nobody had ever questioned her about her age.

The door rattled as she pushed it open and entered to the familiar bleeping of massacred aliens. Kathy Chalmers and Hazel Kirk were engrossed in the game, while Anne

Downes looked on coolly. She was a bookish girl, plain and bespectacled, but she wanted to be liked; and if that meant hanging around with video-game players, then so be it. The others teased her a bit, but never maliciously, and she was blessed with a sharp, natural wit that helped her hold her own.

The other two were more like Sally, if not as pretty. They chewed gum, applied make-up (unlike Sally, they did this badly) and generally fussed about their hair and clothes. Kathy had even got away with a henna treatment. Her parents had been furious, but there was nothing much they could do after the fact. It was Hazel, the sultry, black-haired one, who spoke first.

'Look who's here,' she announced. 'And where have you been all weekend?' The glint in her eye implied that she knew very well where Sally had been and who she had been with. Under normal circumstances Sally would have played along, hinting at pleasures she believed Hazel had only read about in books, but this time she ignored the innuendo and got herself a Coke from the unsmiling Greek. The espresso machine was hissing like an old steam engine and the aliens were still bleeping in their death throes. Sally leaned against the column opposite Anne and waited impatiently for a silence into which she could drop her news.

When the game was over, Kathy reached for another coin, a manoeuvre that necessitated arching her back and stretching out her long legs so that she could thrust her hand deep enough into the pocket of her skintight Calvin Kleins. As she did this, Sally noticed the Greek ogling from behind his coffee machine. Choosing her moment for best dramatic effect, she finally spoke: 'Guess what. There's been a murder. Here in the village. They dug up a body under Crow Scar. I've just come from there. I've *seen* it.'

Anne's pale eyes widened behind her thick lenses. 'A murder! Is that what those men are doing up there?'

'They're conducting a search of the scene,' Sally announced, hoping she'd got the phrasing right. 'The scene of the crime. And the forensic team was there too, taking blood samples and tissue. And the police photographer and the Home Office pathologist. All of them.'

Kathy slid back into her seat, forgetting the game. 'A murder? In Helmthorpe?' She gasped in disbelief. 'Who was it?'

Here Sally had to admit lack of information, which she disguised neatly by assuming that Kathy meant 'Who was the murderer?' 'They don't know yet, you fool,' she replied scornfully. 'It's only just happened.' Then she hurried on, keen not to lose their attention to further fleets of aliens. 'I saw the superintendent close up. Quite a dish, actually. Not at all what you'd expect. And I could see the body. Well, some of it. It was buried by the wall up in Tavistock's field. Somebody had scraped away some of the loose soil and then covered it with stones. There was a hand and a leg sticking out.'

Hazel Kirk tossed back a glossy raven's wing of hair. 'Sally Lumb, you're a liar,' she said. 'You couldn't see that far. The police wouldn't have let anyone get that close.'

'I did,' Sally countered. 'I could even see the wet patches under the superintendent's arms.' She realized too late that this outburst clashed with her more romantic image of the 'superintendent' and rushed on, hoping nobody would notice. Only Anne wrinkled her nose. 'And old man Tavistock was there. I think he discovered the body. And all the policemen from miles around. Geoff Weaver was there.'

'That pink-faced pansy,' Kathy cut in.

'It wasn't so pink today, I can tell you. I think he'd been sick.'

'Well, wouldn't you be if you'd just found a dead body?' Anne asked, coming to the defence of young Weaver, on whom she had had a schoolgirl crush for nearly six months. 'It was probably all decomposed and rotten.'

Sally ignored her. 'And there was another inspector, or whatever they call them. He wasn't in uniform anyway. Tall, strawy hair – a bit like your dad, Kathy.'

'That'll be Jim Hatchley,' Anne said. 'Actually, he's only a sergeant. My father knows him. Remember when the social club was broken into last year? Well, they sent him from Eastvale. He even came to our house. My dad's treasurer, you know. Hatchley's a coarse pig. He's even got hairs up his nose and in his ears. And I'll bet that other chap was Chief Inspector Banks. He had his picture in the paper a while back. Don't you ever read the papers?'

Anne's stream of information and opinion silenced everyone for a moment. Then Sally, who read nothing but *Vogue* and *Cosmopolitan*, picked up the thread again. 'They're here now. In the village. They drove down before I came.'

'I'm surprised they didn't give you a lift,' Hazel said, 'seeing as how you're on such good terms.'

'Shut up, Hazel Kirk!' Sally said indignantly. Hazel just smirked. 'They're here. They'll be questioning everybody, you know. They'll probably want to talk to all of us.'

'Why should they want to do that?' Kathy asked. 'We don't know anything about it.'

'It's just what they do, stupid,' Sally retorted. 'They do

house-to-house searches and take statements from every-one. How do they know we don't know anything till they ask us?'

Sally's logic silenced Kathy and Hazel.

'We don't even know who the victim was yet,' Anne chimed in. 'Who do you think it was?'

'I'll bet it was that Johnnie Parrish,' Kathy said. 'He looks like a man with a past to me.'

'Johnnie Parrish!' Sally sneered. 'Why, he's about as interesting as a . . . a . . .'

'A dose of clap?' Anne suggested. They all laughed.

'Even that would be more interesting than Johnnie Parrish. I'll bet it was Major Cartwright. He's such a miserable, bad-tempered old bugger there must be lots of people want to kill him.'

'His daughter, for one,' Hazel said, and giggled.

'Why?' Sally asked. She didn't like to think she was excluded from what appeared to be common knowledge.

'Well, you know,' Kathy stalled. 'You know what people say.'

'About what?'

'About Major Cartwright and his daughter. How he keeps such a tight rein on her since she came back to the village. Why she ran off in the first place. It's unnatural. That's what people say.'

'Oh, is that all,' Sally said, not quite sure she under-stood. 'But she's got her own place, that cottage by the church.'

'Maybe it was Alf Pringle,' Hazel suggested. 'Now there's a nasty piece of work. Be doing us all a favour if somebody did away with him.'

'Wishful thinking.' Kathy sighed. 'Do you know, he chased me off his land the other day. I was only picking wild flowers for that school project. He had his shotgun with him, too.'

'He sounds more like a murderer than a victim,' Anne chipped in. 'Who do you think did it?'

'Well, it might not be anyone from around here,' Kathy answered. 'I mean, we don't know, do we? It could have been a stranger.'

'Of course it was someone from around here,' Sally said, annoyed at the way her discovery seemed to have become common property. 'You don't think somebody would drive a body all the way from Leeds or somewhere like that just to dump it under Crow Scar, do you?'

'They could have done.' Kathy defended herself without much conviction.

'Well, I'm not going out after dark until he's been caught.' Hazel hugged herself and shuddered. 'It might be one of those sex murderers, another Ripper. It could even be Major Cartwright's daughter up there, for all we know. Or that Mrs Caret, the new barmaid at the Dog and Gun.'

'I shouldn't worry,' Kathy said. 'Nobody would want to sex murder you.' She spoke in the usual spirit of friendly banter, but somehow her joke flopped and the girls seemed distracted, each wrapped in her own thoughts. Kathy blushed. 'Still,' she said, 'we'd better be careful.'

'I'll bet it was Jack Barker that did it,' Anne suggested.

'Who? That writer bloke?' Sally said.

'Yes. You know what kind of books he writes.'

'I'll bet you haven't read any,' Kathy taunted her.

'Yes, I have. I've read *The Butcher of Redondo Beach* and *The San Clemente Slasher*. They're lurid.'

'I've read one too,' Hazel said. 'I can't remember what it was called but it was about this man who went to his beach house somewhere in America and he found two people he'd never seen before chopped to pieces in his living room. It was grisly. I only read it because he lives here.'

'That's *The Butcher of Redondo Beach*,' Anne informed her patiently. 'That's what it's called.'

Sally was bored by the direction the conversation was taking, and, besides, she thought Jack Barker looked far too handsome and debonair to be a murderer. He was a bit like one of those old film stars her mother was always going on about – Errol Flynn, Clark Gable or Douglas Fairbanks – the ones who all looked the same with their oily, slicked-down hair and little moustaches. He was the type, she thought, who might shoot his adulterous wife (if he had one) in a fit of passion, but he certainly wouldn't carry her body all the way up to Crow Scar afterwards, that was for sure. He was far too much of a gentleman to do that, whatever kind of books he wrote.

Sally finished her Coke and turned to leave, but before she did so she whispered, 'The police will see me. I can tell you that for sure. I know something. I don't know who's dead or who the killer is yet, but I know something.'

And with that she exited quickly, leaving the others to gape after her and debate whether she was telling the truth or simply trying to draw attention to herself.

THREE

There are two routes to York from Helmthorpe. The first winds up through Gratly, continues diagonally across the dales, more or less as the crow flies, and eventually joins the main road a couple of miles outside the city; the second, longer but quicker, involves taking the main road back to Eastvale, then driving south-east on the busy York Road. Because it was a beautiful day and he was in no real hurry, Banks took the first route on his visit to Ramsden.

He slipped the cassette back into the player and to the strains of 'O, Sweet Woods' drove up the hill, turned left past the Steadman house and followed the road as it climbed the dale side slowly. He passed through the tiny hamlet of Mortsett and paused with his window down to look at an attractive cottage with a post office sign above its door and a board advertising Wall's Ice Cream propped outside. Insects hovered and hummed in the still, warm air; it seemed unreal, an image of England from before the First World War.

Beyond Relton, at the junction with the Fortford road, he seemed to leave civilization behind. Soon, the greens of the hillsides gave way to the darker hues of the heather-covered moors, which continued for about two miles before dropping slowly into the next dale. It was like a slow roller coaster ride, and the only obstacles were the sheep that sometimes strayed on to the unfenced road, itself only a thin band hardly distinguishable from the landscape around it. Banks saw a few hikers, who stepped on to the rough grass when they heard his car, smiling and waving as he drove by.

The main road, busy with lorries and delivery vans, came as a shock. Following Mrs Steadman's directions, Banks found the turn-off, a narrow track with a lonely red phone box on the corner, about a mile from York's boundary. He turned left and, after a quarter of a mile, came to the converted farmhouse. He pulled into the smooth dirt driveway and stopped outside the new-looking garage.

Ramsden answered the door shortly after the first ring and asked who he was. When Banks showed some identification, he slipped off the chain and invited him in.

'Can't be too careful,' he apologized. 'Especially in such an isolated place as this.'

Ramsden was tall and pale, with the melancholic aspect of a Romantic poet. He had light-brown hair and, Banks soon noticed, a nervous habit of brushing back the stray forelock even when it hadn't slid down over his brow. The jeans and sweatshirt he wore seemed to hang on him as if they were a size too big.

'Please excuse the mess,' he said as he led Banks into a cluttered living room and installed him by the huge empty fireplace. 'As you can see I'm decorating. Just finished the first coat.' A clear polythene sheet covered half the floor, and on it stood a stepladder, a gallon of pale blue paint, brushes, tray and rollers. 'It's not about that woman, is it?' he asked.

'What woman?'

'An old lady not far from here was murdered by thugs a few months ago. I had a policeman around then.'

'No, sir, it's not about the woman. That would have been York Region. I'm from Eastvale CID.'

Ramsden frowned. 'I'm afraid I don't understand then. Pardon me, I don't mean to seem rude, but . . .'

'I'm sorry, sir,' Banks apologized, accepting the whisky and soda Ramsden had poured for him without asking. 'This isn't easy for me. Would you care to sit down?'

Ramsden looked alarmed. 'What is it?' he asked, fitting himself awkwardly into a small armchair.

'You were expecting Mr Steadman to visit you last night?'

'Harry? That's right. We had some notes to go over

before today's field trip. Why? Has something happened?'

'Yes, I'm afraid it has,' Banks said as gently as he could, aware of the muscles in his stomach clenching tightly. 'Mr Steadman is dead.'

Ramsden brushed back the phantom forelock. 'I don't follow. Dead? But he was coming here.'

'I know that, Mr Ramsden. That's why I wanted to tell you myself. Weren't you surprised when he didn't show up? Weren't you worried?'

Ramsden shook his head. 'No, no, of course I wasn't. It wasn't the first time he hadn't come. But are you *sure*? About Harry, I mean. Can't there have been some mistake?'

'I'm afraid not.'

'What on earth happened?'

'We're not certain about that yet, sir, but a farmer found his body this morning in a field under Crow Scar. It looks as if he was murdered.'

'Murdered? Good God! Harry? I can't believe it.'

'You know no one who'd have a reason?'

'Absolutely not. Nobody. Not Harry.' He rubbed his face and stared at Banks. 'I'm sorry, Chief Inspector, I can't really think straight. I'm having trouble taking this all in. I've known Harry for a long time. A long time. This is such a shock.'

'I realize it must be, sir,' Banks persisted, 'but if you could just spare the time to answer a couple of questions, I'll be on my way.'

'Yes, of course.' Ramsden got up and made a drink for himself.

'You said it had happened before, that he hadn't turned up?'

'Yes. It wasn't a formal arrangement. More casual, really.'

'Why didn't he come?'

'Once when Emma wasn't too well he couldn't make it. And one time he had a stomach upset. Things like that. We were very close, Chief Inspector. There was always a bed made up for him, and he had a key in case I had to go out.'

'Didn't it cross your mind to phone and ask what was wrong?'

'Not at all. I've already told you our arrangement was casual. I don't have a phone. I spend enough time on the blasted thing at work. The nearest public call box is on the main road.' He shook his head. 'I just can't believe this is happening. It's like a bad dream. Harry, dead?'

'Did you go out last night?'

Ramsden looked at him blankly.

'You said Mr Steadman had a key in case you were out,' Banks pressed on. 'Were you out last night?'

'No, I wasn't. Actually, when Harry hadn't arrived by eleven o'clock, I was rather – I mean, don't get me wrong – a little relieved. You see, I'm working on a book of my own. A historical novel. And I was glad of the opportunity to get some writing done.' He looked embarrassed about it.

'Didn't you like working with Mr Steadman?'

'Oh, of course I did. But it was his baby, really. I was just the editor, the research assistant.'

'Where were you planning to go today?'

'We were going to visit an old lead mine in Swaledale. Quite a distance really, so we wanted to get an early start. Emma!' he exclaimed suddenly. 'Emma must be in a terrible state.'

'She's upset, of course,' Banks said. 'Mrs Stanton, the neighbour, is looking after her.'

'Should I go?'

'That's up to you, Mr Ramsden, but I'd say best leave her for today at least. She's in good hands.'

Ramsden nodded. 'Of course, of course . . .'

'What about you? Will you be all right?'

'Yes, I'll be fine. It's just the shock. I've known Harry for more than ten years.'

'Would it be possible to talk to you again about this? Just to get some background, that kind of thing?'

'Yes, I suppose so. When?'

'The sooner the better, really. Tuesday morning, perhaps? We might know a bit more by then.'

'I'll be at work. Fisher and Faulkner. We're not ter- rifically busy at the moment. If you want to drop by . . .'

'Yes, that'll be fine.'

Banks asked directions to the publishers, then left Ramsden and returned to Eastvale by the quickest route. At the station, an invitation to call at Superintendent Gristhorpe's for tea awaited him. He phoned Sandra, who wasn't at all surprised at his absence, checked that no important news had come in while he had been at Ramsden's, and set off for Helmthorpe for the second time that day. It was only three o'clock, and, as he wasn't expected at Gristhorpe's until five, he would have plenty of time to see how the locals were coping.

The Helmthorpe police station was a converted cottage on a narrow cobbled road that forked from the eastern end of the High Street towards the river. There, Weaver, who was running off more copies of the request for informa- tion, told him that three constables were still making door-to-door enquiries along Hill Road and another had been dispatched to the campsite.

That was the biggest headache, Banks realized. They

would have to try and find out who had been staying at the campsite on Saturday night. Most of the campers would have moved on by now and it would be damn near impossible to get comprehensive or reliable information.

There was also the press to deal with. Besides Reg Summers of the local weekly, two other reporters were still hanging around outside the station, as Hatchley had warned, thrusting their notebooks at everyone who entered or left. Banks certainly liked to maintain good relations with the press, but at such an early stage in the investigation he could give them little of value. However, to gain and keep their goodwill – because he knew they would be useful eventually – he told them what he could in as pleasant a manner as possible.

At twenty to five, he left Weaver in charge and drove off to see Gristhorpe. On the way, he decided he would visit the Bridge that evening to see what he could get out of Steadman's cronies. More, he hoped, than he'd managed to pick up so far.

3

ONE

Banks pulled into the rutted drive at five to five and walked towards the squat stone house. Gristhorpe lived in an isolated farmhouse on the north dale side above the village of Lyndgarth, about halfway between Eastvale and Helmthorpe. It was no longer a functioning farm, though the superintendent still held on to a couple of acres where he grew vegetables. Since his wife had died five years ago, he had stayed on there alone, and a woman from the village came up to do for him every morning.

The building was too austere for Banks, but he could see it was ideally suited to the environment. In a part of the country windswept and lashed by rain much of the year, any human dwelling had to be built like a fortress to provide even the most basic domestic comforts. Inside, though, Gristhorpe's house was as warm and welcoming as the man himself.

Banks knocked at the heavy oak door, surprised at how the hollow sound echoed in the surrounding silence, but got no answer. On such a fine afternoon, he reasoned, he was more likely to find Gristhorpe in his garden, so he walked around the back.

He found the superintendent crouching by a heap of stones, apparently in the process of extending his wall.

The older man got to his feet, red-faced, at the sound of footsteps and asked, 'Is that the time already?'

'It's almost five,' Banks answered. 'I'm a few minutes early.'

'Mmm . . . I seem to lose all track of time up here. Anyway, sit down.' He gestured towards the rough grass by the stones. The superintendent was in his shirtsleeves, his ubiquitous Harris tweed jacket lying on the grass beside him. A gentle breeze ruffled his thick mop of silver hair. Below it, a red pockmarked face, upper lip all but obscured by a bristly grey moustache, grinned down at Banks. The oddest thing about Gristhorpe's appearance – and it was a facet that disconcerted both colleagues and criminals alike – was his eyes. Deep set under bushy brows, they were those of a child: wide, blue, innocent. At odds with his six-foot-three wrestler's build, they had been known to draw out confessions from even the hardest of villains and had made many an underling, caught out in a manufactured statement or an over-enthusiastic interrogation, blush and hide in shame. When all was well though, and the world seemed as fresh and clear as it did that day, Gristhorpe's eyes shone with a gentle love of life and a sense of compassion that would have given the Buddha himself a good run for his money.

Banks sat for a while and helped Gristhorpe work on the drystone wall. It was a project that the superintendent had started the previous summer, and it had no particular purpose. Banks had made one or two attempts at adding pieces of stone but had at first got them the wrong way around so that the rain would have drained inwards and cracked the wall apart if a sudden frost came. Often, he had chosen pieces that simply would not fit. Lately, however, he had improved, and he found the occasional wall-building afternoons with Gristhorpe almost as relaxing and refreshing as playing with Brian's train set. A silent understanding had developed between them about what stone would do and who would fix it in place.

After about fifteen minutes, Banks broke the silence: 'I suppose you know that somebody dismantled one of these walls last night to cover a body?'

'Aye,' Gristhorpe said, 'I've heard. Come on inside, Alan, and I'll make a pot of tea. If I'm not mistaken there are still a few of Mrs Hawkins's scones left, too.' He rhymed 'scones' with 'on', not, like a southerner, with 'own'.

They settled into the deep worn armchairs, and Banks cast his eyes over the bookcases that covered one entire wall from floor to ceiling. There were books on all kinds of subjects – local lore, geology, criminology, topography, history, botany, travel – and shelves of leather-bound classics ranging from Homer, Cervantes, Rabelais and Dante to Wordsworth, Dickens, James Joyce, W. B. Yeats and D. H. Lawrence. Jane Austen's *Pride and Prejudice* lay on the table; the position of the bookmark indicated that Gristhorpe had almost finished it. As always when he visited the superintendent, Banks mentally reminded himself that he should read more.

Gristhorpe's office in Eastvale was much the same: books everywhere, and not all of them relevant to police work. He came from old dales farming stock, and his decision to join the police after university and army service had caused trouble. Nevertheless, he had persevered, and he had also helped out on the farm in his spare time. When Gristhorpe's father saw that his son's natural aptitude and capacity for hard work was getting him places, he stopped complaining and accepted the situation. Gristhorpe's father had been sad to see the farm dwindle to little more than a large back garden before he died, but his pride in his son's achievement and the status it gave him locally eased him, and his death was without acrimony.

Gristhorpe had told Banks all this during their frequent meetings, usually over a good single malt whisky after a wall-building session. The older man's candour, along with more practical advice, made Banks feel like an apprentice, or protégé. Their relationship had developed this way since the Gallows View affair, Banks's dramatic introduction to northern police work. As he told what he knew about the Steadman murder, he was alert for any tips that might come his way.

'It's not going to be easy,' Gristhorpe pronounced after a short silence. 'And I won't say it is. For one thing, you've all those tourists and campers to consider. If Steadman had an enemy from the past, it would be an ideal way of doing the job. They never keep records at campsites as far as I know. All they care about is collecting the money.' He nibbled at his scone and sipped strong black tea. 'Still, the killer could be a lot closer to home. Doesn't look like you've got much physical evidence, though, does it? Somebody might have heard a car, but I doubt they'd have paid it much mind. I know that road. It swings north-east all the way over to Sattersdale. Still, I don't suppose I need tell you your job, Alan. First thing is to find out as much as you can about Steadman. Friends, enemies, past, the lot. Nose about the village. Talk to people. Leave the donkey work to your men.'

'I'm an outsider, though,' Banks said. 'I always will be as far as people around here are concerned. I look out of place and I sound out of place. Nobody's going to give much away to me.'

'Rubbish, Alan. Look at it this way. You're a stranger in Helmthorpe, right?' Banks nodded. 'People notice you. They'll soon get to know who you are. You don't look like a tourist, and no villager will mistake you for one. You're even a bit of a celebrity – at least for them as reads the papers around here. They'll be curious, interested in the new copper, and they'll want to find out what makes you tick. You'll be surprised what they'll tell you just to see how you react.' He chuckled. 'Before this is all over you'll feel like a bloody priest in his confessional.'

Banks smiled. 'I was brought up C. of E.'

'Ah. We're all Methodists or Baptists hereabouts,' Gristhorpe said. 'But some of us are more lapsed than others, and most of the daftest sects – your Sandemanians, for example – have all but disappeared.'

'I hope I won't have the same obligation to secrecy as a priest.'

'Heavens, no!' Gristhorpe exclaimed. 'I want to know everything you find out. You've no idea what an opportunity this is for me to catch up on Helmthorpe gossip. But seriously, Alan, do you see what I mean? Take Weaver. He's a pleasant enough lad. Trustworthy, competent, thorough. But as far as the villagers are concerned he's a fixture, boring as a rainy day – though I shouldn't make that comparison around these parts. See what I mean, though? Half the womenfolk in Helmthorpe probably changed his nappies when he was a nipper, and most of the menfolk've given him a clip around the ear once or twice. Nobody will tell Weaver anything. They won't confide in him. There's nothing in it for them. But you . . . You're the exotic newcomer, the father confessor.'

'I hope you're right,' Banks said, finishing his tea. 'I was thinking of dropping in at the Bridge tonight; Weaver told me Steadman used to drink there regularly with a few friends.'

Gristhorpe scratched his pitted red chin, and his bushy eyebrows merged in a furrow of concentration. 'Good idea,' he said. 'Imagine it'll be a bit of a wake tonight. Good time to pick up stray words. They'll all know who's been killed, of course, and probably how. Would that chap Barker be one of Steadman's cronies, by the way?'

'Yes. Jack Barker, the writer.'

'Writer be damned!' Gristhorpe almost choked on a mouthful of scone. 'Just because he makes money from the claptrap doesn't mean he's a writer. Anyway, it's a good idea. You'll get something out of them, however useless it might seem at first. What time is it now?'

'Ten to six.'

'Supper?'

'Yes, any time you're ready.' Banks had almost forgotten how hungry he was.

'It won't be owt special, you know,' Gristhorpe called out as he went to the kitchen. 'Just salad and leftover roast beef.'

TWO

Sally and Kevin raced the last few yards and collapsed, panting, by Ross Ghyll. They were high up on Tetchley Fell, on the south side of the dale, having walked to the source of one of the numerous becks that meander their way down to the Swain.

When they had caught their breath, Kevin kissed her,

thrusting his tongue deep into her mouth, and they lay down together on the pale springy grass. He touched her breasts, felt the nipples harden through thin cotton, and slowly let his hand slide down between her legs. She was wearing jeans, and the pressure of the thick seam against her sex made her tingle with excitement. But she broke free and sat up, distracted.

'I'm going to tell the police, Kevin,' she said.

'B-but we—'

She laughed and hit him lightly on the arm. 'Not about this, stupid. About last night.'

'But then they'll know about us,' he protested. 'They'll be sure to tell.'

'No, they won't. Why should they? You can tell them things in confidence, you know, like Catholics and priests. Besides,' she added, twirling a strand of hair between her slim fingers, 'my mum and dad know we were together. I told them we were at your house and we forgot about the time.'

'I just don't think we should get involved, that's all. It could be dangerous, being a witness.'

'Oh, don't be daft. I think it's rather exciting, myself.'

'You would. What if the killer thinks we really saw something?'

'Nobody knew we were up there. Nobody saw us.'

'How do you know?'

'It was dark, and we were too far away.'

'He might see you going to the police station.'

Sally laughed. 'I'll wear a disguise, then. Now you're being really silly. There's nothing to be afraid of.'

Kevin fell silent. Once again he felt he'd been outwitted and outreasoned by a mere girl.

'I won't tell them who you are if it bothers you so

much,' Sally went on, reassuring him. 'I'll just say that I was with a friend I'd rather not name. Talking.'

'Talking!' Kevin laughed and reached for her. 'Is that what we were doing?'

Sally giggled. His hand was on her breast again, but she pushed him away and stood up, brushing the grass from her jeans.

'Come on, Sally,' he pleaded. 'You know you want it as much as I do.'

'Do I now?'

'Yes.' He made a grab for her ankle but she stepped nimbly aside.

'Maybe,' she said. 'But not now. Especially with someone who's ashamed to admit he was with me last night. Besides, I have to be home for tea or my dad'll kill me.' And she was off like the wind. Sighing, Kevin got to his feet and plodded along behind her.

THREE

'When you hit someone over the head, Doc,' Jack Barker asked, 'does the blood gush, pour or just flow?'

'That's a pretty tasteless question at a time like this, isn't it?' Barnes said.

Barker reached for his pint. 'It's for my book.'

'In that case, I shouldn't think accuracy matters, then, does it? Use the most violent word you can think of. Your readers won't know any more than you do.'

'You're wrong there, Doc. You should see some of the letters I get. There's plenty of ghouls among the reading public. Do you know how many of those little old ladies are hooked on gruesome forensic details?'

'No. And I don't want to, either. I see enough blood in my line of work as it is. And I still think you're showing poor taste talking like that before poor Harry's even in the ground.'

It was early, and Barnes and Barker were the only members of the informal group sitting in the snug.

'Death comes to us all in the end, Doc,' Barker replied. 'You ought to know that. You've helped enough people shuffle off their mortal coils.'

Barnes scowled at him. 'How can you be so bloody flippant? For God's sake, have a bit of decency, Jack. Even you've got to admit that his death was an untimely one.'

'It must have been timely enough for the killer.'

'I don't understand you, Jack. Never in a million years . . .' Barnes sighed over his beer. 'Still, I have to keep reminding myself you write about this kind of thing all the time.'

'It's just shock,' Barker said, reaching for a cigarette. 'Believe it or not, I didn't personally witness every murder I've written about. And as you well know, I've never set foot on American soil either.' He ran a hand across his slicked-back hair. 'It's a bloody sad business, all right. I know we used to tease the poor bugger about his rusty nails and pigs of lead, but I'll miss him a lot.'

Barnes acknowledged the eulogy with a curt nod.

'Have the police been talking to you yet?' Barker asked.

The doctor seemed surprised. 'Me? Goodness, no. Why should they?'

'Oh, come off it, Doc. I know you're an eminent GP, pillar of the community and all that crap. But that kind of thing doesn't cut much ice with the CID, old man. And it doesn't alter the fact that you were here last night with the rest of us and you left quite a bit earlier than usual.'

'You surely don't think the police would . . .' he began. Then he relaxed and mumbled almost to himself, 'Of course, they'll have to check every angle. Leave no stone unturned.'

'Cut the clichés,' Barker said. 'They hurt.'

Barnes snorted. 'I can't see why; you write enough of them yourself.'

'It's one thing giving the public what it wants and the publishers what they pay for, but quite another to spout them out in intelligent company. Anyway, you look worried, Doc. What skeletons will they find in your cupboard?'

'Don't be ridiculous,' Barnes said. 'And I don't think you should joke about a matter as important as this. After all, poor Harry *is* dead. And you know damn well where I had to go last night. Mrs Gaskell is already a week overdue with her delivery and, frankly, I'm getting a bit worried.'

'I suppose she can give you an alibi, then?'

'Of course she can, should it ever come to that. Besides, what possible motive could I have for harming Harry?'

'Oh, still waters run murky and deep,' Barker replied, mimicking the doctor's own style of speech.

At that moment, Teddy Hackett arrived, looking every inch the flamboyant entrepreneur. He was a vain dresser, always wearing a shirt with a monogram or an alligator embroidered on its top pocket, gold medallion and expensive designer jeans. He tried to look younger than he was, but his dark hair was receding fast at the temples and a flourishing beer belly hung over his belt, almost obscuring a hand-wrought silver buckle depicting a growling lion's head.

It was well known around the village that when Hackett wasn't making money or drinking with his cronies, he was living it up in nightclubs in Leeds, Darlington or Manchester, turning on the charm for any attractive young woman who came his way. He had certainly done well for himself – the garage, a couple of gift shops – and he kept a keen eye open for anything else that came on the market. He was the kind of businessman who, given free rein, would probably buy up the whole dale and turn it into a gigantic funfair.

'Bloody hell,' he said, easing into his chair with a brimming pint grasped in his fist. 'What a turn-up for the book, hey?'

Barnes nodded and Barker stubbed out his cigarette.

'Got any details?' Hackett asked.

'No more than anyone else, I should think,' Barker replied. 'I bet the doc'll find out a thing or two after the autopsy.'

Barnes reddened with anger. 'That's enough, Jack,' he snarled. 'These things are confidential. It'll be done in Eastvale General by the pathologist, Glendenning. They're bloody lucky to have him up here. One of the best in the country, or so I've heard.' He looked at his watch. 'I wouldn't be surprised if he's at it already. Dead keen, they say.' He faltered, catching the unintentional pun a moment after he'd let it out. 'Anyway, you can be sure it'll go no further.'

'Like young Joanie Lomax's recent dose of clap, eh?'

'You're going too far, Jack. I know you're upset like the rest of us. Why can't you admit it instead of behaving like some bloody actress waiting for opening night reviews?'

Barker shifted uncomfortably in his chair.

'Has anyone been questioned yet?' Hackett asked.

The other two shook their heads.

'It's just that I saw that detective fellow – I'm sure I recognize him from that photo in the local rag last autumn. He's at the bar right now.'

They all looked over and saw Banks leaning against the bar, foot on the rail, apparently enjoying a quiet pint alone.

'That's him,' Barker confirmed. 'I saw him leaving Emma's this morning. What are you so nervous about anyway, Teddy? You've got nothing to hide, have you?'

'Nothing, no. But we were all here last night with him, weren't we? I mean, they're sure to want to question us. Why haven't they done it yet?'

'You left after Harry, as I remember,' Barker said.

'Yes. It was Saturday night, wasn't it? Had to get up to Darly for Freddy's new club opening. Bloody good night it was, too. There were some real corkers around, Jack. Why don't you come along with me sometime? Handsome young bachelor like yourself ought to get around and about a bit more.'

'Ah,' Barker replied, shaking his head. 'Better things to do with my time than chase scrubbers in a disco, mate. A writer's life . . .'

'Writer, my arse!' Hackett said. 'I could turn out that junk in my coffee break.'

Barker raised an eyebrow and grinned. 'Maybe so, Teddy, but you don't, do you? There's the difference. Besides, I hear you've had to hire a secretary with a BA in English to translate your business letters for you.'

'My English would hardly be a handicap if I was in your line of work. Anyway, there's no room for fancy footwork in a business letter. You know that, Jack. Short and to the point.'

'That's what the reviewers said about my last book.' Barker sighed. 'Well, perhaps not in so many words.'

And even Doc Barnes had to laugh at that.

After that brief and traditional exchange the three of them fell silent, as if they knew that they had been talking and joking as usual just to fill the void of Harry's absence, to pretend for as long as possible that nothing had changed, that nothing so brutal and final as murder had touched the cosy little group.

Barker volunteered to buy another round and went to stand next to Banks at the bar. 'Excuse me,' he said, 'but aren't you the policeman investigating Harry Steadman's death?' When Banks nodded, Barker stuck out his hand. 'Jack Barker. I'm a friend of his.'

Banks offered his condolences.

'Look,' Barker went on, 'we were wondering – I mean, we were all pals of Harry's and we spent a good deal of yesterday evening with him – would you care to join us in the snug? It'll be a sight more comfortable and convenient than hauling us all in to the station individually for questioning.'

Banks laughed and accepted the offer. 'I reserve the right to haul you in if I want to, though,' he added, only half in jest.

Banks had been intending to drop in on them all along. He had been imitating the vampire, who will not enter his victim's room until invited, and was pleased that his little trick had worked. Perhaps there was something in Gristhorpe's advice after all. Curiosity had got the better of them.

Barker looked happy enough to be bringing him back in tow, but the other two appeared uneasy. Banks, however, was experienced enough not to read too much into their reaction. He knew what discomfort the arrival of the police always caused. Even the most innocent of men and women begin to worry about that forgotten parking ticket or the little income tax fiddle as soon as a copper comes in range.

A tense silence followed the introductions, and Banks wondered if they expected him to begin a formal inter-rogation, notebook in hand. Instead, he began to fill his pipe, glancing at them in turn as he did so. Barker looked suave in a forties film star kind of way, and Barnes was a little balding grey man with glasses. He had the shabby look of a backstreet abortionist about him, Banks thought. Finally, Hackett, the flashy one, started to chat nervously.

'We were just talking about Harry,' he said. 'Sad business. Can't think who'd want to do such a thing.'

'Is that what you all think?' Banks asked, keeping his eyes on the pipe.

They all murmured their agreement. Hackett lit an American cigarette and went on: 'It's like this. Harry might have been a bit of a dotty professor type, and I don't deny we teased him a bit, but it was all in good humour. He was a fine man, good-tempered, even-natured. He had a sharp mind – and a tongue to match when it came to it – but he was a good man; he never hurt a soul, and I can't think why anyone would want to kill him.'

'Somebody obviously felt differently,' Banks said. 'I hear he inherited a lot of money.'

'Over a quarter of a million. His father was an inventor. Patented some electronic device and opened a factory. Did very well. I suppose the wife'll get it now?'

'That's how it usually goes. What's your opinion of Mrs Steadman?'

'I can't say I really know her well,' Hackett answered.

'She only came down here occasionally. Seems a good woman. Harry never complained, anyway.'

Barnes agreed.

'I'm afraid I can't add anything,' Barker said. 'I know her slightly better than the others – we were, after all, practically neighbours up in Gratly – but she seems unremarkable enough to me. Not much interested in Harry's work. Stays in the background mostly. But she's not stupid – and she knows how to cook a good dinner.'

Banks noticed Barker look over his shoulder at the bar and turned to see what the attraction was. He was just in time to see a young woman with glossy black hair down to her waist. She wore a blue shawl over a white silky blouse, and a long loose skirt that curved from her slim waist over the graceful swell of her hips. He only glimpsed her face in profile for a moment as she walked out. It looked good: angular, high cheekbones, straight nose, like a North American Indian. Half obscured by her hair, a crescent of silver flashed where her jaw met her long neck.

'Who's that?' he asked Barker.

Barker smiled. 'Oh, you noticed, I see. That's Olicana.' He pronounced the foreign word slowly.

'Olicana?'

'Yes. At least that's what Harry used to call her. Apparently it's what the Romans called Ilkely, the spirit of the place, the *genius loci*. Her real name is Penny Cartwright. Not half as exotic, is it?'

'What happened last night?' Banks asked with an abruptness that startled Barker. 'Was it a normal evening's drinking as far as you were all concerned?'

'Yes,' Barker answered. 'Harry was on his way to York and dropped in for a couple of swift halves.'

'He didn't drink any more than usual?'

'A little less, if anything. He was driving.'

'Did he seem unusually excited or worried about anything?'

'No.' Barker assumed the role of spokesman. 'He was always excited about his work – some rusty nail or broken cartwheel.'

'Rusty nail?'

'Yes. That's how we used to joke about it. It was his field of study. Industrial archaeology. His one great passion, really. That and the Roman occupation.'

'I see. I've been told that Mr Steadman was supposed to visit an old lead mine in Swaledale today. Know anything about that?'

'I think he mentioned it, yes. We tried not to let him get away with too much shop talk, though. I mean, it's not everyone's cup of tea, is it, rusty nails?'

'What time did he leave here last night?'

Barker concentrated for a moment. 'It'd be about a quarter to nine,' he answered finally, and the others nodded in agreement.

'When did you leave?'

Barker glanced at Barnes and Hackett before answering. 'I left about ten fifteen. I was alone by then and it was no fun.'

Banks turned to the other two and they gave him their stories.

'So you see,' Barker concluded, 'any one of us could have done it. Our alibis are all weak.'

'Just a minute!' Barnes cut in.

'Only joking, Doc. Sorry, it was in poor taste. But it is true, isn't it? Are we suspects, Inspector? It *is* Inspector, isn't it?'

'Chief Inspector,' Banks answered. 'And no, there aren't any suspects yet.'

'I know what that means. When there are no suspects, everybody's a suspect.'

'You write detective stories, don't you, Mr Barker?' Banks asked mildly. Barker flushed and the others laughed.

'Defective stories, I always call them,' Hackett chipped in.

'Very droll,' Barker growled. 'There's hope for you yet.'

'Tell me,' Banks went on, pushing the pace now he'd got them going. 'You're all well off. Why do you drink in a dump like this?' He looked around at the peeling wallpaper and the scored, stained tables.

'It's got character,' Barker replied. 'Seriously, Chief Inspector, we're not quite so well off as you think. Teddy here's been living on credit ever since he bought up Hebden's Gift Shop, and the doc's making as much as he can fiddle from the NHS.' Barnes just glared, not even bothering to interrupt. 'And I'm just dying for someone to buy the film rights to one of my books. Harry was loaded, true, but when it came, it came as a bit of a surprise to him, and he didn't know what to do with it. Apart from quitting his job and moving up here to devote himself to his studies, he didn't change his way of life much. He wasn't really interested in money for its own sake.'

'You say it came as a surprise to him,' Banks said. 'I thought he inherited it from his father. Surely he must have known that he was in for a sizeable inheritance?'

'Well, yes he did. But he didn't expect as much as he got. I don't think he really paid much mind to it. Harry was a bit of an absent-minded prof. Took after his father.

It seems that the old man had patents nobody knew about tucked away all over the place.'

'Was Steadman mean, stingy?'

'Good heavens, no. He always paid for his round.'

Hackett smiled tolerantly while Barnes sighed and excused Barker's flippancy. 'What he's trying to say in his charming manner,' the doctor explained, 'is that none of us feel we belong to the country club set. We're comfortable here, and I'm not being facetious when I say it's a damn good pint.'

Banks looked at him for a moment then laughed. 'Yes, it is, isn't it?' he agreed.

This was another thing Banks had picked up during his first year in the north – the passion a Yorkshireman has for his pint. The people in Swainsdale seemed to feel the same way about their beer as a man from, say, Burgundy would feel about wine.

Banks got himself another drink and, by directing the conversation away from the murder, managed to get everyone talking more openly on general matters. They discussed ordinary things, it turned out, just like anyone else: politics, the economy, world affairs, sport, local gossip, books and television. They were three professionals, all more or less the same age, and all – except perhaps Barnes – just a little out of place in a small community that had its roots deep in agriculture and craftsmanship.

FOUR

Penny Cartwright locked and bolted the sturdy door behind her, drew the thick curtains tight and switched on the light. After she had put down her package and dropped her shawl over a chair, she went around the room lighting candles that stood, at various lengths, on saucers, in empty wine bottles and even in candlesticks.

When the room was flickering with tiny bright flames which made the walls look like melting butter, she turned out the electric light, slipped a tape in the cassette player and flopped down on the sofa.

The room was now as private and cosy as a womb. It was the kind of place that looked bright and happy in sunlight, and warm and intimate by candlelight. There were a few things tacked to the walls: a postcard-size reproduction of Henri Matisse's *The Dance*, which a friend had sent her from New York; a framed copy of Sutcliffe's photograph, *Gathering Driftwood*; and a glossy picture showing her singing at a concert she and the band had given years ago. Shadowed by candlelight, the alcoves at both sides of the fireplace overflowed with personal knick-knacks such as shells, pebbles and the kind of silly keepsakes one buys in foreign lands – things that always seem to bring back the whole atmosphere of the place and details of the day on which they were bought: a plastic key ring from Los Angeles, a miniature slide viewer from Niagara Falls, a tiny porcelain jar emblazoned with her zodiac sign, Libra, from Amsterdam. Mixed in with these were earrings, which Penny collected, of all shapes and colours.

Penny took out papers and hash from a battered Old Holborn tin and rolled a small joint; then she unwrapped the half-bottle of Bell's. There seemed no point getting a glass, so she drank straight from the bottle, and the whisky burned her tongue and throat as it sank to stir a warm glow deep inside her.

The tape played unaccompanied traditional folk songs – a strong clear woman's voice singing about men going off to war, lifeboat disasters, domestic tragedies and supernatural lovers of long ago. With part of her mind, Penny studied the vocal style critically; she admired the slight vibrato, but winced at the blurring on some of the high notes. As a professional, or an ex-professional, it was second nature to her to listen that way. Finally, she decided that she liked the woman's voice, flaws and all. It had enough warmth and emotional response to the lyrics to make up for the occasional lapses in technique.

One song, about a murder in Staffordshire over two hundred years ago, she knew well. She had sung it herself many times to appreciative audiences in pubs and concert halls. It had even been on the first record she had made with the band, and its modal structure had stood up well to the addition of electric guitars and percussion. But this time it sounded fresh. Though the song had nothing to do with the bad news she had heard that afternoon, murder was murder, whether it had been committed the previous night or two hundred years ago. Perhaps she would write a song herself. Others would sing it or listen to it in warm secure rooms hundreds of years in the future.

The whisky and hash were doing their work; Penny was drifting. Suddenly, the memory of that summer so many years ago sprang clear as yesterday into her mind. There had been many good years, of course, many good times before the craziness of fame spoiled it all, but that summer ten years ago stood out more than the rest. As she relived it, she could smell the green warmth of the grass and catch the earth and animal scents on the feather-light breeze.

Then the general memory crystallized into one

particular day. It was hot, so hot that Emma had refused to move out of the shade for fear of burning her sensitive skin. And Michael, who was sulking for some reason, had stayed at home reading Chatterton's poems. So it was just Penny and Harry. They had walked all the way over to Wensleydale, Harry, tall and strong, leading the way, and Penny keeping up the best she could. That day, they had sat high on the valley side above Bainbridge, below Semerwater, where they ate salmon sandwiches and drank chilled orange juice from a flask as they basked in the heat and looked down on the tiny village with its neat central green and Roman fort. They could see the white-washed front of the fifteenth-century Rose and Crown, and the River Bain danced and sparkled as it tripped down the falls to join the gleaming band of the Ure.

Then the scene dissolved, broke apart and shifted back in time. So vividly had Harry recreated the past in her mind that she felt she had been there. The valley bottom was marshy and filled with impenetrable thickets. Nobody ventured there. The hillmen built circular huts in clearings they made high on the valley sides near the outcrops of limestone and grits, and it was there that they went about the business of hunting, raising oats, and breeding a few sheep and cattle. A Roman patrol marched along the road just below where they sat, strangers in a cold alien landscape but sure of themselves, their helmets shining, heavy cloaks pinned at the chest with enamelled brooches.

The two scenes overlapped: ten years ago and seven-teen hundred years ago. It had all been the same to Harry. She could sense the stubborn pride of the Brigantes and the confidence of the Roman conquerors. She could even, in a way, understand why Queen Cartimandua had sided with the invaders, who brought new, civilized ways to that barbaric outpost. The tension spread throughout the dales as Venutius, the Queen's ex-husband, and his rebellious followers prepared for their last stand at Stanwick, north of Richmond. Which they lost.

Harry brought it all alive for her, and if there had been, sometimes, an inexplicable awkwardness and uneasiness between them, it had always disappeared when the past became more alive than the present. How bloody innocent I was then, Penny thought, laughing at herself, and all of sixteen, too. How long it took me to grow up, and what a road it was.

Then she remembered the coins they had gone to see in the York museum – VOLISIOS, DUMNOVEROS and CARTIMANDUA, they were marked – and the pigs of lead stamped IMP, CAES: DOMITIANO: AVG. COS: VII, and, on the other side, BRIG. The Latin words had seemed like magical incantations back then.

And so she drifted. The joint was long finished, the tape had ended, the level in the whisky bottle had gone down and the memories came thick and fast. Then, as suddenly as they had started, they ceased. All Penny was left with was blankness inside; there were vague feelings but no words, no images. She worked at the bottle, lit new cigarettes from the stubs of old ones, and at some point during the evening the tears that at first just trickled down her cheeks turned into deep, heart-racking sobs.

4

ONE

Monday morning dawned on Helmthorpe as clear and warm as the five previous days. While this wasn't exactly unprecedented, it would have been enough to dominate most conversations had there not been a more sensational subject closer at hand.

In the post office, old bent Mrs Heseltine, there to send her monthly letter to her son in Canada ('Doin' right well for 'imself . . . 'E's a full perfesser now!'), was holding forth.

'Strangled by a madman,' she repeated in a whisper. 'And right 'ere in our village. I don't know what the world's coming to, I don't. We're none of us safe any-more, and that's a fact. Best keep yer doors locked and not go out after dark.'

'Rubbish!' Mrs Anstey said. 'It was 'is wife as done it. Fer t' money, like. Stands to reason. Money's t' root of all evil, you mark my words. That's what my Albert used ter say.'

'Aye,' muttered Miss Sampson under her breath. 'That's because 'e never made any, the lazy sod.'

Mrs Dent, having read every lurid novel in Helmthorpe library and some especially imported from Eastvale and York, was more imaginative than the rest. She put forward the theory that it was the beginning of another series of moors murders.

'It's Brady and Hindley all over again,' she said. 'They'll be digging 'em up all over t' place. There was that Billy Maxton, disappeared wi'out a trace, and that there Mary Richards. You'll see. Digging 'em up all over t' place, they'll be.'

'I thought they'd run off to Swansea together, Billy Maxton and Mary Richards,' chipped in Letitia Stanford, the spindly postmistress. 'Anyway, they'll be questioning us all, no doubt about that. That little man from Eastvale, it'll be. I saw 'im poking about 'ere all day yesterday.'

'Aye,' added Mrs Heseltine. 'I saw 'im, too. Looked too short for a copper.'

''E's a southerner,' said Mrs Anstey, as if that settled the matter of height once and for all.

At that moment, the bell jangled as Jack Barker walked in to send off a short story to one of the few magazines that helped him eke out a living. He beamed at the assembled ladies, who all stared back at him like frightened prunes, bid them good morning, conducted his business, then left.

'Well,' sighed Miss Sampson indignantly. 'And 'im a friend of Mr Steadman's too. I'd like to see what the poor man's enemies is doing.'

'He's an odd one, all right,' Letitia Stanford agreed. 'Not the killing type, though.'

'And how would you know?' asked Mrs Dent sharply. 'You should read some of 'is books. Fair make you blush, they would. And full of murder, too.' She shook her head and clucked her tongue slowly at the sprightly figure disappearing down the street.

TWO

Sally Lumb sat in her best underwear before the dressing table mirror. Her long honey-blonde hair was parted in the middle and brushed neatly over her white shoulders. A short, carefully maintained fringe covered just enough of her high forehead. As she studied her milky skin, she decided it was about time she did some sunbathing. Not too much, because she was so fair and it made her red and sore, but just an hour or so each day to give her skin a deep golden hue.

She had a good face, and she knew all her weak points. Her eyes were fine – big, blue and beguiling – and her nose was perfectly in proportion, with just a hint of a bob at its tip. If anything was wrong, it was her cheeks; they were a little too plump and her cheekbones weren't well enough defined. It was only puppy fat, though. Like that around her hips and thighs, it would disappear completely in time. Nevertheless, there were ways to play down its effect right now, so why wait? The same with her mouth. It was too full – voluptuous would be the kindest word – and that wasn't likely to change by itself.

Sally studied the array of tubes, palettes, brushes, sticks and bottles in front of her, then made her skilful choice of the correct shades and tints calculated to high-light the best and obscure the worst of her facial features. After all, Chief Inspector Banks was from London, so she'd heard, and he would naturally expect a woman always to look her best.

As she applied the cosmetics, she ran through the scene in her mind, imagining what she would say, and how he would jump up and dash off to make an arrest.

Her name would be in all the papers; she would be famous. And what better start could an aspiring star wish for? The only thing better than that, she thought, carefully drawing her eyeliner, would be to catch the killer herself.

THREE

Banks sat in his office and gazed out over the market square with its ancient cross and uneven cobbles. The gold hands of the blue-faced clock on the church stood at ten fifteen. A small group of tourists stood in front of the plain sturdy building taking photographs, and shoppers in twos and threes ambled along narrow Market Street. Banks could hear occasional calls of greeting through his open window. He had been at the office for almost two hours, keen to read and digest all the information on the Steadman case as it came in.

After leaving Barker and company at the Bridge the previous evening, he had driven straight home, enjoyed a mug of hot chocolate and gone to bed. Consequently, on Monday morning he felt unnaturally fresh and wide awake, much to the surprise of Sandra and the children, who had been half asleep at the breakfast table as usual.

On his arrival at Eastvale station, he first found a message from Constable Weaver informing him that the house-to-house had produced negligible results. One person reported hearing a motorcycle at about eleven thirty and two cars between midnight and twelve forty-five (he had been eating Indian food in Harrogate and the resulting heartburn kept him awake later than usual). Everybody else was either away on holiday or fast asleep. One woman, who had spotted the request for information in Helmthorpe parish church at evening service, had dropped in early to rant about the Devil, Hell's Angels, skinheads and the price of local produce. When the patient Weaver had tried to pin her down to specifics, so the laughing Sergeant Rowe reported to Banks, it turned out that she had spent all Saturday, including the night, with her married daughter in Pocklington.

Banks fiddled with his pipe and frowned, annoyed at how little there was to go on. Every good policeman knew that the first twenty-four hours of an investigation were the most crucial ones. As time went on, the trail cooled. The press, of course, had been pestering him again on his way in, and he regretted that he had nothing to tell them. As a rule, for every piece of information he passed on to the papers, he had four more up his sleeve.

There was always the chance that visitors at the camp-site might have seen something. Banks doubted it, though. Most of the ones questioned on Sunday afternoon and evening had either just arrived that day or had heard nothing at all. Many of Saturday's guests had left before the discovery of the body, according to the site manager, who explained that they had to be out by ten o'clock in the morning or pay an extra day's rent. Unfortunately, he kept no register of names and addresses, and he hadn't noticed anyone running around waving a bloodstained candlestick or hammer.

Banks had asked Sergeant Hatchley to check Dr Barnes's alibi and to issue an appeal for information in the *Yorkshire Post*, but his hopes were slim. One problem was that the campsite was on the northern bank of the River Swain, next to the cricket pitch, and the car park was on the south side, well set back from High Street and prac-tically surrounded by trees and tall hedges. It was an ideal secluded place for a murder after dark, except between eleven and half past, when the pubs were emptying. It was possible, according to Dr Glendenning's unchanged estimation of the time of death, that Steadman had been killed between nine and ten o'clock, shortly after he left the Bridge. At that time it would have been just about dark enough, and the car park would have been quiet. Drinking hours being what they were, most people arrived between eight and nine and stayed until closing time.

So far, a thorough search had failed to find any traces of blood on the car park's pitted macadam surface. In fact, forensic had turned up little of interest at all. Glendenning, however, had proved as conscientious as usual. He had spent half the night on a thorough autopsy, and a clear, jargon-free report was waiting in Banks's in tray at eight a.m.

The wound had been made by a metal object with at least one sharp edge, and was indeed the cause of death. Stomach contents revealed a low alcohol level, consistent with the evidence of the Bridge crowd, and the remains of an earlier dinner. The blow itself could have been inflicted by either a man or a woman, Glendenning had added, as the actual strength required to kill with such a weapon was minimal. Also, the killer was probably right-handed, so it would do Banks no good to follow the fictional detective's procedure of watching out for a left-handed suspect. It did, however, appear to rule out Emma Steadman, who was left-handed, but she had a solid alibi anyway.

Hypostasis indicated, as Banks had suspected, that Steadman had been killed elsewhere and his body driven to the field. Much of the lividity had formed on his right side but he had been buried on his back.

There were no traces of blood in the car, but Vic Manson found plenty of prints. The trouble was that the few clear ones proved to be Steadman's. The prints on the steering wheel and the door handle were smudged, as they almost always were. When people drive or open and close doors, their fingerprints slide against the smooth plastic or metal surface of the handle, and the result is a mess.

What fibres remained on the vinyl-covered seats were so common as to implicate half the dale, if taken seriously. They indicated nothing so unique as a personally imported Italian suit or a yak's-wool sweater supplied by an exclusive local outfitter. Nor was there, on the tyres, any trace of mud, soil or clay that could only be found in one specific place. There wasn't even, wedged in the tread, a chip of gravel from an easily identifiable driveway.

Banks had little faith in forensic evidence, anyway. Like most detectives, he had convicted criminals on fingerprints and blood groups, but he had found that if the criminal had any brains at all, forensic evidence, though it might narrow the field of suspects, was useless until he had been caught by other means; then it might help to ensure a guilty verdict. It was surprising how many jury members still seemed to trust the experts, even though a skilled defence lawyer could easily discredit almost any scientist's testimony. Still, Banks supposed, if the public were willing to accept the 'scientifically proven' superiority of certain toothpastes or breakfast cereals that advertisers claimed, then nothing was surprising.

Just after eleven o'clock, Sergeant Hatchley poked his head around the door. Although the station coffee had improved greatly since the introduction of an automatic filter system, the two men had established a tradition of walking across to the Golden Grill for their morning break.

They weaved through the groups of strolling tourists, called hellos to the few locals they recognized, and walked into the café. The only available table was at the back, by the toilets. The petite waitress shrugged apologetically when she saw them take it.

'Usual?' she called out.

'Yes please, Gladys love,' Hatchley boomed back.

The usual was coffee and toasted teacakes for both of them.

Hatchley put his buff folder on the red checked tablecloth and ran his hand through his hair. 'Where the bloody hell's Richmond these days?' he asked, fishing for a cigarette.

'He's on a course. Didn't you know?'

'Course? What bloody course?'

'The super sent a memo round.'

'Never read them.'

'Maybe you should.'

Hatchley scowled. 'Anyway, what course is this?'

'Something to do with computers. It's down in Surrey.'

'Jammy bastard. Probably at the seaside with his bucket and spade.'

'Surrey doesn't have a coast.'

'He'll find one. When's he due back?'

'Two weeks.'

Hatchley cursed, but their order arrived before he could say anything else. He would have, Banks knew, two objections to Richmond's absence: in the first place, the sergeant had often said that he thought education was about as useful as a rubber with a hole in it; and secondly, even more serious, with Detective Constable Richmond away, Hatchley would have to do most of the legwork on the Steadman case himself.

'I checked on Doc Barnes's alibi this morning, like you asked,' Hatchley said, reaching for his teacake.

'And?'

'It's true – he was there with that Mrs Gaskell, all right. Seems she's having a difficult pregnancy.'

'What times?'

'Arrived about nine thirty, according to the husband, and left at ten fifteen.'

'So he could still have easily killed Steadman first and stuffed him in the boot of his car, or done it later.'

'No motive,' Hatchley said.

'Not that we know of yet. What's that?' Banks pointed at the folder.

'Gen on Steadman,' Hatchley mumbled, his mouth half full of toasted teacake.

Banks browsed through the report as he ate. Steadman had been born in Coventry almost forty-three years ago, at a time when his father was busy setting up his electronics business. Educated at a local grammar school, he won a scholarship to Cambridge, where he got a first in history. After that, he did postgraduate work at Birmingham and Edinburgh, then landed a teaching job at Leeds University at the age of twenty-six. There he began to develop and pursue his interest in industrial archaeology, a new field then, and in local history. In his first year of teaching, two important things happened. First, just before Christmas that year his mother died, and second, at the end of the final term he married Emma Hartley, whom he had known for two years. Emma was the only daughter of a Norwich shopkeeper, and she had been working as a librarian in Edinburgh when Steadman was studying there. She was five years younger than her husband. They had no children.

The couple honeymooned in Gratly, staying at the house they now owned. Hatchley had put an asterisk by this piece of information, and when Banks turned to the note at the bottom of the page, it read: 'Check with Ramsden. The house belonged to his parents.' Banks knew this already, but he praised Hatchley's thoroughness; it was so unusual it deserved encouragement.

As Steadman's career continued to flourish – publications, praise, promotion – his father's health steadily declined. When the old man had finally died two years ago, the son inherited a considerable fortune. He first took his wife on a European tour, then, after seeing out the university year, he bought the house in Gratly, left his job and began to concentrate on his own interests.

'What do you make of it?' Banks asked Hatchley, who had finished eating and was now picking his teeth with his fingernails.

'Well, what would you do with all that money?' the sergeant said. 'I'm damned if I'd buy a house around here and spend all my time poking about ruins.'

'You think it was foolish of him?'

'Not much of a life, is it?'

'But it's what he wanted: independence to pursue his own studies.'

Hatchley shrugged as if there were no answer to such a silly statement. 'You asked what I'd do.'

'But you didn't tell me.'

Hatchley slurped down the last of his coffee; it was syrupy at the bottom with undissolved sugar. 'I reckon I'd make a few choice investments first. Just enough so I could live comfortably off the interest, like. Nothing risky.

Then I'd take a few thousand and have a bloody good holiday.'

'Where?'

'Everywhere. Fleshpots of the world.'

Banks smiled. 'And then?'

'Then I'd come back and live off the interest.'

'But what would you do?'

'Do? Nowt much. Bit of this, bit of that. Might even go and live in Spain or the south of France. Or maybe one of those tax havens like Bermuda.'

'You'd leave your job then?'

Hatchley looked at Banks as if he was insane. 'Leave my job? Course I'd leave my job. Wouldn't anyone?'

'I suppose so.' But Banks wasn't sure what he would do himself. A holiday, yes. But afterwards? To him, Steadman had made an admirable choice; he had extricated himself from the pedestrian and stultifying elements of his work and turned to concentrate on its essence. Perhaps I'd set myself up like Sherlock Holmes – a dalesman, himself – Banks thought, if I suddenly found myself with a private income. Take only the most interesting cases . . . wear a deerstalker.

'Come on,' he said, shaking off the fantasy. 'It'll be a cold day in hell before you and I have to worry about problems like that.'

When Banks got back to his office, he found Emma Steadman waiting for him. She had just been to identify her husband's body and was still distraught. There was little expression in her pale face, but the owlish eyes magnified by the lenses of her spectacles showed traces of recent tears. She sat upright on the hard chair, her hands clasped together on her lap.

'I won't keep you long,' Banks said as he took his seat

opposite her and started filling his pipe. 'First, I'd like to know if your husband had any enemies. Is there anyone you can think of who might have wanted to do him harm?'

'No,' she answered quickly. 'Not that I can think of. Harold wasn't the kind of man who made enemies.'

Banks decided not to point out the lack of reason in that statement; the bereaved relatives of murder victims frequently assumed that there could be no possible motive for the crime.

'Was there anybody he argued with, then? Even a slight disagreement? It could be important.'

She shook her head, frowning. 'No, I told you. He wasn't . . . Just a minute. There was something. I don't know how important it was though.'

'Tell me.'

'He had complained a bit about Teddy Hackett recently.'

'Hackett? When was this?'

'About a week ago. They were friends really, I know, but they had some kind of ongoing feud about land. Oh, I suppose it was just silly. Men often are, you know. Just like little boys. Anyway, I'm afraid I don't know all the details. You'll have to ask Mr Hackett.'

'Do you have any idea what it was about?'

Mrs Steadman frowned again, this time in concentration. 'I think it might have been something to do with Crabtree's Field. That's just a bit of overgrown land by the river. Harold was certain he'd located some Roman ruins there – he had some coins and bits of pottery he said were evidence – but Teddy Hackett was trying to buy the land.'

'Why? What did he want with it?'

'Knowing Hackett, it would be some vulgar project for

making money. I don't know exactly what he had in mind – a discotheque perhaps, or a fairground, video arcade, supermarket . . .'

'Let me get this clear.' Banks said, leaning forward. 'What you're saying is that Hackett wanted some land for development and your husband was trying to get it preserved as a historic site? Is that right?'

'Yes. It wasn't the first time, either. Last year, Harold wanted to start a small local museum in a shopfront on High Street, but Hackett bought the place up quickly and turned it into a gift shop. They argued about that, too. Harold was too trusting, too . . . nice. He wasn't aggressive enough.'

'There's no one else you can think of? What about Dr Barnes? Did your husband ever say anything about him?'

'Like what?'

'Anything.'

'No.'

'Jack Barker?'

'No. He thought Jack Barker was a bit of a cynic, a bit too flippant, but that's all.'

'What about visitors to the house? Did you have many?'

'Just friends we entertained.'

'Who?'

'Locals, mostly. We seem to have lost touch with the crowd from Leeds. Barker, Penny Cartwright, Hackett and Dr Barnes occasionally. Sometimes Michael Ramsden came over from York. Some of the teachers and kids from Eastvale Comprehensive – Harold gave guest lectures and took classes on field trips. That's all I can think of.'

'There'll be a lot of money,' Banks said casually.

'Pardon?'

'A lot of money. Your husband's. You'll inherit, I should imagine.'

'Yes, I suppose so,' she said. 'I hadn't really thought . . . I don't know if Harold made a will.'

'What will you do with it all?'

Mrs Steadman looked startled behind her glasses, and more than a little disapproving. 'I've no idea. As I said, I haven't really given the matter much thought.'

'What about your relationship with your husband? Were you on good terms? Was the marriage stable?'

Mrs Steadman froze. 'What?'

'I have to ask.'

'But I don't have to answer.'

'That's true.'

'I don't think I like what you're insinuating, Chief Inspector,' she went on. 'I think it's a very impertinent question. Especially at a time like this.'

'I'm not insinuating anything, Mrs Steadman. Just doing my job, that's all.' Banks held her cold gaze and remained silent.

'If that's all, then . . .' She stood up.

Banks followed her to the door and shut it quietly behind her before breathing a sigh of relief.

FOUR

After shocking the old ladies in the post office, Jack Barker set off down Helmthorpe High Street. It was only about ten thirty, but already clusters of tourists sauntered along the pavements, cardigans draped over their shoulders to keep off the morning chill. They would stop now and then, holding on to impatient children, to glance at displays of local craftware in shop windows. Crow Scar loomed to the north, and the shadow of an occasional wispy cloud drifted across its limestone face.

Barker hesitated for a moment outside the tiny second-hand bookshop run by Mr Thadtwistle – at ninety-eight the village's oldest inhabitant – then hurried on and turned into the narrow street of cottages opposite the church. At number sixteen he paused and knocked. Nothing happened. He knocked again. Then he heard stirrings inside and smoothed back his hair as he waited. The door opened a few inches.

'Oh, it's you,' Penny Cartwright said, squinting at him closely.

'My God, you look awful,' said Barker. 'Old man not around, is he?'

Penny began to shake her head but immediately thought better of it.

'Can I come in?'

Penny stood aside and let him enter. 'If you'll make me a strong cup of coffee.'

'It's a deal. And I didn't mean what I said earlier. You look as lovely and fresh as a white rose in the morning dew.'

Penny pulled a face and flopped down on the couch. Her long jet-coloured hair was uncombed and the whites around her blue eyes looked greyish and bloodshot. She had dark puffy bags under her eyes, and her lips were cracked and dry. She held a bottle-green kimono-style dressing gown closed at her throat. A red dragon reared and breathed fire on the back.

Barker busied himself in the small untidy kitchen and soon came out carrying two steaming mugs of coffee. He sat in the battered armchair at right angles to Penny. As she reached forward to pick up her mug from the low table, he could see her lightly freckled cleavage. The folds of her silky gown also revealed a long delightful curve of thigh as she crossed her legs. She seemed entirely oblivious to the way she was making Jack Barker's pulse race.

'I suppose you've heard about Harry,' he began, lighting a cigarette.

Penny reached out for one too. 'Yes.' She nodded, blowing out a lungful of smoke and coughing. 'I've heard. These things'll ruin my voice.' She glared at the cigarette.

'Have the police been to see you yet?'

'Why should they?'

'That chief inspector – Banks his name is – he was at the Bridge last night,' Barker explained. 'He talked to us for quite a bit. Anyway, he saw you – at least he saw me glancing over at you and asked who you were.'

'And you told him?'

'Yes.'

'You told him I was a friend of Harry's?'

'Had to. He'd have found out sooner or later, wouldn't he? Then he'd have been suspicious about why I didn't tell him in the first place.'

'So what? You've got nothing to hide, have you?'

Barker shrugged.

'Anyway,' Penny went on, 'you know how I feel about the police.'

'He's not a bad sort. Quite friendly, really. But sharp as a knife. Doesn't miss a trick. He's the kind who'll spend a pleasant evening buying you drinks, then ask you hard questions when you're sozzled.'

'Sounds awful.' Penny pulled a face and ground out her half-smoked cigarette in the ashtray. 'Still, they're all much the same.'

'What will you tell him?'

She looked at him and frowned. 'What is there to tell?'

'The old man?'

She shook her head.

'He's sharp,' Barker repeated.

Penny smiled. 'Well, then, he'll be able to find out all he wants to know, won't he?'

Barker leaned forward and took her hand. 'Penny . . .'

She shook him off gently. 'No, Jack, don't. Not now.'

Barker slumped back in his chair.

'Oh come on, Jack,' Penny chided him. 'Don't behave like a sulky boy.'

'I'm sorry.'

Penny gathered her gown around her and stood up. 'Think nothing of it. You'd better go, though; I'm a bit unsteady on my pins today.'

Barker got to his feet. 'Are you singing this week?'

'Friday. If my voice holds out. You'll be there?'

'Wouldn't miss it for the world, love,' Barker answered. Then he left.

FIVE

The police station didn't look at all like Sally expected. For one thing, the old Tudor-fronted building was modern inside, and the walls weren't papered with 'wanted' posters. Instead, it was more like one of those pleasant open-plan offices with potted plants all over the place and nothing but screens separating the desks behind the reception area. It smelled of furniture polish and pine-scented air-freshener.

She told the polite young man at the front desk that she

wanted to see Chief Inspector Banks, the man in charge of the Helmthorpe murder. No, she didn't want to tell the young man about it, she wanted the chief inspector. She had important information. Yes, she would wait.

Finally, her persistence paid off and she was shown upstairs to a network of corridors and office doors with things like 'Interview Room' stencilled on them. There she was given a seat and asked if she would mind waiting a few moments. No. She folded her hands in her lap and stared ahead at a door marked, disappointingly, 'Stationery Supplies'.

The minutes dragged on. She wished she had brought a copy of *Vogue* to flip through like at the dentist's. Suddenly sounds of scuffling and cursing came from the stairwell and three men fell into the corridor only feet from where she was sitting. Two of them were obviously police, and they were struggling with a handcuffed third who wriggled like an eel. Finally, they dragged him to his feet again and hauled him off down the hall. He was squirming and swearing, and at one point he managed to twist free and run back down the hall towards her. Sally was terrified. At least half of her was. The other half was thinking how exciting, how much like *Hill Street Blues* it was. The policemen caught him again before he got too close and hustled him into a room. Sally's heart beat fast. She wanted to go home, but the chief inspector came out of his office and ushered her inside.

'I'm sorry about that,' he apologized. 'It doesn't happen often.'

'Who is he?' Sally asked, wide-eyed and pale.

'A burglar. We think he broke into Merriweather's Stereo Emporium last week.'

Sally found herself sitting before a flimsy metal desk

littered with paper clips, pens and important-looking folders. The air was thick with pipe smoke, which reminded her of her father. She coughed, and Banks, taking the hint, went to open the window. Fragments of conversation drifted up on the warm air from Market Street.

Banks asked Sally what she wanted.

'It's private,' she whispered, looking over her shoulder and leaning forward. She was unsettled by what she had just witnessed and found it much harder to get started than she had imagined. 'I mean,' she went on, 'I want to tell you something but you have to promise not to tell anyone else.'

'Anyone?' The smile disappeared from his lips but still lingered in his lively brown eyes. He reached for his pipe and sat down.

'Well,' Sally said, turning up her nose at the smoke like she always did at home, 'I suppose it's up to you, isn't it? I'll just tell you what I know, shall I?'

Banks nodded.

'It was last Saturday night. I was up below Crow Scar in that little shepherd's shelter – you know, the one that's almost collapsed.' Banks knew it. The derelict hut had been searched after the discovery of Steadman's body. 'Well, I heard a car. It stopped for about ten or fifteen minutes, then drove off.'

'Did you see it?'

'No. I only heard it. I thought it was maybe a courting couple or something at first. But they'd stay longer than that, wouldn't they?'

Banks smiled. It was clear from the girl's desire for secrecy and her knowledge of the temporal requirements of courting exactly what she had been doing in the shepherd's shelter.

'Which direction did the car come from?' he asked.

'The village, I think. At least, it came from the west. I suppose it could have come from over the dale, up north, but there's nothing much on that road for miles except moorland.'

'Where did it go?'

'Up along the road. I didn't hear it turn round and come back.'

'The road that leads to Sattersdale, right?'

'Yes, but there's plenty of other little roads that cross it. You could get almost anywhere from it.'

'What time was this?'

'It was twelve fourteen when it stopped.'

'Twelve fourteen? Not just after twelve, or nearly quarter past twelve? Most people aren't so accurate.'

'It was a digi—' Sally stopped in her tracks. Banks was looking down at her wrist, on which she wore a small black watch with a pink plastic strap. It wasn't digital.

'Better tell the truth,' he said. 'And don't worry, your parents needn't know.'

'I wasn't doing anything wrong,' Sally blurted out, then she blushed and calmed down. 'But thank you. I don't think they'd understand. Yes, I was with somebody. My boyfriend. We were just talking.' This didn't sound convincing, but Banks didn't regard it as any of his business. 'And then this car came,' Sally continued. 'We thought it was getting late anyway, so Kev, my boyfriend, looked at his watch – it's a digital one with a light in it – and it said twelve fourteen. I knew I should have been home hours ago, but I thought I might as well be hung for a sheep as a lamb. We just stayed where we were not paying it much mind really, then when we heard it go Kevin looked at his watch again and it said twelve twenty-nine. I remember because it was funny. Kevin said they hadn't much time to . . .'

Sally stopped and reddened. It had been all too easy, once she got going, to forget who she was talking to. Now, she realized, she had not only told this strange man with the pipe her boyfriend's name but had also given him the impression that she knew all about what men and women did together at night in cars on lonely hillsides.

But Banks didn't pursue her romantic activities. He was far more concerned about the accuracy of the infor-mation he was getting than about her love life. Besides, she looked at least nineteen – old enough to take care of herself, whatever her parents thought.

'I imagine Kevin, your boyfriend, could confirm these times?' he asked.

'Well . . . if he had to,' she answered hesitantly. 'I mean, I told him I wouldn't mention his name. We don't want any trouble. My mum and dad wouldn't like it, see. I told them we were at his house watching telly. They'd tell his mum and dad where we really were and they'd stop us seeing each other.'

'How old are you, Sally?'

'Sixteen,' she answered proudly.

'What do you want to do with your life?'

'I want to be an actress. At least, I want to be involved in films and theatre, that kind of thing. I've applied to the Marion Boyars Academy of Theatre Arts.'

'I'm impressed,' Banks told her. 'I hope you get accepted.' He noticed that she was already a dab hand at make-up. He had thought she was nineteen. Most girls of her age never seemed to know when enough was enough, but Sally obviously did. Her clothes sense was good too. She was dressed in white knee-socks and a deep-blue skirt, gathered at the waist, that came to just above her dimpled knees. On top she wore a white cotton blouse and a red ribbon in her gold-blonde hair. She was a beautiful girl, and Banks wouldn't have been at all surprised to see her on stage or on television.

'Is it true you're from London?' Sally asked.

'Yes.'

'Did Scotland Yard send you?'

'No. I moved here.'

'But why on earth would you want to come up here?'

Banks shrugged. 'I can think of plenty of reasons. Fresh air, beautiful countryside. And I had hoped for an easier job.'

'But London,' Sally went on excitedly. 'That's where it all happens. I went there once on a day trip with the school. It was fabulous.' Her wide eyes narrowed and she looked at him suspiciously. 'I can't understand why anyone would want to leave it for this godforsaken dump.'

Banks noted that in about twenty seconds Sally's opinion had undergone a radical reversal. At first she had been coquettish, flirtatious, but now she seemed disdainful, almost sorry for him, and much more brusque and businesslike in her manner. Again, he could hardly keep from smiling.

'Did you know Harold Steadman?'

'Is that who . . . the man?'

'Yes. Did you know him?'

'Yes, a bit. He often came to the school to give lectures on local history or geology. Boring stuff mostly about old ruins. And he took us on field trips sometimes to Fortford, or even as far as Malham or Keld.'

'So the pupils knew him quite well?'

'As well as you can know a teacher.' Sally thought for

a moment. 'But he wasn't really like a teacher. I mean, I know it was boring and all that, but he liked it. He was enthusiastic. And he even took us to his home for hot dogs and pop after some of the trips.'

'Us?'

'Yes, the pupils who lived in Helmthorpe or Gratly. There were about seven of us usually. His wife made us all some food and we just sat and talked about where we'd been and what we'd found. He was a very nice man.'

'What about his wife, did you know her?'

'Not really. She didn't stick around with us. She always had something else to do. I think she was just shy. But Mr Steadman wasn't. He'd talk to anybody.'

'Was that the only time you saw him? At school, on trips?'

Sally's eyes narrowed again. 'Well, apart from in the street or in shops, yes. Look, if you mean was he a dirty old man, the answer's no.'

'That's not what I meant,' Banks said. But he was glad that she had reacted as if it was.

He made her go through the story again while he took down all the particulars. She gave the information unwillingly this time, as if all she wanted was to get out of the place. When she finally left, Banks slouched back in his chair and grinned to think that all his appeal, all his glamour, had been lost in his move from London to Eastvale. Outside in the market square the clock chimed four.

5

ONE

On Tuesday morning, having sent Sergeant Hatchley to Helmthorpe to check on Weaver's progress, search Harold Steadman's study and bring in Teddy Hackett for questioning, Banks set off for York to visit Michael Ramsden again.

He drove into the ancient Roman city at about eleven o'clock through suburbs of red-brick boxes. After getting lost in the one-way system for half an hour, he found a parking space by the River Ouse and crossed the bridge to Fisher & Faulkner Ltd, a squat ugly brick building by the waterside. The pavements were busy with tourists and businessmen, and the huge Minster seemed to dominate the city; its light stone glowed in the morning sun.

A smart male receptionist pointed him in the right direction, and on the third floor one of Ramsden's assistants called through to the boss.

Ramsden's office looked out over the river, down which a small tour boat was wending its way. The top deck was bright with people in summer holiday clothes, and camera lenses flashed in the sun. The boat left a long V of ripples, which rocked the rowing boats in its wake.

The office itself was small and cluttered; beside the desk and filing cabinets stood untidy piles of manuscripts, some stacked on the floor, and two bookcases displaying a set of Fisher & Faulkner's titles. Even in a dark business suit, Ramsden still looked as if his clothes were too big for him; he had the distracted air of a professor of nuclear physics about to explain atomic fission to a layman while simultaneously working out complex formulae in his mind. He brushed back an invisible forelock and asked Banks to sit down.

'You were a close friend of Harold Steadman's,' Banks began. 'Could you tell me a little about him? His background, how you met, that kind of thing.'

Ramsden leaned back in his swivel chair and crossed his long legs. 'You know,' he said, looking sideways towards the window, 'I was always just a little bit in awe of Harry. Not just because he was nearly fifteen years my senior – that never really mattered – but because I don't think we ever really got over the student–professor relationship. When we met, he was a lecturer at Leeds and I was just about to begin my studies in London, so we weren't even at the same university. We weren't in the same field, either. But these ideas get fixed in one's mind nonetheless. I was eighteen and Harry was nearly thirty-three. He was a very intelligent, very dedicated man – an exact role model for someone like me at that time.

'Anyway, although I was, as I said, just about to go to university in London, I always came home at Christmas and in summer. I'd help around the house, do odd jobs, make bacon and eggs for the guests. And I loved being at home, being in the Yorkshire countryside. It was best when Harry and Emma came to stay for their annual holidays. I'd walk for hours, sometimes alone, sometimes with Harold or Penny.'

'Penny?' Banks cut in. 'Would that be Penny Cartwright?'

'Yes, that's right. We were very close until I went off to London.'

'Go on.'

'We used to go out together, in a casual sort of way. It was all very innocent. She was sixteen and we'd known each other nearly all our lives. She'd even stayed with us for a while after her mother died.'

'How old was she then?'

'Oh, about ten or eleven. It was tragic, really. Mrs Cartwright drowned in a spring flood. Terrible. Penny's father had a nervous breakdown, so she stayed with us while he recovered. It seemed only natural. Later, when . . . well, you know, we were a bit older . . . Anyway, Harold was very knowledgeable and enthusiastic about the area. He took to Swainsdale immediately, and pretty soon he was teaching me more than I'd learned living there all my life. He was like that. I was impressed, of course, but as I was about to study English at university I was insufferably literary – always quoting Wordsworth and the like. I suppose you know he bought the house when my mother couldn't afford to keep it on?'

Banks nodded.

'Yes,' Ramsden went on, 'they came every year, Harry and Emma, and when father died they were in a position to help us out a great deal. It was good for Harry, too. His work at the university was too abstract, too theoretical. He published a book called *The Principles of Industrial Archaeology*, but what he really wanted was the opportunity to put those principles into practice. University life didn't give him time enough to do that. He fully intended to teach again, you know. But first he wanted to do some real pioneering work. When he inherited the money, all that became possible.

'When I graduated, I went to work for Fisher and Faulkner in London first. Then they opened the northern branch and offered me this job. I missed the north and I'd always hoped to be able to make a living up here some day. We published Harold's second book and he and I developed a good working relationship. The firm specializes in academic books, as you can see.' He pointed towards the crowded bookshelves, and most of the titles Banks could make out had *principles* or *a study of* in them. 'We do mostly literary criticism and local history,' Ramsden went on. 'Next Harry edited a book of local essays, and since that we've been working on an exhaustive industrial history of the dale from pre-Roman times to the present. Harry published occasional essays in scholarly journals, but this was to be his major work. Everybody was looking forward to it tremendously.'

'What exactly is industrial archaeology?' Banks asked. 'I've heard the term quite often lately, but I've only got a vague idea what it means.'

'Your vague idea is probably as clear as anyone else's,' Ramsden replied. 'As yet, it's still an embryonic discipline. Basically, the term was first used to describe the study of the machinery and methods of the Industrial Revolution, but it's been expanded a great deal to include other periods – Roman lead mines, for example. I suppose you could say it's the study of industrial artefacts and processes, but then you could argue for a month about how to define "industrial". To complicate matters even further, it's very hard to draw the line between the subject as a hobby and as an academic discipline. For instance, if someone happens to be interested in the history of steam trains, he can still make a contribution to the field, even though he actually works nine to five in a bank most days.'

'I see,' Banks said. 'So it's a kind of hybrid area, an open field?'

'That's about it. Nobody's yet come up with a final definition, which is partly why it's so exciting.'

'You don't think Mr Steadman's death could be in any way linked to his work, do you?'

Ramsden shook his head slowly. 'I can't see it, no. Of course, there are feuds and races just like in any other discipline, but I can't see any of it going that far.'

'Did he have rivals?'

'Professionally, yes. The universities are full of them.'

'Could he have uncovered something that someone might wish to keep quiet?'

Ramsden thought for a moment, his sharp chin resting in his bony hand. 'You mean the unsavoury past of a prominent family, that kind of thing?'

'Anything.'

'It's an interesting theory. I can't say for certain one way or the other. If he had discovered something, he didn't tell me. It's possible, I suppose. But we're a long way from the Industrial Revolution. You'd have to dig back a very long way if you want to find a descendant of someone who made his fortune by exploiting child labour, for example, which wasn't entirely uncommon back then. I don't think there are many direct descendants of the Romans around who still have anything to hide.'

Banks smiled. 'Probably not. What about enemies, academic or otherwise?'

'Harry? Good Lord, I shouldn't think so. He wasn't the kind to make enemies.'

Again, Banks refrained from stating the obvious. 'Do you know anything about this business with Teddy Hackett?' he asked.

Ramsden glanced sharply at him. 'You don't miss much, do you?' he said. 'Yes, I know about it, for what it's worth. There's a field in Helmthorpe over the river near the cricket pitch – it's called Crabtree's Field because it used to belong to a farmer named Crabtree. He's long dead now, though. There's a small bridge which connects the field with the campsite on the other side, and Hackett wants to provide more "facilities" for the campers – by which he no doubt means junk food and video games. You must have noticed the increasing Americanization of the English countryside, Chief Inspector. McDonald's seems to be springing up everywhere now, even in places as small as Helmthorpe. Harold had good reason to suppose – and I've heard his evidence – that there was once a Roman camp there. It could be a very important discovery. He was trying to persuade the local authorities to protect it for excavations. Naturally, that caused a bit of friction between Harry and Teddy Hackett. But they remained friends. I don't think it was a serious quarrel.'

'Not serious enough to lead to murder?'

'Not in my opinion, no.' Ramsden turned sideways again and looked out over the river at the shining Minster towers. 'They were quite close friends, though God knows why, seeing as their views on just about everything were always diametrically opposed. Harry enjoyed a good argument for its own sake – that was the academic in him – and Hackett is at least a fairly intelligent, if not a very tasteful, adversary. I'm afraid you'll have to ask Harry's friends in the village how serious the quarrel was. I didn't get over there often enough. I suppose you've met the good doctor and the resident scribbler?'

Banks nodded. 'Do you know them?'

'A little. Not very well, though. As I said, I don't get to

Helmthorpe as often as I'd like. Doc Barnes has been around as long as I can remember, of course. And I've had one or two beery evenings in the Bridge. Naturally there was quite a bit of excitement when Jack Barker moved to Gratly three or four years back, but it soon settled down when he proved to be much like everyone else.'

'Where did he come from? What made him choose Gratly?'

'Haven't a clue, I'm afraid. I have a vague notion he's from somewhere in Cheshire, but I couldn't swear to it. You'll have to ask him.'

'Did he know Mr Steadman before he moved to Gratly?'

'Not as far as I know. Harry never mentioned him.'

'Does your company publish his books?'

'Lord, no.' Ramsden made curious snuffling noises through his nose, and Banks took the sound for laughter. 'I told you what we specialize in. I believe Barker writes paperback originals.'

'Did Mr Steadman ever say anything about Dr Barnes or Jack Barker?'

'He said a number of things, yes. What do you have in mind?'

'Anything odd. Did he ever tell you anything about them that you thought they might not want to be common knowledge?'

'Are you trying to suggest that Harry was a black-mailer?'

'Not at all. But if he did know something, they weren't to know what he'd do with the knowledge, were they? You say he was a decent upright man – fair enough. If he knew of anything illegal or immoral anyone was involved in, what do you think he would have done?'

'I see what you mean.' Ramsden tapped a yellow pencil on his bottom teeth. 'He'd have done the right thing, of course. Gone to the authorities. But I still can't help you. He never indicated to me that either Barker or Barnes had ever been involved in anything untoward.'

'What about Penny Cartwright?'

'What about her? Harry certainly never spoke ill of Penny.'

'What about your relationship with her?'

Ramsden paused. 'I'm not sure it's any of your business.'

'Up to you,' Banks said.

'It was all a long time ago. There was certainly nothing odd about it. I don't see how knowing can possibly help you.'

Banks kept silent.

'Oh, what the hell, then,' Ramsden said. 'Why not? I told you – we were good friends, then we drifted apart. We were both in London at roughly the same time, but we moved in very different circles. She was a singer, so she hung around with musicians. She was always a bit of a rebel, too. You know, had to be different, embraced all the causes. She made a couple of records and even toured in Europe and America, I believe. It was traditional folk music they played – at first, anyway – but they jazzed it up with electronic instruments. Then she got tired of life in the fast lane and came home. Her father forgave her and she settled into her cottage. Apart from the old man getting a bit overprotective now and again, she more or less gets on with her own life. Still sings a bit around the local pubs, too.'

'What's her father like?'

'The major? To do him justice, he never really

recovered from his wife's death. He's a strange old bird. Lives right on High Street with his dog. Has a flat over old Thadtwistle's bookshop. There were rumours, you know, when Penny left. Look, I'm not sure I should be telling you this. It's just silly local gossip.'

'I shouldn't worry about that, Mr Ramsden. I know a hawk from a handsaw.'

Ramsden swallowed. His Adam's apple bobbed up and down. 'People said they were a bit too close, father and daughter, living together after the mother died. They say the old man wanted her to take her mother's place in his bed and that's why she took off so young. Do you know what I'm saying? It's not entirely uncommon around these parts.'

Banks nodded. 'Do you believe it?'

'Not for a moment. You know how vindictive gossip can be.'

'But what did anyone have against the Cartwrights?'

Ramsden picked up his pencil again and started rolling it between his fingers. 'People thought they were a bit stuck-up, that's all. The major's always been stand-offish, and his wife wasn't from around these parts. People in the dale used to be a lot more parochial than they are now so many outsiders have moved in. Even now most of them think of Penny as some kind of scarlet woman.'

'You were close to her. Did she say anything?'

'No, she didn't. And I think she would have done if anything unusual had been going on.'

'Was she friendly with Mr Steadman?'

'Yes, they were very good friends. Penny knows a lot about folk traditions through her music, you see, and Harold was always willing to learn. She even taught him some guitar. Also, she was very disorientated for a while after she came back from her brush with fame and fortune, and I think Harry's support meant a lot. He thought the world of her. They both loved going for long walks, watching birds and wild flowers, talking about the past.'

There was plenty to follow up in that, Banks thought. But he had no more questions to ask. He already had more than enough information to digest and analyze.

He thanked Ramsden, said goodbye and walked back over the sluggish Ouse to his car.

He stopped at the first likely-looking village inn he saw and enjoyed a late, leisurely pub lunch of shepherd's pie and a refreshing pint of shandy made from Sam Smith's Old Brewery bitter. As he drove back to Eastvale listening to Purcell's airs, he began to go over the list of involved characters in his mind, trying to imagine motives and opportunities.

First there was Teddy Hackett. That field business might only be the tip of the iceberg, and if Steadman had been blocking similar projects, Hackett would have a good enough reason for wanting rid of him.

Then there was Jack Barker. No obvious motive there but no alibi either, as Barker himself had admitted on Sunday evening. His glance at Penny Cartwright in the Bridge had spoken volumes, and if there was more to her relationship with Steadman than Ramsden had told him, then jealousy may have provided a very strong motive.

As for Dr Barnes, his alibi hadn't been nearly as solid as he had seemed to think, and though there was no motive apparent yet, Banks wasn't willing to consider him out of the running.

It seemed pointless to include Emma Steadman; for one thing she was left-handed, and for another she had been watching television with Mrs Stanton all evening. But there was the money. She did have a great deal to gain from her husband's death, especially if the two weren't seeing eye to eye anymore. She could, possibly, have hired someone. It was unlikely, but he couldn't rule it out.

Ramsden seemed to have neither the motive nor the opportunity. In a way, Steadman was his bread and butter, an important client as well as an old friend. Perhaps he did envy Steadman, but that was no reason to kill him. Banks couldn't quite work Ramsden out. There was the business of the novel, for a start. He sensed that perhaps great things had been expected of Ramsden artistically but had never really materialized. Why? Indolence? Lack of talent? He seemed to have a rather precious personality, and Banks guessed that he had been pampered as a child, most likely by his mother, and led to believe that he was special and gifted. Now he was in his twenties and the talent hadn't really made itself manifest.

Penny Cartwright remained a grey area. She might have had both motive and means, but they had yet to be discovered. Banks wanted very much to talk to her, and he decided to go to Helmthorpe that evening. He would have to see her father, too, at some point.

One problem was that there was so much time to account for. If Steadman had left the Bridge at about a quarter to nine and his body had been dumped at twelve fourteen, where had he been and what had he been doing during those three and a half hours? Surely someone must have seen him?

Slowly, Banks's thoughts faded as the countertenor sang a mournful 'Retir'd from any Mortal's Sight' and the poplars and privet hedges that lined the road gave way to the first houses in Eastvale.

TWO

'So you told him everything then?'

'I didn't mean to, Kevin, honest – not your name and all. But it just slipped out.'

Kevin leered and Sally's expression darkened. She elbowed him in the ribs. 'You've got a filthy mind, you have. It was the time that did it. Twelve fourteen. He could see I hadn't got a digital watch. Why do you have to wear that silly thing anyway?'

Kevin looked down at his watch as if examining it for faults. 'I don't know,' he said.

'It beeps every hour,' Sally went on, her voice soften-ing. 'No matter what you're doing.'

Kevin leaned forward and kissed her. She squirmed beneath him and he slipped his hand under her blouse to hold her soft warm breast. Her body was pressed down hard against the ground, and the moist sickly smell of grass filled the air. Insects buzzed and whined all around. Finally, she broke away and gasped for breath. Kevin lay back with his hands behind his head and stared at the deep-blue sky.

'What did you think of him, then, this hotshot from London?' he asked.

Sally snorted. 'Some hotshot. Fancy leaving London to come up here. The bloke must be barmy.'

Kevin turned to face her, leaning on one elbow and sticking a long stalk of grass between his teeth. 'What did he say?'

'Didn't seem very interested, really. He just asked me a lot of daft questions. I don't know why I bothered. I won't be so fast to go out of my way and help the police next time, that's for sure.'

'What do you mean, "next time"?'

'I mean if I find out anything else.'

'Why should that happen? It was only by chance we heard the car. We didn't even know what it was.'

'But we do now. Aren't you curious? Don't you want to know who did it?'

Kevin shrugged. 'I wouldn't want to get involved. Leave all that to the police. That's what they get paid for.'

'Well, isn't that a typical small-minded attitude?' Sally said scornfully.

'It's a sensible one, though.'

'So? It's no fun being sensible all the time.'

'What are you getting at?'

'Nothing. I just might do a bit of snooping on my own, that's all. I've lived here all my life. I ought to know what's going on in the village.'

'What can you do that the police can't?'

'I don't know yet, but I bet I can do better than them. Wouldn't it be exciting if I solved the case for them?'

'Don't be an idiot, Sally. We've been through this before. You know what I think. It's dangerous.'

'How?'

'What if the killer knew what you were doing? What if he thought you might be getting too close?'

Sally shivered. 'I'll be careful, don't worry. Besides, you never get anywhere if you're frightened of a bit of danger.'

Kevin gave up. Sally smoothed her skirt and lay on her back again. They were high on the southern slope of the dale, overlooking cross-shaped Gratly and Helmthorpe's chequerboard pattern of slate roofs. Sally plucked a buttercup and held it to her chin. Kevin took the flower from her hand and trailed it over her throat and collarbone. She shuddered. He kissed her again and put his other hand up her skirt to caress the tender flesh of her thighs just below her panties.

Suddenly Sally heard a sound: a snapping twig or a thwacking branch. She sat up quickly, leaving Kevin with his face in the grass.

'Someone's coming,' she whispered.

A few moments later, a figure appeared from the small copse by the beck side. Sally put her hand over her eyes to shield them from the sun and saw who it was.

'Hello, Miss Cartwright,' she called out.

Penny walked towards them, knelt on the grass and tossed back her hair. 'Hello. It's a beautiful day, isn't it?'

'Yes,' answered Sally. 'We're just having a breather. We've been walking most of the afternoon.'

'I used to walk around these parts a lot, too, when I was your age,' Penny said quietly, almost to herself. 'It seems like centuries ago now, but it was only ten years. You'll be surprised how quickly time passes. Enjoy it while you can.'

Sally didn't know what to say; she felt embarrassed. After an uneasy silence, she said, 'I'm sorry about your friend, Mr Steadman, really I am. He was a nice man.'

Penny seemed to return from a great distance to focus on her. At first Sally thought the commiseration had gone unheard, but Penny smiled warmly and said, 'Thank you. Yes, he was.' Then she got to her feet and brushed the scraps of grass from her long skirt. 'I must be off, anyway. Mustn't bore you young people with my memories.'

In silence, Sally and Kevin watched her walk up the hillside with a strong, determined stride. She looked a lonely, wild figure, Sally thought, like Catherine in *Wuthering Heights*: a woman of the moors, spirit of the place. Then she felt Kevin's palm against her warm thigh again.

THREE

Further up the hillside, Penny paused as she stood on a stile and looked back on the dale she loved spread out below her. There was the church by her cottage. High Street and the whitewashed frontage of the Dog and Gun. On the other side of the river, past the cricket pitch and Crabtree's Field, the commons sloped up, rougher and rougher, to Crow Scar, which that day was almost too bright to look at.

But she couldn't gaze long without thinking of Harry, for he was the one who had shown her Swainsdale's secrets, given it depth and life beyond its superficial beauties. And now she fancied she could see the collapsed section of Tavistock's wall. The stones that had been used to cover Harry's body seemed darker than the rest.

Looking back the way she had come, Penny saw the two young lovers fuse in a tight embrace on the grass. She smiled sadly. When she'd first approached them, she had noticed how flustered and embarrassed they had looked.

Again she thought of Harry. Suddenly, the memory of a picnic they'd had ten years ago came into her mind. It must have been on the exact spot where Sally and Kevin were lying. She remembered the view of the village clearly, and they had been near a small copse, as Emma had sat in the shade, knitting. The more she concentrated on it, the more details came back. It was just around the time when she and Michael had started drifting apart. He had been reading Shelley's poetry. Penny could even remember the scuffed brown leather of the book's cover; it was a second-hand edition she'd bought him for his birthday. She and Harry had spread the red checked cloth on the grass and started to unload the hamper. Somehow, their hands had touched by accident. Penny remembered blushing, and Harry had busied himself looking for the corkscrew. It was for the Chablis. Yes, they had drunk Chablis, a good vintage, that day, and now, ten years later, she felt the crisp flinty taste of the cool wine on her tongue again.

The picture faded as quickly as it had come. How innocent it had all been, how bloody innocent! Wiping the tears from her eyes with the back of her hand, she jumped down from the stile and strode sharply on.

FOUR

Hackett had already been waiting an hour when Banks got back from York, and he was not at all amused.

'Look here,' he protested, as Banks led him upstairs to the office. 'You can't do this to me. You can't just drag me in like this without an explanation. I've got a business to run. I told you everything last night.'

'You told me nothing last night.' Banks took off his jacket and hung it on the back of the door. 'Sit down,' he said. 'Make yourself at home.'

The room was stuffy, so Banks reopened the window and the smells of Market Street wafted up: exhaust fumes, fresh-baked bread, something sweet and sickly from the chocolate shop. Hackett sat rigidly in his chair and lapsed into a tense affronted silence.

'There's nothing to get excited about,' Banks told him,

taking out his pipe and fiddling with it over the waste-paper basket.

'Then why did your sergeant kidnap me like that and rush me over here, eh? I want my lawyer.'

'Oh, do relax, Mr Hackett! There's really no need for melodrama. You've been watching far too many American films on television. I've not brought you here to lay charges or anything like that. I'm sorry if Sergeant Hatchley seemed a little brusque – it's just his manner. I've got a few questions to ask you, that's all.' He gave Hackett a sharp glance. 'Just one or two little things we'd like to get cleared up.'

'Why pick on me? What about Jack, or the doc?'

'Do you know of any reason they might have had for killing Mr Steadman?'

'Well, no, I didn't mean to imply that. It's just that . . .'

'Did he ever say anything about them to you, give you any reason to think one of them might want him out of the way?'

'No. That's not what I meant, anyway. I'm not trying to put the blame on someone else. I just want to know why you picked on me to haul in like this.'

'Crabtree's Field.' Banks picked up his pipe and reached for the matches.

Hackett sighed. 'So that's it. Someone's been telling tales. I should have known you'd have found out before long.'

Banks lit his pipe and gazed at the ceiling. Some old juices trickled down the stem and caught in his throat; he coughed and pulled a face.

Hackett looked at him angrily. 'You don't give a damn, do you? Anyway, it's nobody's bloody business—'

'It's police business now, Mr Hackett,' Banks interrupted. He put his pipe aside and drained the cold coffee left in his mug. 'If it's all the same to you, the sooner we get it cleared up, the better.'

Hackett shuffled in his chair and smoothed his droopy moustache. 'It was nothing,' he said. 'Just a minor disagreement over an acre or two of land, that's all.'

'Countries have been invaded for less,' Banks remarked, and went on to give Hackett the details as he had heard them.

'Yes,' Hackett agreed, 'that's more or less it. But I wouldn't kill anyone for that, let alone a close friend like Harry. Even if he did want to wrap up the whole bloody dale and give it to the National Trust, I liked the man. I respected his principles, even though they weren't the same as mine.'

'But you did argue about the field?' Banks persisted.

'We argued about it, yes. But it was half in fun. The others will tell you. Harry liked a good argument as well as the next man. It wasn't that important.'

'Money is always important, Mr Hackett. How much did you expect to make from the land if you got it?'

'That's impossible to say. I wouldn't stand to make anything for ages, of course. I'd be out of pocket, in fact. There's the purchase price, construction, publicity . . . It could have been years before I started showing a profit.'

'So you were only in it for the fun?'

'Not only that, no. I mean, I like business. It's a way of life that suits me. I like doing deals. I like building things up. But of course I wouldn't put out good money if I didn't think the eventual returns would be substantial.'

'Can we agree,' Banks asked, 'that you did hope at some point to make a considerable amount from your investment?'

'Hell, yes. Eventually.'

'And now?'

'What about now? I don't understand.'

'Oh, come on, Mr Hackett. Don't play the innocent. The pitch is clear now, isn't it? The field's yours.'

Hackett laughed and relaxed in his chair. 'That's just where you're wrong, I'm afraid. You see, I think Harry pulled it off. At least there's a freeze on the place right now. I suppose young Ramsden will carry on his master's work and wrap it up. A bloody Roman camp! I ask you! What's there but a few broken pots and stones? No wonder the bloody economy's in the state it's in. No room for initiative anymore.'

'Oh,' said Banks, feigning surprise, 'I thought our government wanted to encourage small businesses.'

Hackett glared at him; whether for the slight about his fiscal proportions or for picking up a throwaway comment, Banks wasn't quite sure. 'You know what I mean, Chief Inspector. We're hamstrung by these historical societies and tourist boards. They're all a load of bloody romantics as far as I can see. It's all a myth. The past wasn't like that; it wasn't neat and tidy like they all seem to think, for Christ's sake. Life was nasty, brutish and short, as the man said. Just because I never went to university, it doesn't make me an ignoramus, you know. I've read books, too. If you ask me, Harry walked around seeing the past through rose-coloured glasses. Penny Cartwright, too. In reality, life must have been bloody misery back then. Imagine them poor Roman sods freezing their balls off up north when they could have been lounging around in the sun on the seven hills drinking vino and rogering the local tarts. And as for the bloody Industrial Revolution, it was nothing but exploitation – hard, harsh work for most people. No,

Chief Inspector, Harry hadn't a bloody clue about the past, for all his degrees.'

'Maybe you should move somewhere else,' Banks suggested. 'I doubt they care much for local history in Wigan, for example, or Huddersfield.'

'You'd be surprised,' Hackett said. 'It's all over the bloody place. They call it civic pride. They're even flogging Bradford as the "gateway to Brontë country" now – and if they can get away with that they can do anything. Besides, I like it here. Don't think just because I'm a businessman I lack a finer appreciation of nature. I'm as much for the environment as the next man.'

'What were you doing on Saturday night?' Banks asked, renewing the attack on his pipe with a cleaner.

Hackett scratched his receding hairline. 'After I left the Bridge I went to a new club in Darlington. I drove up there, had a couple of drinks in a local, then went on to the club. I know the owner, like. We've done a bit of business together.'

'So you left the Bridge at what time?'

'About half nine.'

'And drove straight to Darlington?'

'Well, not exactly. I went home first to get changed.'

'What time did you leave for Darlington?'

'About ten to ten.'

'And arrived?'

'About half past, twenty to eleven.'

'And you went to the club when?'

'Half eleven, quarter to twelve.'

'What's it called?'

'The KitKat Klub. Only been open a few weeks. It's a sort of disco place, but not too loud. Caters for the more mature crowd.'

'I suppose you knew people there, people who can corroborate your story?'

'I talked to a few people, yes. And there's Andy Shaw, the owner.'

Banks took down the details, including the name of the pub, and noticed how anxious Hackett looked throughout the process.

'Anything else you can tell us, Mr Hackett?'

Hackett chewed on his lower lip and frowned. 'No, nothing.'

'Right then, off you go,' Banks said. He stood up and walked over to open the door.

As soon as Hackett was out of the building, Banks called Sergeant Hatchley in and asked if he'd found anything in his search of Steadman's study.

'Nowt much of interest, no,' Hatchley said. 'A few manuscripts, letters to historical preservation societies – they're on my desk if you want to look at them.'

'Later.'

'And he had one of those fancy computers – a word processor. I suppose he had to spend his brass on something. Remember how much wheeling and dealing it took us to get central admin to let us have one downstairs?'

Banks nodded.

'And now they send bloody Richmond off t' seaside to learn how to use the bugger.' Hatchley shook his head slowly and left the office.

FIVE

It was about six thirty, after what passed for rush hour in that part of the country, when Banks pulled into Helmthorpe's main car park. He had attended the brief inquest, given the press a snippet or two of information, and managed a quick dinner at home with Sandra and the kids.

Penny Cartwright was washing up the dinner dishes and enjoying the play of evening sunlight as it reflected from the shiny surfaces and skittered about the walls. When she heard a knock at the front door she quickly wiped her hands on her apron and went to answer it. She knew immediately that the dark-haired wiry man standing there was the policeman Barker had told her about. She hadn't expected him to be so good-looking, though, and immediately felt unattractive in her apron with her hair tied back in a long ponytail.

'You'd better come in,' she said. 'We wouldn't want to give the neighbours too much to talk about.' She pointed him to a worn armchair and slipped into the kitchen, where she quickly divested herself of the stained apron, untied her hair and brushed it swiftly so that it fell around her face and spilled over her shoulders.

If Banks was struck by the abrupt casual manner of his hostess, he was also struck by her beauty. She looked good in close-fitting jeans, and her striking hair framed a proud, high-cheekboned face without a trace of make-up. The combination of jet-black hair and sharp blue eyes added to the stunning effect.

Penny sat in a straight-backed chair by a writing table and asked Banks what she could do for him.

He began casually, trying to establish a friendly tone: 'Maybe nothing, Miss Cartwright. I'm just talking to Mr Steadman's friends, trying to get some idea of what he was like.'

'Do you really need to know?' Penny asked. 'I mean, do you care?'

'Perhaps not in the way that you do,' Banks admitted. 'After all, I didn't know him. But it might help me to find out who killed him. And I care about that. Obviously somebody did, but all I've heard so far is how wonderful he was – the kind of man who didn't have an enemy in the whole wide world.'

'What makes you think you'll get anything different out of me?' Penny asked. Her lips curved slightly in a mocking smile.

'Just fishing.'

'Well, you won't catch anything, Inspector. Not from me. It's all absolutely true. I can't imagine for the life of me who'd want to do a thing like that to him.'

Banks sighed. It was going to be a difficult evening. 'Fortunately, Miss Cartwright,' he said, 'it's not your life we're concerned about, it's Mr Steadman's. And somebody brought that to an abrupt and cruel end. Do you know anything about his business affairs?'

'Do you mean that fuss over Crabtree's Field? Really, Inspector, does Teddy Hackett strike you as the murdering kind? He wouldn't have the guts to kill a worm if his life depended on it. He might be a ruthless businessman – though the competition around here isn't much cop and, if you ask me, he's got by more on good luck than good management – but a killer? Hackett? Never.'

'Stranger things have happened.'

'Oh, I know. "There are more things in heaven and

earth, Horatio, than are dreamt of in your philosophy,"'
she quoted.

'It might not be a serious possibility,' Banks went on,
'but it's the only one we've got so far.'

'Typical bloody police, that is,' Penny mocked. 'Crucify
the first poor bastard that comes out less than squeaky
clean. Still,' she added, 'Hackett's no great loss to society.
Not like Harry.'

'How long had you known Mr Steadman?' Banks
asked.

'Depends on what you mean by "know".' Penny lit a
long filter cigarette and went on. 'I first met him years ago
when I was a teenager and he and Emma came up to
Gratly for their holidays. They'd been two or three times
before I got to know them through Michael. That's
Michael Ramsden. They stayed at his parents' bed-and-
breakfast place, the house they live in now. I was about
sixteen, and Michael and I were sweethearts at that time,
so, naturally, I saw them quite often.'

Banks nodded and sucked on his pipe. That archaic
word 'sweethearts' sounded wonderfully erotic coming
from Penny's lips. It seemed unselfconscious, at odds
with her tight and aggressive manner.

'We went on walks together,' she continued. 'Harry
knew a lot about the countryside and its history. That was
his real love. And then . . . well. It was a beautiful
summer, but it passed, as all summers do.'

'Ah, yes. "But where are the snows of yesteryear?"'
Banks quoted back at her.

'It was summer; there wasn't much snow.'

Again Banks noticed that tiny twitch of a smile at the
corners of her pale lips. 'That would be about ten years
ago, wouldn't it?' he asked.

Penny nodded slowly. 'Ten years, almost exactly. Yes. But things changed. Michael went to university. He was eighteen. I went away. Years passed. Harry came into some money and bought the house. I'd been back about eight months then – sort of return of the prodigal daughter. Black sheep. Most people had no time for me, but Harry always did.'

'What do you mean they had no time for you? Where had you been? Why did you come back?'

'That's a long story, Inspector,' Penny said, 'and I'm not sure it comes under the heading of relevant information. Briefly though, I spent about eight or nine years away, in the music business. Mostly I was homesick, despite all the fun and a moderate amount of acclaim. Finally, I got very cynical, and I decided it was time to come home. People weren't friendly because they can't accept anything modern around here and they no longer knew how to behave towards me. I'm sure they made up stories to suit their opinions. They didn't know who or what I was, so they made a lot of assumptions based on what they read in the Sunday papers about the music business – and I don't mean the *Sunday Times*, either. To them I became a degenerate, a scarlet woman. In fact, I always had been – they couldn't admit they'd ever been wrong about me. Does that answer your questions?'

She paused but didn't look at Banks for a response. 'It was very hard for my father, but he took me back. Why don't I live with him? Is that what you were going to ask next? For my sanity, Inspector, my mental health. He's just a bit too solicitous of my welfare, shall we say. And I think I'm a big girl now. It seemed best for both of us if I took this little cottage. Surely you can understand that?'

'Of course. There were rumours, too, weren't there?'

Penny laughed. 'Oh, you know about that as well, do you? See what a nice close little community our village is? Well, don't be embarrassed, Inspector, ask me. Go on, ask me.'

Her bright blue eyes glittered with anger. Banks said nothing. Finally, Penny gave him a scornful look and turned away to pull another cigarette from her packet.

'So only your father and Harold Steadman were kind to you?'

'Yes.' Penny hesitated. 'And Jack Barker, too. He'd been here a year or so by then, but he knew nothing of what had happened. Not that it would have mattered to him. He's a friend, too.'

'And now?'

'Oh, now?' Penny laughed. 'People are beginning to say hello again.'

'Do you still see Michael Ramsden?'

'Not much. Only when he calls in at the Bridge or drops by with Harry. Sometimes when you drift apart you never really drift back together.'

'And you can't think of any reason why anyone would want to harm Mr Steadman?'

'None at all. I've told you.' Penny's smooth brow creased in thought and she shook her head sadly. 'He wasn't greedy or scheming. He never cheated or lied.'

'What did his wife think of your relationship?'

'Emma? Nothing much, I should imagine. Probably glad to get him out of the way.'

'Why do you say that? Were they unhappy together?'

Penny looked at him as if he'd just crawled out from under a stone and blew her smoke out angrily. 'How should I know? Ask her.'

'I'm asking *you*.' Things were taking the kind of turn he had hoped to avoid, but with someone as anti-establishment as Penny Cartwright, he reflected, it was bound to happen. She had been toying with him all along. He pressed on: 'Still no answer?'

'I told you, I don't know,' she said. 'For God's sake, what do you want me to say?'

'Was their marriage normal?'

'Normal! Ha! What the bloody hell does that mean? Yes, I suppose so. I've never been married myself, so I'm hardly the best person to ask.'

'Were they happy?'

'I should think so. As I said, I don't really know. It's not as if I was his confidante or his shoulder to cry on.'

'Did he need one?'

Penny sighed and rested her head in her hands. 'Look,' she protested tiredly, 'this is getting us nowhere. What do you want from me?'

Banks ignored her question and pressed on: 'What were you to Mr Steadman?'

'Harry and I were friends. Just friends; I told you. We had interests in common.'

'And his wife didn't object?'

'She never said anything to me. Why should she? Harry never said anything, either.'

'You do know her, then?'

'Of course I bloody well know her. Harry and I weren't carrying on a clandestine relationship, like you seem to think. I went to their house for dinner plenty of times. She was always very kind and charming. She was a good cook, too.'

'What did you talk about?'

'When Emma was around?'

'Yes.'

'Nothing much. Just the usual stuff. She didn't really share Harry's passions. She likes music – mostly classical, though. Christ, what do you talk about when you go to someone's house for dinner?'

'Were you having an affair with Harold Steadman?'

At last, the inevitable question. And Banks felt a fool the moment it was out. If he had been expecting a burst of pent-up anger or a howl of derisive laughter in reply, he couldn't have been more surprised. His question seemed instead to deflate the interview of all its mounting tension, and Penny gazed at him steadily, a spark of amusement in her sapphire eyes, as if, in fact, she had goaded him into bluntness.

'No, Inspector,' she said, 'I was not having an affair with Harry Steadman, or with anyone else, for that matter. In fact, I'm not having an affair with Emma Steadman, or with my father, either. Everything is exactly as I've told you. I just didn't feel that way about Harry, nor he about me, as far as I could tell.' Banks thought Steadman must have been mad. 'He didn't excite me physically,' she went on, lighting another cigarette and walking around the small room as she smoked it. 'Only my mind, my imagination. And I liked him very much. I think he was a good man, a bright, sweet person. Perhaps I even loved him in a platonic sort of way, but that's as far as it went.' She tossed her hair back and sat down facing him, chin held high. Bright tears shone in her eyes but they never began to flow. 'There you are, Inspector,' she said with dignity. 'I've bared my soul for you. Aren't you pleased?'

Banks was moved by the obvious intensity of her feeling, but he didn't want to let his disadvantage show.

'When did you last see him?' he asked.

Her eyes reflected a chain of options running through her mind. It was a phenomenon Banks had often observed in people who were trying to decide quickly whether to lie or tell the truth.

Penny opened her mouth, then closed it. She took a final drag on her cigarette, ground it out half smoked and whispered, 'Saturday. Saturday evening.'

'What time?'

'About nine.'

'After he'd left the Bridge?'

'Yes. He dropped by here.'

'Then why the hell didn't you tell me before? You knew damn well you were holding back important information.'

Penny shrugged. 'You didn't ask me. I didn't want to get involved.'

'Didn't want to get involved?' Banks echoed scornfully. 'You say you liked the man, that he helped you, and you couldn't be bothered to help us try and find his killer?'

Penny sighed and began to wind a strand of hair around her index finger. 'Look, Inspector,' she said, 'I know it sounds shabby, but it's true. I don't see how his visit to me could help you in any way. And, dammit,' she flashed, 'I don't think I owe the police any bloody favours.'

'That's not the point. I don't care about your personal feelings towards the police. What was important was the time. If nothing else, your information could help us pinpoint the time of the murder. When did he leave?'

'About ten.'

'Did he say where he was going?'

'I assumed he was going to York. He'd mentioned it.'

'But he didn't mention any other calls he wanted to make first, any errands to run?'

'No.'

It was another hour accounted for, anyway. Banks had nothing more to say; his session with Penny had exhausted him. She seemed irritated and the tension grew between them again, as tangible as a tightening hacksaw blade. Finally, Penny broke it.

'Look,' she began, 'I'm sorry, I really am. I do care about Harry. The thing is that in my life involvement with the police has always meant trouble. I've never been involved in a murder investigation before, so I don't know what matters and what doesn't. When you're a musician, young, in with a certain crowd, you get a very warped view of authority – police, customs men, immigration officials, security guards – they all seem against you; they're all such a royal pain in the arse.'

Banks couldn't help but grin. 'Drugs?' he asked.

Penny nodded. 'Not me. I was never into it. Not in a heavy way. But you know how it is in London. There's drugs all around you, whether you take them or not. Sure, I smoked a joint or two, maybe took some amphetamines to keep me awake on tour, but never the heavy stuff. Try and tell the drug squad that.'

Banks wanted to argue, to defend the police, but he was too tired and he knew there would be no point anyway. Besides, he also knew that the police were just like everyone else; a lot were bastards and a few weren't. He had known a high-ranking officer in the drug squad who routinely planted illegal substances on people he wanted out of the way, and that was by no means rare or unusual behaviour. Also, he smelled something familiar in the air of Penny's cottage. He knew what it was, but he

didn't care to pursue the matter any more than he wanted
to tell her that his full title was Chief Inspector. People
often got it wrong.

He stood up, and Penny walked to the door with him.
He felt that she was seeking some kind words of re-
assurance from him, some forgiveness for acting in a way
contrary to her feelings for Steadman. But he didn't know
how to give it. At the door he said, 'I hear you sing, Miss
Cartwright?'

'Actually, it's Ms,' Penny corrected him, a playful smile
lighting her eyes. 'Yes, I sing.'

'Locally?'

'Sometimes. I'm at the Dog and Gun this Friday and
Saturday. Competing with the disco in the Hare and
Hounds.'

'I'll see if I can drop by, then,' Banks said. 'If nothing
turns up.'

'Feel free.' There was a trace of doubt in Penny's voice,
as if she couldn't quite believe that a policeman would be
interested in traditional folk music, or in any kind of
music for that matter.

Banks walked down the narrow cobbled street by the
church wall, and as soon as he got to the corner he heard a
hissing sound behind him and turned. An old woman stood
at the door of the cottage next to Penny's and beckoned
him over. When he got close enough she whispered, 'You'll
be that there policeman they're all talking about.'

'Detective Chief Inspector Banks,' he said, reaching for
his card. 'At your service.'

'Nay, nay lad, there's no need for that. I believe thee,'
she said, waving it aside. 'Been talking to 'er ladyship next
door, I see.' She jerked a shrivelled thumb in the direction
of Penny's cottage. Puzzled, Banks nodded.

'Did she tell 'ee about Sat'day night?'

'What about Saturday night?'

'I thought she wouldn't,' the old woman said triumph-
antly, crossing her arms with great satisfaction. 'A proper
ruckus there were. T' old major near flung 'im down t'
garden path.'

'Flung who?'

'Why, 'im as got 'isself murdered,' she announced with
obvious relish. 'I don't 'old wi' married men sniffing
around young lasses. And she's a flighty one, yon missy
is, you mark my words. There again, though,' she
laughed, 't' major's mad as an 'atter 'isself.'

'What are you talking about, Mrs . . . ?'

'Miss,' she said proudly. 'Lived seventy-one years and
never saw t' need for a 'usband yet. Miss Bamford it is,
young man, and I'm talking about Sat'day night when
Major Cartwright popped in on 'is daughter and caught 'er
wi' that murdered chappie. 'Bout ten o'clock, it were.
Now, don't ask me what they was doing, cos I couldn't
say, but 'e flew off t' handle, t' old man did. Told 'im not
to come around no more.'

'You mean the major physically threw Mr Steadman
out of Penny Cartwright's house?' Banks asked, trying to
get things straight. He was sure that something was bound
to have got lost in translation.

'Well, not in so many words.' Miss Bamford backed
down; her chin retracted deep into the folds of her neck.
'I couldn't see proper, like. Pushed 'im, though – and that
chap so pale and weakly from shutting 'imsen up wi'
books all day and night. I'll bet she didn't tell you about
that, did she, yon Lady Muck?'

Banks had to admit that Penny had not told him about
that. In fact, he had backed away from the whole issue of

her father after she had challenged him to be direct.

'Did she go out afterwards?' he asked.

' 'Er Royal 'ighness? No. T' door banged about eleven, but that were t' major.'

'Surely there's a back door, too?'

'Oh, aye,' Miss Bamford answered. She hadn't missed his meaning.

Banks thanked her. With a smug smile on her wrinkled face, the old woman shut her door. After a quick and puzzled glance back at Penny's cottage, Banks walked towards his car and drove home.

6

ONE

'**So according** to your mate in Darlington—'

'Sergeant Balfour, sir. A good man.'

'According to your Sergeant Balfour,' Banks went on, 'Hackett didn't arrive at the KitKat Klub until after one o'clock in the morning, and nobody in the pub he mentioned remembered seeing him?'

'That's right. The landlord said he often dropped by, but last week it was on Friday, not Saturday.'

'So the bastard's been lying.' Banks sighed. He was becoming more and more irritated with the inhabitants of Helmthorpe, and as many London villains would testify, the more annoyed he got the harder it was all round. 'I suppose we'd better have him in again. No, wait . . .' He glanced at his watch and stood up. 'Better still, let's have a drive into Helmthorpe. There's a couple of things I want to do there.'

Sandra was using the Cortina, so they signed out a car from the pool and Banks let Hatchley drive. The hedgerows by the river were dotted with clumps of white, yellow and purple wild flowers, none of which Banks could name. A few dark clouds skulked about the sky, but the sun pierced through here and there in bright lances of light that picked out green patches on the shadowed dalesides. The effect reminded Banks of some paintings he'd seen in a London gallery Sandra had dragged him to, but he couldn't remember the artist's name: Turner, Gainsborough, Constable? Sandra would know. He made a mental note to look into landscape painting a bit more closely.

'What do you think, then?' Hatchley asked. He drove with one hand and lit a cigarette from the glowing red circle of the dashboard lighter. 'About Hackett, I mean.'

'Could be our man. He's certainly hiding something.'

'What about the others who were with Steadman that night?'

'We just don't know, do we? Any one of them could have done it. They've no real alibis, not even Barnes.'

'But what motive could he have for killing Steadman? He's got a good reputation locally, always has had.'

Banks fiddled with his pipe. 'Could be blackmail. Maybe Barnes had something on Steadman, or vice versa. Maybe Steadman learned something that would ruin the doctor's reputation.'

'It's possible, I suppose,' Hatchley said. 'But Steadman was rich; he didn't need to blackmail anyone, surely? And if he was paying Barnes it'd be daft to kill the goose that laid the golden egg, wouldn't it?'

'Agreed. But it needn't have been money. Perhaps Steadman felt morally bound to tell what he knew. From all accounts, he was just the kind of person who would. I know it's all speculation at this point, but I still think we should look into the doctor's finances and background, and find out if Steadman made any large bank withdrawals recently.'

'Won't do any harm, I suppose. Bloody hell!' Hatchley swerved to avoid a wobbling cyclist and yelled out of the window, 'Watch where you're going, bloody road hog!'

Banks tightened his seat belt; he remembered one of the reasons why he preferred driving his own car on the job.

They arrived safely and parked by the river, where Steadman had left his car, and walked up the alley to High Street. It was about midday; tourists thronged the small ice-cream shop, and the locals were out shopping or gossiping by cottage gates up the narrow cobbled side streets. The two policemen were now well known in the village, and voices lowered as they passed. Banks smiled to himself; he enjoyed the effect his presence had on people. In London, nobody but the criminals he'd put away more than once knew who he was.

They paused by a newsagent's, where racks of coloured postcards, maps and local guidebooks outside on the pavement flapped in the light breeze.

'Let's take Hackett together after lunch,' Banks suggested.

'All right.' Hatchley looked at his watch. 'Want to eat now?'

'Not yet. Why don't you drop in on Weaver and see if anything's turned up? I want a word with Major Cartwright. Then we'll have a pie and a pint at the Bridge and work out how to tackle Hackett.'

Hatchley agreed and walked off to the small local police station.

Nobody, Banks thought, could look more like a retired major than the man who opened the door next to Thadtwistle's bookshop. He was elderly but trim-looking, with silver hair, a brick-red complexion and a grey handlebar moustache. After Banks had identified himself, the major grunted and led him up a narrow staircase. The flat turned out to be directly above the bookshop.

Banks followed him into a sitting room dominated by a huge framed reproduction of a bare-breasted woman carrying a flag over a battlefield of dead and wounded soldiers; she was accompanied by a small boy with a gun in each hand.

'*Liberty Leading the People*,' the major said, catching him staring at it. 'Delacroix. That's what we were fighting for, isn't it?'

Luckily, Banks could recognize a rhetorical question when he heard one. He turned his attention to the terrier sniffing around his ankles and tried subtly shifting his feet to make it go away. Banks didn't like dogs – if anything, he was a cat man – but he liked it even less when their proud owners expected him to fuss over the damned animals as if they were newborn babies. Kicking out a bit harder, Banks finally persuaded the pooch to slink off to its basket, from where it gazed at him with an expression of resentment mingled with arrogance. The major was pouring drinks, so fortunately his back was turned.

Stale smoke made the warm room stuffy. Banks spotted an antique pipe rack on the wall above the fireplace and, hoping to establish a rapport, he sat in a straight-backed chair and coaxed his own briar alight.

The major handed him a small whisky and soda, took a larger one for himself, and sat down in the scuffed leather armchair that had obviously been his since time immemorial.

Some military types, Banks found, regarded the police as fellow professionals, colleagues-in-arms almost, but others looked upon them as upstarts, petty dabblers who had not quite made the grade. Major Cartwright seemed to be of the latter type. He looked at Banks with open hostility, the purple veins around his nose showing a clear predilection for early morning snifters.

'What is it, then?' he asked, as if he had been interrupted in the midst of planning a new assault on the Boers.

Banks explained about the murder, drawing only grunts and sharp nods, and tried as delicately as he could to mention that the major had probably been the last person, apart from the killer, to see Steadman alive.

'When would that be?' Cartwright asked.

'Saturday night, about ten o'clock.'

The major stared at him with icy blue eyes and sipped his whisky. 'Who told you that?'

'It doesn't matter who told me, Major. Is it true?'

'I suppose it was that busybody of a neighbour, eh? Silly old biddy.'

'Did you see him and did you have an argument?'

'You can't be suggesting—'

'I'm not suggesting anything. I'm just asking you a simple question.'

The major swirled the whisky in his glass for a moment, then answered, 'All right, what if I did?'

'You tell me.'

'Nothing to tell, really. Found him hanging about my daughter again and told him to sling his hook.'

'Why did you react so violently?'

'It's not right.' Cartwright leaned forward in his chair. 'A married man, older than her. What would you do? It's not healthy.' He slumped back again.

'Did you assume they were having an affair?'

'Now hold on a minute, young man. Hold your horses. I never said anything like that.'

'Look,' Banks pressed on, 'I'm not making any

accusations or charges. I'm asking you what you thought. If you didn't think your daughter was likely to be involved in anything unsavoury, then why did you practically kick Steadman down the street?'

'She's exaggerating, the old bag.' Cartwright sniffed. He tossed back the rest of his drink, then got up and picked an old briar from the rack and filled it with twist from a pouch. 'We had words, yes, but I never laid a finger – or a toe – on him. Anyway, it's a matter of principle, isn't it? A married man. People talk.'

Banks found it hard to see the link between principle and the fear of gossip, but he ignored the issue. 'Is that why you objected to a harmless relationship that both parties seemed to enjoy?' he asked instead. 'Did you behave the same way over all your daughter's friendships?'

'Dammit, the man was married,' the major repeated.

'He was married ten years ago when they first met, but you didn't object then, did you?'

'That was all in the open. Always someone else around – young Michael. She was just a girl. Look, if they want to meet, they can do it openly, can't they? In a pub with other people there, for example. No reason to shut themselves up in private like that. They're a sharp-tongued lot in this village, lad. You don't know the half of it.'

'Were you worried that they'd talk like they did about you and your daughter? Is that what you wanted to protect her from?'

The major whitened and sagged in his chair. All of a sudden his belligerence seemed to desert him and he looked his age. He got up slowly and mixed himself another drink. 'Heard about that, did you?'

Banks nodded.

'You weren't there,' he said in a sad, bitter tone. 'You can't know what it was like for the two of us after my wife died. I couldn't look after myself, had to go into hospital for a while, had to send Penny away to the Ramsdens. But she came back and cared for me. Selflessly, God bless her. She's an only child, you know. And then the vicious gossip started. It only takes one to start the rumour – just one rotten bastard – then it spreads like the plague until everyone's had enough of it and something better comes along. And it's just a game to them. They don't even care whether it's true or not; it just titillates their imaginations, that's all. I blame them for driving her away. They said it wasn't natural, the two of us together. After she left, I sold the house and moved here.'

'I thought she left to start a career in music?'

'Oh, she'd have gone eventually. But she was too young. She shouldn't have gone so soon; then things wouldn't have turned out the way they did for her.'

'She seems well enough adjusted to me. Maybe a little sharp at the edges.'

'You didn't know her before. Lost a lot of her spirit, her joy. Too young to be a cynic. Anyway, she couldn't stand it here with people staring at her that way. Took a lot of courage for her to come back.'

'So you forgave her?'

'Nothing to forgive, really. She thought she'd let me down, leaving me like that. There'd been rows, fights, yes. But I never stopped loving her. Steadman wasn't a bad sort, I know that. A bit wet, I always thought, but not a bad sort. I just wanted to spare her it all again. She's bitter enough already. But it's not the first time I've had words with him. Ask anyone. My argument with Steadman wasn't new.'

'What happened on Saturday night?'

'Nothing, really. I told him not to call on her alone after dark again. I'd told him before. I suppose I just made things worse, drawing attention to it.'

'What did you do afterwards?'

'When he'd gone?'

'Yes.'

'I stayed and talked to Penny for an hour or so. She was a bit upset with me but we settled things amicably enough.'

'Can you remember what time you left?'

'I can remember the church bells ringing eleven. It wasn't long after that.'

'And Steadman left at ten?'

'That was when I arrived, yes.'

'Did you notice anyone hanging around the area?'

'No. It was quiet. Always is up there. There were a few people on High Street, but nothing unusual.'

'Did Steadman say where he was going? Did he give you any idea at all what he intended to do next?'

Major Cartwright shook his head. 'No, he just left. Sorry I can't be of more help to you, Inspector.'

'Never mind. Thanks for your time, anyway, Major.'

Cartwright turned and walked over to the drinks cabinet, leaving Banks to make his own way back downstairs.

TWO

With her head propped up on cushions, Sally lay in the back garden, sunbathing in her pale blue bikini. It was a luxury she felt entitled to as she had made temporary peace with her parents by breaking a date with Kevin the previous evening in order to visit boring Aunt Madge in Skipton. There, she had sipped tea from tiny fragile china cups with gilded rims and red roses painted on their sides, and had answered politely all the dull and predictable questions about her schoolwork. At least the television had been on – Aunt Madge never turned it off – so she had been able to half-watch an old Elizabeth Taylor film while pretending to pay attention to the conversation, which ranged from the shocking state of the neighbour's garden to news of a distant cousin's hysterectomy. The odd thing was that her parents hadn't seemed to enjoy the evening much either; her father hardly said a word. They all seemed relieved when the goodbyes had been said and they could troop out to the car.

With a sigh, Sally put down *Wuthering Heights* and rolled over on to her stomach. Her skin was already glowing pleasantly, and even with the lotion she would have to be careful how long she spent outside.

She was puzzled and frustrated by the book. In the film – even the old black and white version with Laurence Olivier – Heathcliff had seemed so sexy and tragic. She remembered sharing tissues with her mother while they watched it on television and her father had laughed at them. But the book was different; not the story – that was basically the same – but the character of Heathcliff. True, he loved Catherine passionately, but in the book he was so much more cruel and violent. He seemed to want to destroy everyone around him. And worse, he was even more interested in getting his hands on the house and property. That was the real reason he married Isabella – though he did appear to be taking revenge for Edgar marrying Catherine – and an obsession with acquiring property was hardly romantic. He acted more like a demented (and much more handsome) Teddy Hackett than a true heroic figure.

She reached for her glass of Perrier. It was warm; the ice had all melted and the sparkle had vanished. Pulling a face, she rolled on to her back again and started thinking rather despondently about her sleuthing. There wasn't much to think about. She had no idea who the police suspected, what clues they had, what they knew about motives and opportunities. All she had to go on was what anyone in the village would know about Steadman: that he seemed fond of Penny Cartwright, much to her father's chagrin; that he worked a lot with Michael Ramsden; that he had been able to help the Ramsden family by buying the house when the father died; that he was generally well liked; that he drank in the Bridge with Jack Barker, Teddy Hackett and Dr Barnes. He just didn't seem the type to go around inflaming people's passions, like Heathcliff. But he must have done; somebody had killed him.

It had to be a man. Of that, Sally was sure. Steadman had been quite tall and must have weighed a bit; no woman could have manoeuvred his body over the wall and all that way up the field. But that still left too many suspects. If only she had had the foresight to watch from the shelter that night. Sally began to apply her imagination to the facts. Everyone knew that Michael Ramsden had once courted Penny Cartwright. What if he was still carrying a torch for her, like Heathcliff for Catherine, and was jealous of Steadman's attentions? But she remembered seeing Ramsden – and avoiding him – that evening she went drinking in Leeds with Kevin. He had been with a good-looking woman, and though Sally had only got a fleeting glance while pulling Kevin quickly back out through the door before they were seen, she knew it wasn't Penny. And he'd hardly be going out with someone else if he was still in love with her.

There was Jack Barker. At first she hadn't suspected him, but now she could see him acting in the heat of passion. She'd noticed how often he'd been out walking with Penny around the village lately and wondered if Barker might have seen Steadman as an obstacle. He wrote detective stories, after all, so he must know all about murder. Even though he was a gentleman, he would hardly stand there with the gun smoking in his hand and wait for the police to come. Surely he would try and get rid of the body so he could remain free and win Penny's love. She wondered if he had an alibi and if there was any way of finding out.

And then there was Hackett. No love interest there, of course, but she'd heard rumours of arguments over property. People certainly seemed to get all steamed up about such things in *Wuthering Heights*.

She reached out for her suntan lotion. One more coat, another hour or so, then she'd go in. As far as catching the murderer was concerned, all she could do was try to remember all she'd seen and heard in the village since the Steadmans came to Gratly eighteen months ago. Maybe there was something she'd overlooked: a word or gesture that had meant nothing or made no sense at the time but took on more significance in the light of the murder. She had a good visual memory – it probably came from watching so many films – so she could review facial expressions and body language. Maybe something would click if she worked at it.

The oil felt good as she massaged it slowly into her stomach and thighs, and she wished Kevin's hands were rubbing it on her flushed skin. A bee droned around the neck of the open bottle, then floated away. Sally picked up her book again, leaving oily fingerprints on the pages.

THREE

The two men walked slowly along Helmthorpe High Street deep in conversation. Banks had one hand in his trouser pocket, and the other held a light sports jacket slung casually over his shoulder. The sleeves of his white shirt were rolled up above the elbows and he had loosened his tie enough to allow him to open his top button. Banks hated ties, and wearing them loosely was his way of compromising. He walked with his head bowed, listening to Hatchley, who towered beside him. The sergeant had both hands clasped behind his back and his head was tilted back on his thick neck as if he were examining the rooftops; a well cultivated beer belly hung over his tight belt. The weather was still undecided, and the sun popped in and out between quick-moving clouds that raced over on the wind and cast their shadows across the bright face of Crow Scar.

'Said he was in a bit of a state,' Hatchley went on. 'Shook up, like. Downed a quick double Scotch and went on his way.'

The scrap of information Constable Weaver had been so eager to impart was that the barman of the Dog and Gun had told him Steadman had dropped in just after ten o'clock on Saturday night. He hadn't come forward earlier because he had been away fishing in Scotland and hadn't even heard about the murder.

'I can tell you the reason for that,' Banks said, and

proceeded to tell Hatchley about his interview with Major Cartwright. This took some of the wind out of the sergeant's sails, and he muttered a surly 'No' when Banks asked him if there had been any other developments.

Hatchley began to smile again, however, as soon as he sniffed the beer fumes and tobacco smoke in the Bridge. They sat at the same scarred table as they had on their previous visit, and soon had two pints of Theakston's bitter before them and two steak and mushroom pies on order.

'Steadman could have gone back to the cottage though, couldn't he?' Hatchley said. 'Maybe he came to the boil when he thought about how he'd let the major walk all over him, so he went back to settle things. We can't rule him out yet, or the girl.'

'No, we can't. Steadman could have waited for the coast to clear and gone back to finish what he and Penny had started before they were interrupted. The major's certainly very protective towards her.'

'From what I hear,' Hatchley said with relish, 'she always was a bit of a wild 'un. Running off to London, hanging about with those freaks and musicians. There were probably drugs involved, too, and I doubt she was very careful about who she hopped in and out of bed with. I think if she were a daughter of mine I'd keep her on a short leash after that.'

'But the woman's twenty-six years old. Besides, Steadman was a safe enough companion, wasn't he?'

Hatchley shrugged. 'As far as we know he was. But there could be more to it.'

'Oh, there's more to it all right. There's always more to things like this. As far as Penny Cartwright's concerned, there are two points in her favour. First, the old woman didn't hear anyone else call at the cottage later, and she says Penny didn't go out either; and second, I doubt that she was strong enough to drag the body to its hiding place.' Banks was about to add that he had also been convinced by Penny's genuine display of affection for Steadman, but he knew it wasn't the kind of evidence Sergeant Hatchley would appreciate. Besides, the spell of her presence had worn off, and he was beginning to wonder if she was not just a consummate actress. 'Still,' he went on, 'she could have had help with the body; and there is a back door, so the old woman might not have heard if she was in the front room.'

'Do you think the Cartwright girl really was having it off with Steadman, then?' Hatchley asked.

'I don't know. You can never tell about things like that. Sometimes couples can be having affairs for years and nobody knows.'

'Why else would he be hanging around her?'

'There is such a thing as friendship, you know.'

'In a pig's eye,' Hatchley muttered.

The pies came and the two men ate silently until their plates were empty.

'Steadman had a lot of money,' Banks said, reaching for his second pint. 'And his wife stands to inherit. I'd say that was a pretty good motive, wouldn't you?'

'But we know she couldn't have done it,' Hatchley objected. 'I mean, why complicate something that's difficult enough already?'

'She could have hired someone.'

'But Helmthorpe isn't New York or London.'

'Doesn't matter. I once knew of a chap in Blackpool who had a price list – arms fifty quid, legs seventy-five and so on. Mind you, his rates have probably gone up a bit with inflation now. It's naïve to think that kind of thing is restricted to the south, and you should bloody well know that as well as anyone. Are you telling me there's no one in Eastvale would take a job like that? What about Eddie Cockley, for one? Or Jimmy Spinks? He'd slit his own mother's throat for the price of a pint.'

'Aye,' said Hatchley, 'but how would a woman like Mrs Steadman get mixed up with the likes of Cockley and Spinks?'

'I admit it's unlikely, but hardly more than anything else in this bloody business. Put it this way: we don't know much about the Steadmans' marriage. It seemed ordinary enough on the surface, but what did she think about him and Penny Cartwright, for example? Maybe she was mad with jealousy. We just don't know. And even if we ask them, they'll lie. For some reason, they're all protecting one another.'

'Perhaps they suspect each other.'

'I wouldn't be surprised.'

Hatchley guzzled his pint.

'You know what the trouble with this case is, Sergeant?' Banks went on. 'Everyone except Major Cartwright seems to think the sun shone out of Steadman's arse.'

Hatchley grinned. They drained their glasses and set off to see Hackett.

FOUR

Teddy Hackett sat in his office, part of an old mill that looked out on the River Swain behind the garage. The window was open and scents of flowers floated in with the sound of water rushing over pebbles. Occasionally a bee strayed from the clematis that clung to the stone wall, buzzed into the room and, finding nothing of interest in human affairs, meandered out again.

Hackett was nervous and sweaty right from the start. He sat behind the defence of his cluttered desk, back to the window, and toyed with a letter opener as Banks faced him from a chair. Hatchley leaned against the wall by the window. Banks filled his pipe, got it going, then brought up the subject of Hackett's false alibi.

'From what we've been able to discover, you arrived at the KitKat Klub alone and after one o'clock, a little later than you said.'

Hackett squirmed. 'I'm not very good at times. Always late for appointments, that's me.'

Banks smiled. 'That's not a very good habit for a businessman, is it? Still, that's no concern of mine. What I want to know is what you were doing before then.'

'I told you,' Hackett said, slapping his palm with the letter opener. 'I went to a pub and had a couple of drinks.'

'But closing time on Saturday is eleven o'clock, Mr Hackett. Even on the most liberal of premises you'd be out in the street by eleven thirty. What did you do between eleven thirty and one o'clock?'

Hackett shifted his weight from cheek to cheek and rubbed his chin. 'Look, I don't want to get anyone into trouble. Know what I mean? But when you get pally with the bar staff you can sometimes get in an extra drink or two. Especially when the local copper's there, too.' He winked. 'I mean, if young Weaver ever wanted to—'

'I don't want to hear about Constable Weaver,' Banks cut in. 'I want to hear about you, and I'm getting impatient. What you're saying is that the publican broke the licensing laws by serving you after hours, as late as one o'clock. Is that what happened?'

'I wouldn't put it quite like that. It was more in the nature of a drink or two together. Privacy of his own home, like. There's no law says a man can't have a mate in for a drink whenever he wants, is there?'

'No, not at all,' Banks answered. 'Let's say you weren't breaking any laws, then. If you were so pally with the manager you'll remember the name of the pub, won't you?'

'I thought I told you already. Didn't I?'

Banks shook his head.

'I thought I did. I meant to. It was the Cock and Bull on Arthur Street, near the club.' Hackett put down his letter opener and lit a cigarette, taking deep noisy drags.

'No, it wasn't,' said Banks. 'It wasn't the Cock and Bull on Arthur Street. The manager says he knows you, right enough, and that you'd been in on Friday, but not Saturday. Where were you, Mr Hackett?'

Hackett looked crestfallen. 'He must have been mistaken. Got a bad memory, old Joey. I'm sure if you ask him again, jog his memory a bit, he'll remember. He'll tell you it's true. I was there.'

'Come off it, man, tell us where you were!' Hatchley's loud voice boomed out from behind Hackett, unnerving him completely. During the preliminary part of the inter-rogation, the sergeant had remained so quiet that Hackett must have forgotten he was in the room. Now he half-turned and looked terrified to find a new, more aggressive adversary towering over him. He got to his feet but Hackett still had the advantage of height.

'I don't know what you're getting at—'

'We're not getting at anything,' Hatchley said. 'We're

telling you loud and clear. You never went to the Cock and Bull, did you? That was just a cock and bull story, wasn't it? You never went to any pub in Darlington. You waited for Steadman outside the Bridge, followed him to Penny Cartwright's, waited there, then followed him to the Dog and Gun and back to the car park. There, where it was dark and quiet, you hit him on the head and hid him in the boot of your car. Later, when the whole village was asleep, you dumped him in the field on your way over the dale to Darlington, didn't you? The timing's just right, Hackett, we've checked. What with all the lies you've told us and the traces we'll find in the boot of your car, we've got you by the short and curlies, mate.'

Hackett turned to Banks for sympathy and support. 'You can't let him bully me, accuse me like this,' he spluttered. 'It's not . . .'

'Not cricket?' said Banks. 'But you must admit, Mr Hackett, it is a possibility, isn't it? A very strong possibility.'

Hackett flopped back down into the chair behind his desk and Hatchley walked over to stand in front of him. 'Look, sir,' the sergeant began softly, 'we know you didn't arrive at the club until after one o'clock, and that gives you plenty of time to dump Steadman's body and get there. Don't you think it would be easier all round if you told us what happened? Perhaps it was manslaughter? Perhaps you had an argument and came to blows; you didn't mean to kill him. Is that how it happened?'

Hackett stared at him, wary of his apparent friend-liness. Banks got up and walked over to the window, through which he appeared to be gazing at the river.

'I walked around,' Hackett said. 'That's all. I set off for Darlington as soon as I'd left the Bridge and got changed, then I stopped on the way. It was a lovely evening. I didn't feel like a drink just then, so I went for a walk. I wanted to be alone.'

'You and bloody Greta Garbo,' Banks snarled from behind him, turning quickly from the window and knocking his pipe out in the thick glass ashtray. 'I'm fast losing patience with you,' he rushed on, raising his voice and glaring. It was a measure of Hackett's terror and confusion that he now looked to the huge Hatchley as a benign presence.

'But I—'

'Shut up,' Banks ordered him. 'I don't want to hear any more lies from you, Hackett. Get it? If I'm not satisfied your next story's true I'll have you in Eastvale nick before your feet touch the ground. Understand?'

Hatchley, enjoying himself tremendously, played the role of kindly uncle. 'Best do as the chief inspector asks, sir,' he advised the pale Hackett. 'I'm sure it can't do any harm if you've nothing to hide.'

Hackett stared at Hatchley for a good half-minute, then came that visible relaxation of tension, the moment that signalled the truth. Banks could feel it in his veins; he recognized it well from years of experience. Hackett was still so mixed up that he glowered at Hatchley and directed his statement toward Banks, who smiled and nodded at various points with benevolent understanding.

All in all, it was a great disappointment, but it did get one red herring out of the way. After leaving the Bridge, Hackett had gone home to shower and change, then he had driven to Darlington, where he first spent about two hours of uninhibited carnal bliss with a young married woman whose husband worked the night shift at the local colliery. After that, he had gone on to the KitKat Klub alone because he didn't want to be seen with her locally. People would talk. Banks finally extracted her name and address from him, along with pleas and warnings about not letting her muscle-bound husband find out.

'Please,' he begged, 'if you must talk to Betty, do it after ten at night. I'll get her to come in. That'll be even better, won't it?'

'If you don't mind, Mr Hackett,' Banks replied, 'we'll do it our way.'

'Have a heart, Chief Inspector. Haven't you ever had a bit on the side?'

The muscles in Banks's jaw tightened. 'No,' he answered sharply. 'And even if I had it wouldn't make a jot of difference to your situation.' He put his hands on the desk and leaned forward so that his face was only inches from Hackett's. 'What you don't seem to realize is that this is a murder investigation. A friend of yours has been murdered, or don't you remember, and all you're concerned with is some bloody tart you've been poking in Darlington.'

'She's not a tart. And there's no reason to ruin a perfectly good marriage, is there? That's what you'll be doing, you know.'

'No. That's what you've done. It's what she's done too. If I thought for a moment that you cared more about the marriage than about your own skin, I might just consider doing things differently.'

Banks nodded to Hatchley and the two of them left Hackett biting his fingernails and cursing the day he met nubile little Betty Fields in the Cock and Bull.

'Fancy a trip to Darlington, Sergeant?' Banks asked when they reached High Street. 'Best if you check it out yourself.'

'Yes, sir,' Hatchley replied, grinning.

'Right then. After ten o'clock tonight, if you can make it.'

'What? But . . .'

'If you don't mind.'

'It's not that I mind. I've got a couple of mates up there I've not seen in a while. But what about Hackett?'

'Simple really. Hackett's right; I don't see any point putting unnecessary strain on a marriage, even one as flimsy as Betty Fields's. But he doesn't know that, does he? By the next time he hears from his young lady he'll be a gibbering wreck. Some of these miners are big chaps, so I've heard.' He smiled as comprehension dawned on Hatchley. 'You have to balance your cruelty with compassion, Sergeant. Come on, just one more visit to make then home. And by the way . . .'

'Yes, sir?'

'That was a terrible pun back there. Cock and bull story.'

'Oh, I thought it was quite good myself.'

Taking advantage of the fine weather, Banks and Hatchley walked to Gratly. They took the short cut through the cemetery and along a narrow path through a field. Lynchets led down to the beck like a broad flight of green velvet stairs. Sheep grazed under a clump of ash trees in the lush green grass by the water.

This time, Banks was struck by the tranquillity and individuality of Gratly. At the centre of the hamlet was a low stone bridge under which a broad stream ran over several abrupt terraces and descended in a series of small waterfalls past a disused mill and down the valley side to the all-consuming Swain.

Gratly itself radiated like a cross from this central point, and ginnels and snickets here and there led to twisting backstreets and hidden outhouses. The houses were all old, built of local stone, but their designs varied. Some, originally weavers' cottages, had many windows in their upper stories, while others looked like old farmhouses or labourers' quarters. The sun on the light stone and the steady music of water as it trickled relaxed Banks, and he found himself thinking that this was no day and no place for his kind of business. The hamlet was silent and still; there were no signs of life at all.

Emma Steadman, wearing a brown apron over her shirt and slacks, answered the door at the second ring and invited them inside, apologizing for the mess. She stopped at the entrance to the front room and ushered the two men in, running a grimy hand over her moist brow. Banks saw immediately what she meant. All Steadman's books had been taken down from the shelves and stood in untidy, precariously balanced piles on the floor.

The widow moved forlornly into the middle of the room and gestured around. 'They're all his. I can't stand it, having them all over the place. I don't know what to do with them.' She seemed less frosty than when they had parted on Monday afternoon, vulnerable among the detritus of a shared life.

'There's a book dealer in Eastvale,' Banks advised her. 'I'm sure he'll come out and appraise them if you give him a call. He'll give you a fair price. Or what about Thadtwistle in Helmthorpe?'

'Yes, that's an idea. Thank you.' Mrs Steadman sat down. 'It'll have to wait though, I'm afraid. I can't face that kind of thing yet. I don't know what I'll do with all his things. I never realized he'd collected so much junk. I wish I could just get up and leave Gratly, go somewhere else.'

'You'll not be staying here?' asked Hatchley.

She shook her head. 'No, Sergeant, I don't think so. There's nothing for me here. It was Harold's work, really. His place.'

'Where will you go?'

'I haven't really thought. A city, I suppose. Maybe London.' She looked at Banks.

'I shouldn't worry about it yet,' he said. 'You need a bit of time. It'll all get taken care of.'

Silence followed. Mrs Steadman offered to make a cup of tea, but Banks, much to Hatchley's distress, refused for them both. 'No thanks. It's just a flying visit. We were in the area.'

She raised her eyebrows, hinting that he should get to the point.

'It's about Penny Cartwright,' Banks began, noting that her expression didn't alter a jot at the mention of the name. 'I gather that she and your husband were rather close. Didn't that bother you at all?'

'What do you mean, "bother me"?'

'Well,' Banks went on cautiously, 'she's an attractive woman. People talk. People have talked about her before. Weren't you worried that your husband might have been having an affair with her?'

It was immediately clear that the suggestion surprised rather than annoyed Emma Steadman, as if it were something she had never even thought of. 'But they'd been friends for years,' she answered. 'Ever since she was a teenager, when we first came up here for our holidays. I don't— I mean, I never really thought of her as anything else, really. A teenager. More like a daughter than a rival.'

Banks felt that it was short-sighted in the extreme to look upon a woman only twelve or thirteen years one's junior as a child, especially if that woman was over the age of sixteen. 'It didn't bother you at all, then?' he went on. 'It never caused any trouble, any jealousy?'

'Not on my part it didn't, no. As I said, Chief Inspector, she's been a friend of the family for years. I suppose you know that she and Michael Ramsden used to go out together ages ago? He brought her up here quite often – after all, it was his home then; we were only summer visitors. I think she had a lot in common with Harry. She looked up to him as a teacher, a man of knowledge. So did Michael, for that matter. I'm sorry, I'm afraid I can't really see what you're getting at.'

'I simply wondered whether you suspected your husband of having an affair with Penny Cartwright.'

'No, I didn't. First you cast doubts on my marriage, now you accuse my husband of adultery. What's going on? What is all this about?'

Banks held up his hand. 'Wait a minute. I'm not making any accusations; I'm asking questions. It's my job.'

'That's what you said last time,' she said. 'It didn't make me feel any better then, either. Don't you realize they're burying my husband tomorrow?'

'Yes I do, and I'm sorry. But if you want us to carry out a thorough investigation into his death, you've got to be prepared for some awkward questions. We don't find the truth by skating over the surface or by skirting difficult patches.'

Mrs Steadman sighed. 'I understand that. It's just . . . so soon.'

'Did you see much of Penny after she left Helmthorpe?' Banks asked.

'Not much, no. Sometimes, if we were in the same

place – London, say – we'd have dinner together. But you could count the times on the fingers of one hand.'

'What did she seem like during that period?'

'Like herself.'

'She never seemed depressed, on drugs, strung out?'

'Not when we saw her.'

'How well did your husband know Jack Barker?'

'Jack? I'd say they were fairly close. As close as Harry could be to someone who didn't share his enthusiasms.'

'How long had Barker been living in Gratly?'

'I don't really know. Before us. Three or four years.'

'How long had your husband known him?'

'They got to know each other over the past eighteen months. We'd met before, on our visits here, but it wasn't till we moved in that Harold really spent much time with the locals.'

'Where did Barker come from?'

'He's from Cheadle, in Cheshire. But I think he lived in London for a while.'

'And neither your nor your husband knew him when you first visited Gratly?'

'No. I don't think anyone in Helmthorpe or Gratly did. Why this fascination with the past, Chief Inspector?'

Banks frowned. 'I'm not really sure, Mrs Steadman. I'm just trying to get a sense of the pattern of relationships: exits and entrances.'

'And that's why you were asking me about Harry and Penny?'

'Partly, yes. Major Cartwright didn't seem too pleased about their friendship.'

Mrs Steadman made a sound halfway between a sneeze and a guffaw. 'The major! Everybody knows he's a crackpot. Mad as a March hare. She's all he's got, you know, and she did desert him for a long time.'

'You know about the rumours?'

'Who doesn't? But I don't think you'll find anyone who takes them seriously these days.'

'Forgiven and forgotten?'

'Something like that. People tire easily. Surely you don't think . . . the major?'

Banks didn't answer.

'You policemen have such wild imaginations,' Emma Steadman went on. 'What do you think happened? Do you think the major found out about this mythical affair and killed Harry to protect his daughter's virtue? Or do you think I did it in a jealous rage?'

'You couldn't have done it, could you? You were watching television with your neighbour at the time. We don't rely entirely on imagination, Mrs Steadman. I know it's a difficult period for you right now, and I apologize if I seem to be pestering you, but I'm simply trying to build up as complete a picture as I can of your husband and his circle. This is a difficult and vital time for us, too. Memories fade and stories change with every hour that goes by. As yet, I don't know what's important and what isn't.'

'I'm sorry for mocking you,' Mrs Steadman apologized. 'I know you have your job to do, but it is upsetting, you coming around talking about Harold having affairs and suggesting our marriage was in trouble. You must try and see it from my point of view. It's almost as if you're accusing me.' She paused and smiled weakly. 'He just wasn't that kind of man, and if you'd known him you'd see what I mean. If there's anything Harry was having an affair with, it was his work. In fact, sometimes I thought he was married to his work and having an affair with me.'

She said this with good humour, not in bitterness, and Banks laughed politely. 'I'm sure my wife thinks the same,' he said, then called to Hatchley, who had turned to browse through the decimated bookshelves.

'I won't trouble you any further,' Banks said at the door, 'but there is one small piece of information you might be able to help me with.'

'Yes?'

'Your husband taught at Leeds in the history department, am I right?'

She nodded. 'Yes. That was his field.'

'Who were his colleagues? Who did he spend most time with during your years there?'

She thought for a moment before replying. 'We didn't socialize a great deal. Harry was too intent on his career. But let me see . . . there was Tom Darnley, he was a fairly close friend, and Godfrey Talbot. I think he knew Harry at Cambridge, too. That's about all, except for Geoffrey Baynes, but he went off to teach in Winnipeg, in Canada, before Harry left. That's all I can think of.'

'Thank you, Mrs Steadman,' Banks said as the door closed slowly. 'That'll do fine for a start. See you tomorrow.'

They walked back the same way to the car, which was hot from standing in the sun most of the day, and drove back to Eastvale. Banks regretted not having the Cortina; the landscape inspired him to listen to music. Instead, Hatchley drove too fast and droned on about never having seen so many bloody books outside Gristhorpe's office. 'Funny woman, that Mrs Steadman, don't you think?' he asked finally.

'Yes,' Banks answered, staring at a pattern of six trees on a distant drumlin, all bent in the same direction. 'She makes me uncomfortable, I've got to admit. I can't quite make her out.'

7

ONE

Had an adventurous fell-walker found himself on top of Crow Scar at eleven o'clock that Thursday morning, he would have seen, to the south, what looked like two shiny black beetles followed by green and red aphids make their way slowly down Gratly Hill and turn right at the bottom into Helmthorpe village.

Pedestrians on High Street – locals and tourists alike – stopped as the funeral cortège crawled by. Some averted their gaze; others doffed their caps; and one or two, clearly visitors from afar, even crossed themselves.

Harold Steadman had been a believer because belief was, for him, inextricable from the men and the actions that had helped shape and mould the area he loved; therefore, the funeral was a traditional, if nowadays rare, graveside ceremony conducted by a visiting minister from Lyndgarth.

On the hottest day of the year thus far, the motley group stood uneasily around the grave as the Reverend Sidney Caxton recited the traditional words: 'In the midst of life we are in death; of whom may we seek succour but Thee, O Lord . . . Thou knowest, Lord, the secrets of our hearts; shut not Thy merciful ears to our prayer; but spare us, Lord most holy.' He followed this, at Mrs Steadman's request, with the twenty-third Psalm: 'The Lord is my shepherd; I shall not want. He maketh me to lie down in green pastures: he leadeth me beside still waters . . . Yea, though I walk through the valley of the shadow of death, I will fear no evil: for Thou art with me; Thy rod and Thy staff they comfort me . . . Surely goodness and mercy shall follow me all the days of my life: and I will dwell in the house of the Lord forever.' It was a sombre and eerily appropriate farewell for a man like Harold Steadman.

To Sally Lumb, representing Eastvale Comprehensive School along with Hazel, Kathy, Anne and Mr Buxton, the headmaster, it was a gloomy and uncomfortable affair indeed. For one thing, in the tasteful navy-blue outfit her mother had made her wear, she was far too hot; her blouse was absolutely stuck to her back, and the beads of sweat that occasionally ran down her spine tickled like spiders.

Reverend Caxton took a handful of earth and cast it down on the coffin. 'For as much as it hath pleased Almighty God of His great mercy to receive unto Himself the soul of our dear brother here departed; we therefore commit his body to the ground . . .'

To pass the time, Sally studied the others covertly. Penny Cartwright was the most striking. Dressed in black from head to foot, her pale face in stark contrast, she wore just enough make-up to hide the bags under her eyes from all but the most discerning of onlookers, and to highlight her tragic, romantic cheekbones. She really did look extraordinarily beautiful, Sally thought, but in an intense, frightening and overwhelming way. On the other hand, Emma Steadman, in a conservative, unfashionable, charcoal-grey suit, didn't look much. She could have done herself up a bit, at least for the funeral, Sally thought, mentally adding a touch of blusher, eyeliner and a slash of lipstick. Immediately, though, she felt ashamed of herself for thinking such worldly thoughts at a time like this; after all, Mrs Steadman had always been nice to her.

'Earth to earth, ashes to ashes, dust to dust; in sure and certain hope of the Resurrection to eternal life, through our Lord Jesus Christ, who shall change our mortal body . . .'

Between the two grieving women stood Michael Ramsden, who looked, to Sally, rather like one of those doomed tubercular young men in the black and white gothic films her mother liked to watch on Channel Four. At Penny's other side was Jack Barker in a dark suit with a black armband. He really did look dashing and dangerous – that Errol Flynn moustache, the glint in his eyes – and Sally lost herself for a few moments in a swashbuckling fantasy.

The policeman, Banks, didn't detain her for long. True, he was handsome in a lean and bony kind of way and the scar was mysterious, but she had seen his true colours and found them lacking. He was soft; he had lived in London, had adventure all around him, countless opportunities for heroism, and he had given it all up to retire to this godforsaken part of the country. Old before his time, obviously. Dr Barnes looked as grey and insignificant as ever, and Teddy Hackett wore an ostentatious gold medallion which glinted in the sun against the background of his black shirt whenever he shifted from foot to foot.

'. . . that it may be like unto His glorious body, according to the mighty working whereby He is able to subdue all things to Himself.'

When Sally turned her attention back to the ceremony, it was all over. Slowly, as if reluctant to leave the deceased once and for all, the mourners edged away. Penny and Emma had their handkerchiefs out, and each hung on to the arm of the nearest man. In Penny's case that was Jack Barker, and Sally noticed what an attractive couple they made. The others left in groups of two or three, and the policeman sidled away alone. Harold Steadman, lowered to rest, had become a part, in death, of the dale he had loved so much in life.

TWO

At one o'clock, after having spent an hour discussing their lack of progress with Constable Weaver in the Helmthorpe station, Banks sat alone at a white table in the back garden of the Dog and Gun sipping a pint of shandy. The tables around him were all full. Tourists chatted about their holidays, the weather, their jobs (or lack of them), and children buzzed around unhindered like the wasps that flitted from glass rims to the remains of gateaux and sticky buns left on paper plates.

Banks didn't mind the squealing and the chatter; he was always able to shut out distracting background noise when he wanted to. He sat in his shirtsleeves and fiddled with his pipe, dark suit jacket slung over the back of a chair. The pipe was a blasted nuisance. It kept going out or getting clogged up, and the bitter juices trickled down the stem on to his tongue. It suited him, though; it was a gesture towards establishing the kind of identity and image he wanted to develop and project.

A wasp droned on to his sleeve. He brushed it away. Across the dazzling river with its overgrown banks the local club was playing cricket on a field of freshly mown grass. The slow pace of the game made it look like a Renaissance pavane. The harmony of white against green, the sharp crack of willow against leather, and the occasional smatterings of applause seemed to blend with the scent of the grass and enhance the sensation of peace. He rarely went to matches these days – and if he did, got bored after a few overs – but he remembered the famous England cricketers of his school days: Ted Dexter, 'Fiery' Fred Trueman, Ken Barrington, Colin Cowdrey; and the classroom games he had played with dice and paper, running his own county championship and Test Match series. The clichés about cricket were true, he reflected; there was something about the game that was essentially English – it made one feel that God was in his heaven and all was well with the Empire.

Far from it, though, he realized with a jolt. Beyond the pitch, the valley side sloped up gently at first, veined with drystone walls, then steepened and peaked into the long sheer curve of limestone, Crow Scar, above which Banks actually fancied he could see crows wheeling. And about halfway between the pitch and the scar, as far as the eye's imperfect perspective could make out, was the spot where Steadman's body had been found.

Banks didn't like funerals, and in a way it seemed a pointless convention to attend the funerals of people he had never known. Not once had he caught a murderer that way: no graveside confessions, no mysterious stranger lurking behind the yew trees. Still, he did it, and when he probed his motives he found that it was because of a strange and unique bond he felt with the dead man, perhaps more intimate even than if he had known him. In a sense, Banks saw himself as the victim's appointed avenger, and, in an odd way, he worked together with the dead man to redress the balance of nature; they were co-workers of light against darkness. In this case, Steadman was his guide from the spirit-world: a silent and shapeless guide perhaps, but present nonetheless.

Banks looked back at the game just in time to see the batsman swipe a badly paced off-spinner towards the boundary. The bowler found his length in the next two deliveries though, and play slowed down as the batsman was forced to switch to defensive tactics. Banks, aided by the warm air, drifted back into a reverie about his first year and a half in Yorkshire.

The landscape, it went without saying, he found beautiful. It was wild and rough, unlike the southern downs, but its scale inspired awe. And the people. Whatever he had heard about the stubborn intractability of the Yorkshire character, the gruffness, the slowness in taking to strangers, was all true to some extent, but like all generalizations didn't do justice to the full reality. He had grown to appreciate the stoic humour, the quick wit and instinctive good sense, the friendliness beneath the crusty surface.

Banks also liked the feeling of being an outsider. Not a stranger, as he had been among the anonymous international crowds of London, but an outsider. He knew he always would be, no matter how deep he put his roots.

Knocking out his pipe, he tried to bring his mind to bear on the case again. It had the same sordid elements as any murder, but in such an environment it seemed even more of a blasphemy. The whole way of life in the small dale – the people, their priorities, beliefs and concerns – was different from that in London, or even in Eastvale. Gristhorpe had said that being an outsider would give him an advantage, a fresh perspective, but Banks wasn't too sure; he seemed to be getting nowhere fast.

He turned as a long shadow brushed across the white table and saw Michael Ramsden disappearing into the pub.

'Mr Ramsden!' he called after him. 'A word, if you've got a moment to spare.'

Ramsden turned. 'Chief Inspector Banks. I didn't see you there.'

Banks thought he was lying, but it meant nothing. As a policeman, he was used to being avoided. Ramsden perched on the very edge of a chair, indicating through his body language that he had no intention of staying for more than a minute or two.

'I thought you'd be at the funeral lunch,' Banks said.

'I was. You know what those things are like: all that false humour and bonhomie to cover up what's really happened. And someone inevitably drinks too much and get silly.' He shrugged. 'I left. Was there something you wanted to ask me?'

'Yes. Are you certain you didn't go out on Saturday night?'

'Of course I'm certain. I've already told you.'

'I know, but I want to make absolutely sure. Not even for half an hour or so?'

'You've seen where I live. Where would I go?'

Banks smiled. 'A walk? A run? I've heard that writers get blocked sometimes.'

Ramsden laughed. 'That's true enough. But no, not me, not on Saturday anyway. I was in all evening. Besides, Harry had a key; he would have let himself in and waited.'

'Had he done that before?'

'Once, yes, when I had to work late at the office.'

'He wouldn't, say, visit another friend in the area and come back later?'

'I don't think Harry really knew anyone else in the York area. Not well enough to drop in on, at least. Why do you want to know all this, if you don't mind me asking?'

'We need to know where Mr Steadman was between ten fifteen and the time of death. But there's something else,' Banks went on quickly, sensing Ramsden's restlessness. 'I'd like to talk to you a bit more about the past – your relationship with Penny Cartwright.'

Ramsden sighed and made himself more comfortable. A white-coated waiter passed by. 'Drink?' Banks asked.

'Might as well, if you intend to keep me here a while. But it's all so long ago – I don't see how you expect me to remember. And I can't imagine what any of it has to do with Harry's death.'

Banks ordered two pints of lager. 'Just bear with me, that's all. Ten years ago,' he went on, 'was a very important time in your life. It was summer, and you were eighteen, all set for university, courting the prettiest girl in Swainsdale. Harold and Emma Steadman came to stay at your parents' guest house for a month, as usual. By all accounts that was a memorable summer – long walks, expeditions to local sites of interest. Surely you remember?'

Ramsden smiled. 'Yes, of course I do, now you put it like that. I just hadn't realized it was so long ago,' he said wistfully.

'Time does seem to pass quickly,' Banks agreed. 'Especially when you lose your sense of continuity, then look back. Anyway, it came to an end. Things changed. What happened between you and Penny?'

Ramsden sipped his lager and brushed away a trouble-some wasp. 'I've told you before. Like most teenage lovers, we just drifted apart.'

'Did you ever regret it?'

'What?'

'The turn of events. Perhaps you could have been happily married to Penny now, and none of this would ever have happened.'

'None of what? I fail to see the connection.'

'Everything: Penny's adventures in the music business, your bachelorhood.'

Ramsden laughed. 'You make it sound like a disease, Chief Inspector. I may be a bachelor, but that doesn't mean I live a celibate life. I have lovers, a social life. I enjoy myself. As for Penny . . . well, it's her life. Who's to say things haven't turned out for the best for her, too?'

Banks tried to coax his pipe alight. A baby in a high chair two tables away started to cry. Its cheeks were smeared with strawberry jam. 'Perhaps if Steadman hadn't come along, though, and spirited her away . . . ?'

'What are you suggesting? That Harry and Penny were involved?'

'Well, he was older, more mature. You have to admit it's a possibility. She certainly spent a lot of time with him. Isn't that why you split up? Didn't you argue about Steadman?'

Ramsden was on the edge of his seat again. 'No, we didn't,' he said angrily. 'Look, I don't know who's been telling you all this, but it's lies.'

'Did you split up because Penny wouldn't give you what you wanted? Maybe she was giving it to Steadman?'

This time Ramsden seemed on the point of getting up and hitting Banks, but he took a deep breath, scratched the back of his ear and smiled. 'You know, you really are irritating,' he said. 'I should imagine people tell you things just to make you go away.'

'Sometimes,' Banks admitted. 'Go on.'

'Maybe there's some truth in the first part of your question. A man can only wait so long, as you probably know yourself. I was definitely ready, and Penny was a very beautiful girl. It's only natural, isn't it? We were both a bit naïve, scared of sex, but it didn't help that she kept saying no.'

Banks laughed. 'It certainly wouldn't,' he said knowingly. 'I dare say I'd have been climbing the walls myself. But why do you think she kept saying no? Was it something to do with Steadman? Or did she have another boyfriend?'

Ramsden thought, frowning, before he answered. 'No, there wasn't another boyfriend, I'm sure of that. I think it was just a matter of morality. Penny was brought up to be a nice girl, and nice girls don't. As for Harry, I don't think he did what you're suggesting. I'm sure I'd have known, somehow. I suppose at times I was a bit peeved about how close they were. Not that I thought there was anything going on, mind, but they did spend a lot of time together, time she could have spent with me. Harry was so much more sure of himself than I was. I was shy and clumsy. So yes, I might have been a bit envious, but I didn't feel the kind of jealousy you have in mind.'

'Oh? What kind of jealousy do I have in mind?'

'You know. The kind that eats away at you and ends in murder,' he answered, deepening his voice for dramatic effect.

Banks laughed. Ramsden had nearly finished his drink and looked anxious to leave, but there were a couple more areas Banks wanted to probe. 'What about her father, the major? Do you think he had anything to do with you two drifting apart?'

'I don't think so, no. As far as I know, he approved of me. He's a bit cracked, but he never really gave us any trouble.'

'Did you ever get together with Penny again later? You were both in London at times, weren't you?'

'I suppose so. But I never saw her. Once it was over, that was it.'

'What did you do while she was off with Steadman?'

'It wasn't the way you make it sound, Chief Inspector. Often we all went together; sometimes I just didn't want to go with them. I read a lot. I'd just discovered the pleasures of literature. My sixth-form English teacher, Mr Nixon, was a brilliant inspiring man, and he managed to undo, in one year, all the damage that the others had done. For the first time, I could enjoy Shakespeare, Eliot, Lawrence, Keats, and the rest with a joy I'd not known before. What I'm saying is that I was a very romantic and introspective young man; I was happy enough to sit by a "babbling brook" and read Wordsworth.'

'When you weren't trying to get Penny into bed,' said Banks, who had once, on Gristhorpe's recommendation, tried Wordsworth and found him an insufferable bore.

Ramsden blushed. 'Yes, well . . . I was a normal adolescent; I don't deny that.' He looked at his watch. 'Look, I don't mean to seem rude, but I do have to get back to the office. Tell me, before I go, why this fascination with past events?'

'I'm not really sure,' Banks said, reaching for his glass. 'I'm just following my instincts.'

'And what do your instincts tell you?'

'That Harold Steadman's death wasn't a spur-of-the-moment affair; it was premeditated and it probably had its roots in the past. You see, you were all together ten years ago – you, Penny Cartwright, her father, the Steadmans – and now you're all back in more or less the same place. Eighteen months after Steadman comes to live in Gratly, he's dead. Doesn't that strike you as odd?'

Ramsden brushed back his forelock, which this time actually had slipped over his eyes, then he drained his glass and stood up. 'Put that way, I suppose it does,' he said. 'But I think your instinct is wrong. Things aren't the same as they were before. For one thing, there are other people around now, too. If you think Harry's death had anything to do with Penny, I suggest you follow your instinct to Jack Barker. He's been hanging around with her a lot lately, so I hear. Now good day, Chief Inspector, and thanks for the drink.'

Banks watched Ramsden thread his way between the tables and turned his attention back to the cricket match just in time to see a wicket fall dramatically. The bails flew high in the air and the bowler threw up his arms and yelled, 'Owzat!'

Banks thought about his talk with Ramsden and wondered if there was anything in what he'd said about Barker. 'Men have died from time to time, and worms have eaten them, but not for love.' So his daughter Tracy, playing the fair Rosalind, had said in *As You Like It*, which had been Eastvale Comprehensive's school play that term. But it wasn't true; many had killed and many had died for love. And Penny Cartwright was certainly the kind of woman to stir up such strong feelings.

Suddenly, the air roared and screamed as two F-111s from a nearby US airbase shot overhead. They flew so low that Banks could almost see the pilots' faces. It was a common enough occurrence in the dales; jet bombers frequently ripped through the peaceful landscape and shattered the idyll as they broke the sound barrier. On the hillside below Crow Scar, scared sheep huddled together and ran for the cover of a drystone wall. People at the tables put their hands over their ears and screwed up their faces.

The planes broke the spell for Banks. There was paperwork to be done that afternoon. Grabbing his jacket, he drained his glass and left the cricketers to finish their game.

THREE

Dinner in the Banks household that evening was a lively affair. It seemed like ages since the family had all sat down together and enjoyed one of Sandra's delicious concoctions: chicken in tarragon and white-wine sauce. She had a wonderful knack of making the most inexpensive cuts of meat taste like gourmet creations. This skill, Banks thought, was characteristic of someone with inborn good taste and a poor working-class background. All it took, said Sandra, clearly delighted with the compliments, was the right cooking method and a little care with the sauce.

Most of the conversation was taken up by the children's accounts of their day trip to York.

'The Minster was smashing,' enthused Tracy, the bright fourteen-year-old with a passion for history. 'Do you know, Daddy, there's more stained glass in there than in any other cathedral in Europe?'

Banks expressed interest and surprise. Architecture had not, so far, been one of his interests, but it was becoming more and more appealing. At the moment he was still reading up on the geology of the dales.

'And the Five Sisters are simply stunning,' Tracy went on.

'Five Sisters?' Banks asked. 'In a minster?'

'Oh, Daddy,' Tracy laughed, 'you don't know anything, do you? The Five Sisters are lancet windows in the north transept. They're made of grisaille glass. Thirteenth century, I think. And the Rose Window—'

'It was boring,' cut in Brian, who all the while had been feeling left out. 'Just a lot of old statues of dead kings and stuff. Junk, it was. Boring.'

'You're just a philistine,' Tracy retorted, pronouncing the word with both difficulty and authority. 'I'll bet you didn't even notice that monument to Archbishop Scrope.'

'Scrope? Who's he?' Banks asked. While sympathizing with Brian, he didn't feel justified in cheating Tracy out of her excitement. She was at an age now when one of her great thrills was to educate her parents, whom she thought dreadfully ignorant of the past that surrounded them. Very soon, Banks mused sadly, all that would be forgotten, at least for a few years, and life would be all clothes, pop music, make-up, hairstyles and boys.

'He was a rebel,' Tracy informed him. 'Henry the Fourth had him executed in 1405.'

'Oh shut up with all them dates, clever clogs,' Brian burst out. 'You think you know it all.' And before Tracy could respond, he turned to his father and launched into his own account.

'We went on a boat down the river, Dad, and she felt seasick.' He cast a look of pitying contempt at his sister. 'And we passed this big chocolate factory. Me and some of the boys wanted to go on a tour but the teacher wouldn't let us. She just wanted to show us history and stuff and all those silly old narrow streets.'

'The Shambles,' Tracy interrupted. 'And Stonegate and Petergate. Anyway, the chocolates would only have made you sick.'

'It didn't need chocolates to make *you* sick, did it?' Brian taunted her.

'That's enough, Brian!' Sandra cut in. 'Stop it, both of you!'

And so it went on; Brian sulked and Tracy scowled at him until they both went upstairs to watch television while Sandra cleared the table and Banks helped her with the dishes. Finally, still arguing, they were packed off to bed, and Banks suggested a nightcap.

'I've got a new job,' Sandra said, pouring the Scotch. 'Well, not really new, just different.'

Banks asked what it was. Sandra worked as a dentist's receptionist three mornings a week in Eastvale.

'Mr Maxwell's going on holiday, shutting up shop for three weeks, and Peggy Matthews – that's Mr Smedley's receptionist – is off at the same time, too.'

'Not together, I hope?'

Sandra laughed. 'No. Fine bedfellows they'd make, I'm sure. Maxwell's going to the Greek Islands and Peggy's off to Weymouth. Anyway, apparently Smedley asked if he could borrow me while the boss was away. Maxwell asked me and I said yes. It's all right, isn't it? I didn't think we had any plans.'

'Yes, it's fine if you want to. I can't really plan anything until this Steadman business is settled.'

'Good. Smedley's a real perfectionist, so I hear. Especially when it comes to fitting caps and crowns, matching the colours and all that. They say he's one of the best in Yorkshire.'

'You might get to meet the local gentry, then. Who knows?'

Sandra laughed. 'Well, Peggy did say that Mrs Steadman goes there. She's having some root canal work done. She's a bit of a local celebrity now.'

'It's amazing, isn't it?' Banks said. 'The husband gets murdered and people suddenly line up to look at the wife as if she were bloody royalty.'

'It's only natural, though. We all have some morbid curiosity.'

'Not me. Look,' Banks said, 'we haven't been out for a long time, and there's supposed to be a good folk singer on in Helmthorpe tomorrow. Do you fancy going?'

'Changing the subject, eh? Helmthorpe? Isn't that where the Steadmans live?'

'Yes.'

'This isn't work, is it, Alan? It's not connected to the case?'

'Cross my heart. We'll just go and listen to some good folk music like we've done plenty of times before. Ask Harriet and David along, too.'

'If they can get a sitter. It's such short notice. What about Jenny Fuller? Think she might like to come?'

'She's in France,' Banks said. 'Don't you remember? That wine-tasting tour. Took off as soon as term ended.'

'Lucky her. All right, then, I'll call Harriet. As long as you promise it's nothing to do with work! I don't much fancy sitting there like a spare part while you grill some suspect.'

'Scout's honour. And I'm not sure I like what you're implying. I don't grill people.'

Sandra smiled. Banks moved closer and put his arm around her. 'You know—' he began.

'Ssshhh . . .' Sandra put her finger to his lips. 'Let's go to bed.'

'What's wrong with the sofa?' Banks asked, and pulled her gently towards him.

FOUR

Sally Lumb was finding it difficult to get to sleep. She had put aside *Wuthering Heights* because her eyes were getting tired, but sleep just would not come.

First she thought of Kevin. She would have to give in soon or he'd be off after someone more experienced. He was right on the edge and she couldn't tease him for much longer. She didn't want to, anyway. The last time they'd been together, the day they saw Penny Cartwright, she had let him put himself close to her sex; she had felt his heat and hardness right at her very entrance and it made her tremble and go all wet, just like it said in the books. It had been cruel to stop him then, she knew, but they had no protection; she didn't want to get pregnant. There were ways around that, though. Next time . . .

Turning over and praying for sleep to come, she started thinking about the implications of what she had remembered that afternoon. Not the car on Saturday night – that was nothing – but something she hadn't fully perceived at the time that now had more sinister far-reaching possibilities. It was her first real clue, and she had to decide what to do about it. She wouldn't go to the police, that was for certain – a proper fool she'd make of herself if she was wrong! Besides, she was already determined to solve the affair herself. Perhaps she might even become a heroine.

And the police were fools anyway; she could easily one-up them. That man from London had treated her like a silly child. And what had he done that was so wonderful? Given up an exciting metropolitan life for the boredom of Swainsdale, that's what he'd done. Lord, the man could have been working for Scotland Yard!

And so, as her mind tossed and turned towards sleep, the first step became clear. If she was right, then someone was in danger; a warning had to be given. She would arrange a secret meeting, and maybe after that, if her suspicions were proved correct, she could go about setting a trap. That thought worried her, as she really would be making herself vulnerable. But she could always rope Kevin in; he was a big strong lad, and he'd do anything for her.

As Sally finally drifted into the dream world that usually puzzled and irritated her, she could see the lights of London strung out before her like a diamond necklace. Why stop there? the dream insisted. And the images progressed, built up from magazine photographs and television programmes: *Vogue* models sashayed down the Champs Elysées, famous actresses stepped out of limousines under the neons of Sunset Strip, and all the well-known television personalities she had ever seen chatted over cocktails at a party in Manhattan . . . But soon it all faded, and what she remembered in the morning was a rather absurd image of being in Leeds, a place she had visited several times on shopping exped-itions with her mother. In the dream it felt like a foreign city. There were uniformed policemen all over the place, and Sally had to push her bicycle because she didn't have a licence – at least, not one that was valid in Leeds. She was there, she vaguely remembered, because she was searching for a bird, a white one that had flown from her garden, a vast dark expanse like a tilled field after rain. She didn't know if the bird had been her pet, her responsibility, or just a wild creature she had taken a fancy to, but it was important, and she was there in an alien familiar city pushing her bicycle among the policemen looking for it . . .

FIVE

Banks slipped Finzi's choral setting of 'Intimations of Immortality' into the car stereo as he turned off the A1 at the Wetherby roundabout and took the A58 to Leeds. It was eleven thirty on Friday morning, just five days after the discovery of Steadman's body. Hatchley, under the weather on Thursday morning after his visit to Darlington, had checked Hackett's alibi thoroughly and found that it held. Barnes, too, was out of the running; though he was unmarried and had no one to confirm that he went straight home after visiting Mrs Gaskell, his finances were in order and there had never been even the slightest hint of malpractice or wrongdoing of any kind during his twenty years as a doctor in Helmthorpe.

In his office earlier that morning, Banks had completed the mass of paperwork he had started the day before: transcripts of interviews, maps and timetables of people's movements, lists of unasked or unanswered questions. He had gone over the forensic evidence again, but found nothing new. Constable Weaver and his reinforcements were still asking questions around the village, the campsite and outlying farms, but the likelihood of their turning up new evidence after so long was fast diminishing.

The hushed choir entered, repeating the opening theme, 'There was a time when meadow, grove, and stream . . .' over the baritone's solo line, and Banks forgot his frequently distasteful job for a few moments. Finzi's music made Wordsworth's poem bearable.

The drive, which he took slowly, turned out to be quite pleasant once he'd left the Great North Road and its never-ending stream of lorries. It was the quickest way, the same route as he had taken on his last trip to Leeds, to interview a pawnbroker in connection with a series of robberies. But that had been a grey, rainy day in late October. Now it was summer and he drove through the kind of peaceful green countryside one so often finds close to large English cities.

Banks puffed at his pipe as Finzi played on, not bothering to relight it after the second time it went out, and soon found himself in the Seacroft area. He had to concentrate hard on directions; the tower blocks all looked much the same and there were few landmarks to go by. He came out finally through an underpass near the city centre and parked close to the Town Hall. From there, he could see the high white tower of the library building, something Gristhorpe had told him about that morning in his potted history of the city and its architecture.

Banks had no fixed ideas about how to approach the academics; he intended to play it by ear. He had called earlier and arranged to have lunch with Darnley and Talbot in a pub near the university. Though term was officially over, they still travelled to their offices almost every day to carry on with their research or simply to get out from under their wives' feet. Darnley, to whom Banks had spoken, seemed quite excited by the prospect of a chat with the police, or so he had said in a rather detached way, as if he were discussing the mating habits of lemurs.

Banks still had an hour to kill, so he decided to take Gristhorpe's advice and take a look at the Town Hall. It was an impressive Victorian edifice, complete with fluted columns, huge domed roof, clock and a pair of lions guarding the entrance by the broad flight of stone steps. The stone, sandstone by the look of it, seemed light and clean. Gristhorpe had told him it had been sandblasted a few years ago, as few such structures had withstood a hundred years or more of industry without turning black.

Banks admired the bulk of the place and the bold classical lines of its design. He felt he could grasp, just by looking, some of the civic pride that had gone into its construction. Queen Victoria herself had attended the grand opening. She must have spent a lot of time opening buildings, Banks reflected.

He ventured inside past the statues of Victoria and Albert in the foyer and into the main hall, which appeared to have been recently restored. Enormous pillars of what looked like marble streaked with pink, green and blue were spaced along the walls, and the ceiling was divided into brightly coloured square panels, gilded around their edges. Mottoes and proverbs beloved of the pious Victorians adorned the high places: EXCEPT THE LORD BUILD THE HOUSE, THEY LABOUR IN VAIN THAT BUILT IT; EXCEPT THE LORD KEEP THE CITY, THE WATCHMAN WATCHETH BUT IN VAIN; WEAVE THE TRUTH WITH TRUST; and LABOUR OMNIA VINCIT. At the end stood a majestic pipe organ.

Banks glanced at his watch and walked out slowly; his footsteps echoed in the silence. Yes, it was impressive, and he could begin to see what Steadman found so fascinating about northern history.

But he also remembered Hackett's outburst about false romanticized views of the past. The wealthy city officials and merchants had gone to great trouble to make sure that Queen Victoria's route avoided the more squalid areas of the city: row upon row of overcrowded back-to-backs with leaky roofs and damp walls where the nameless masses lived. It was from their labours and in their name, the name of civic pride, that such glories as the Town Hall were built, yet they were condemned to live in squalor and then accused of becoming animals. There had even been one man, a chemist according to Gristhorpe, who had perfumed the air outside his shop as the royal progress passed. It all depended on what side you were on, Banks thought, as to what your perspective was.

He consulted his pocket map and walked up between the Town Hall and the library, carried on along Caverley Street past the Civic Hall, a white building with twin pointed towers and colourful gardens, then past the General Infirmary and Leeds Polytechnic and into the outer reaches of the university campus. Finally, he came to a quadrangle surrounded by modern office-style buildings. It was a long way from the dreaming spires of Oxford and Cambridge, but Leeds was supposed to be a red-brick university, even if there were no red bricks in sight.

He found Darnley's office in the History Department with the help of an angular bespectacled secretary. After a quick firm handshake, Darnley was ready for a pub lunch. 'Talbot's going to meet us there,' he explained. 'He's got a session with one of his doctoral students right now.'

He led Banks across a dirt path behind the building and on to a narrow cobbled street. The pub was actually part of a hotel, and it stood back from the road at the end of a short driveway. As it was such a warm sunny day, they sat at one of the outside tables.

Darnley was a tall man about forty, well built and fit. He had a trace of a northern accent and did not seem at all the absent-minded professor type that Banks had expected. His short brown hair was neatly combed and although his suit seemed half a size too big, it was of good quality. It had probably been a perfect fit when he bought it, Banks guessed, but like many men of his age, fearing heart attacks and other plagues of the sedentary life, he had begun to exercise.

The two men sipped draught Guinness, squinting in the bright sun, and Banks laid his pipe, tobacco and lighter on the table.

'Aha, a pipe-smoker, I see,' Darnley noted. 'Touch of the Maigret, eh? Thought of taking it up myself but it's too much trouble. Wasted years trying to stop smoking, cutting down, switching to milder brands, and in the end I found the only way to bloody well stop was cold turkey.'

'It can't have been as easy as you make it sound,' Banks said, stuffing his pipe with rubbed flake and tamping it gently.

'No, no, it wasn't.' Darnley laughed. 'I had a few relapses. But I've been playing a lot of squash and tennis lately and running a few miles each day. You'd be surprised how that kind of thing puts you off smoking. You'd never believe it, but a year or so ago I was overweight, drinking too much – ugh!'

'Doctor's orders?'

'Told me point-blank. "Go on like you are doing, and I'll give you another ten years at most." It was a toss-up which would go first – heart, liver or lungs. Anyway, he said if I shaped up the sky's the limit. Well, not in so many words, but I got the point.' He watched Banks light his pipe. 'Still,' he said, 'I suppose you need props in your business. False sense of security and all that.'

Banks smiled and admitted it helped. He liked the look of curiosity and intelligence in Darnley's eyes.

'I hope you don't think you need it with me? I mean, I'm not a suspect, am I?' He was smiling, but the tension showed in the tight set of his lips.

'Not yet,' Banks replied, returning his gaze.

'Touché. You mean if I start to put myself forward as one, all offers are welcome?'

'I shouldn't worry about it,' Banks assured him. He was still trying to work out the best approach to this edgy intelligent man whose quick playful exterior no doubt masked a mind like a steel trap and covered up a complex, perhaps even devious, personality.

He decided to play along a little longer, certain that the arrival of Talbot would alter the light-hearted mood. 'You might as well tell me where you were last Saturday night, though,' he asked.

Darnley looked at him, bright eyes twinkling but hard. 'Do you know, Chief Inspector, I have no alibi at all for last weekend. I had a lot of work to do so I stayed in all Saturday evening marking examination papers and reading a new account of the Peterloo massacre. Of course, my wife was at home too, but I don't suppose she counts, does she?'

Banks laughed. 'I wouldn't know till I asked her, would I?'

'You're a canny man, as the Scots say. No, I don't suppose you would.'

'Why weren't you at the funeral yesterday?'

'Wasn't invited, was I? Neither of us. Actually, I didn't even know about it. I only knew about Harry because I read it in the *Yorkshire Evening Post*.'

'You'd lost touch?'

'Sort of, yes.'

After a little more banter and a good draught of stout, Darnley seemed to relax more. Trying to establish the conversation as one between professionals, Banks asked the professor about his job: 'I suppose you need props, too? It can't be easy standing up there alone in front of a hundred or so students and just talking for an hour.'

'Put like that, it does sound rather awful,' Darnley conceded. 'You get used to it, of course, but you're right, there's always a bit of stage fright till you get going. I've always got my notes to fall back on, though. No teacher worth his salt dries up in front of a class. You can always waffle and students would never know the difference. Sometimes I think I could tell them that Adolf Hitler was one of the heroes of twentieth-century politics and they'd just write it down without question. But props . . . yes . . . One tends to find a position one is comfortable in. Funny thing, that. Some people pace back and forth, some hunch over the lectern, and others sit on the edge of a desk and fold their arms. One chap I knew always used to play with his keys while he was lecturing. Trouble was, they were in his trouser pocket and the students all thought he was playing with himself.'

They both laughed. 'What about Harry Steadman?' Banks asked casually.

Darnley squinted. 'Harry was good,' he answered. 'It's true we've been out of touch and I've not seen much of him since he left, but we were quite close at one time, and I was sorry to hear about his death. I'd say we were colleagues rather than friends, if there's a difference. He was exceptionally bright – but I suppose you know that already. Ambitious, yes, but only in his field. He genuinely believed in what he was doing: teaching, research, breaking new ground. He thought it all had some real value for society. And, believe me, that's rare these days. There's so much cynicism around in education, especially as the government doesn't seem to set much store by us any more.'

Banks nodded. 'It's the same with crime. You're fighting a losing battle, or so it seems most of the time, and that's no good for anyone's professional pride.'

'But at least the government believes in your value: pay rises, recruitment, modern equipment.'

'True,' Banks agreed. 'But it's all long overdue.' He didn't want to get sidetracked into an argument, especially as he had many objections to the way the government seemed to look upon the police as a private army of paid bully boys to pit against people with genuine grievances and a constitutional right to air them. A copper with humanist socialist leanings would be a bit hard for Darnley to take, he thought. Besides, he was a detective – CID, a paid thinker – and he didn't have to go on crowd control, bashing the bonces of the proletariat.

'I'm envious,' Darnley said. 'That's all. I just wish we could get a larger slice of the cake, too. Academics are very big on pride as well, believe me. Harry was a good lecturer and he always managed to stimulate enthusiasm among his students. That's hard to do these days when you're in competition with television, video games and God knows what. Stop me if I'm beginning to sound too much like a good reference for him, but it's true. Most of all, he loved research, real field work, and that's why he left. When he found himself with enough money to do as he pleased, that's exactly what he did. Some chaps might have packed it all in and buggered off to the south of France for a life of idleness, sin and luxury, but not Harry. He was a dedicated man.'

At this point they were joined by a smaller, pudgy man, bald except for a few wisps of grey hair above his ears. He had a deeply ingrained frown in his broad brow and a tiny pursed mouth that gave him, overall, a surly and miserly look. His cultured voice was surprisingly soft, and Banks wondered how he managed with a large room full of students. He proved rather taciturn, and after they had ordered roast beef sandwiches and another round of stout, he simply sat and listened as Banks and Darnley went on talking.

'I think I've got a fairly clear picture of Mr Steadman's professional life now,' Banks said. 'It's something everyone seems to agree on – bright, dedicated, obsessed even.'

At this Talbot tut-tutted, and when he spoke his voice was redolent of Cambridge quadrangles, effete dons and afternoon glasses of amontillado. 'Surely, er, Chief Inspector, an obsession is something we might define as intrinsically unhealthy, wouldn't you say? I don't mean to nit-pick over semantics, of course, but one must admit that the term has definite connotations of mental imbalance. Harold Steadman was most certainly not unbalanced; therefore, he was not obsessed.' And all the time he talked he frowned, as if the usage really upset him.

Banks apologized. 'I didn't mean to imply anything as drastic as that. No, I realize that there's a difference between dedication and obsession. What I'd like to know is whether he found time for other pursuits. Social life, for example. Did he mix, go to parties, drink?'

Talbot returned in moody silence to his drink, perhaps

to contemplate the exact *OED* definition of 'obsessed', as if such eccentricities as 'social life' were best left to the lower classes.

'Do you know, Godfrey,' Darnley said cheerfully, oblivious to his colleague's disdain, 'the chief inspector might not be far wrong.' He turned to Banks and winked. 'Yes, Harry liked a few drinks now and then, and he went to the occasional faculty party. But he was never really at ease socially – especially when he was out of his element, so to speak, when there was nobody to talk to about his field. He didn't care much for sports, never watched television, and he certainly wasn't a woman chaser.'

'Do you mean he was uncomfortable in the presence of non-academics?'

'Oh no, not that at all. I didn't mean to give you that impression. Harry certainly wasn't an academic snob. As a matter of fact he invited me up to Gratly once, shortly after he'd moved, and we spent a very pleasant evening in a dingy local with a thriller writer and some other chaps. No, Harry would talk to anybody. That was one of his beefs against academic life, the rampant intellectual snobbery. What I mean is that his heart was in his work and his work was basically to do with people, so he enjoyed their company. There's a strong human element in his field, you know. It's not all abstract. He was interested in ordinary people, their background and ways of life. I suppose you know that his main fields were industrial archaeology and the Roman occupation? But he also loved folk music, local lore, things like that. He was fascinated by the history of trade unions, the early working class radicals. So you could say that Harry was quite at home with the common man, he'd just no time for petty chit-chat like you so often get at parties. He always tended to edge conversations in the direction of his interests.'

Talbot nodded in grudging agreement and lit a cigarette. 'Let me put it this way, Chief Inspector Banks,' he said in a tone of professor to lowly student. 'If you were to – if you were able to – sit down now and talk to Harold Steadman, he would probably begin by asking you about your job, how you feel about it, just to get things going. He would discover where you come from and find out about your family background. Then, depending on how interesting he found all that, he would either question you further – say, if your father had been a union man or a farm labourer in the dales – or he would proceed to tell you about the history of your area, how it fits in with the rest of the country, what the Romans did there, and so on. People usually enjoyed his company. He could sense when he was becoming a bore and would usually stop and listen politely for a while. Of course,' Talbot added, with a deft flick of ash, 'if he found you boring, then you wouldn't get much out of him. Am I right, Darnley?'

Darnley nodded.

'What about Mrs Steadman?' Banks asked. 'Did you see much of her when she was in Leeds?' He addressed the question to Talbot, who seemed to have become quite garrulous, but it was Darnley who answered.

'At first we did, yes. Quite a pretty little thing, really. Naturally, they were in a new environment and wanted to meet people and settle in. But like many faculty wives, she soon withdrew. It's common enough, believe me. My wife, for example, wouldn't be seen dead at an academic gathering these days. It bores them, you see. And they let themselves go over the years. You know, not bothering much about their appearance any more.'

Banks couldn't be sure whether Darnley was talking about his own wife or about Emma Steadman.

The conversation moved on to generalities again, with Darnley doing most of the entertaining, and Banks soon realized he wasn't going to learn anything more of value.

When he left, he carried away with him the image of a young couple – perhaps not unlike Sandra and himself in the old days – newly married, the husband beginning what was likely to be a distinguished academic career. There were long summer holidays in Gratly at the Ramsden house; there was the young ambitious Michael courting Penny, the flower of the dale; it was pure peace and innocence with nothing but a bright future ahead for them all.

For Steadman, things seemed to get better and better; for Emma, there was withdrawal from the dull academic life into domestic boredom; for Penny, a wild exciting fling in the fast lane which left her isolated and cynical, cut off from her roots; and for Ramsden, a steady advance up the publishing ladder and a return to his beloved north. It all sounded so idyllic, but one of them was dead. What had gone wrong and why?

An hour later he was no closer to the solution, but his spirits felt lighter, despite the clouds, as he drove into the dales countryside and sang along with Britten's versions of old English folk songs.

SIX

They were sipping Coke and talking about boys under the scornful lascivious eyes of the old Greek. Hazel Kirk had had her first date with Terry Preston, son of the local grocer, the previous night, and she was titillating her friends with an account of her attempt to keep his wandering hands from her most private parts. Once in a while she would blush while describing the indefinable feelings she had had when she failed in her task.

But Sally Lumb, usually so interested – not to mention condescending – during such discussions, seemed pre-occupied. The others noticed, but Hazel, for one, was not going to be done out of her moment of glory simply because madam was sulking.

Anne Downes, perhaps more sensitive to mood and certainly less interested in boys and their inexplicable desires, waited patiently until Kathy Chalmers had stopped giggling and tried to change the subject.

'They haven't caught him yet, you know,' she announced, adjusting her glasses on the bridge of her nose.

'Who?' Hazel asked abruptly, annoyed at being dragged away from other, more important thoughts.

'The killer, of course. Who else? The man who killed Mr Steadman.'

'How do you know it was a man?' Hazel asked. It was a question she'd heard on countless television programmes.

'Stands to reason, doesn't it,' Anne snorted. 'It'd have to be a pretty strong woman to slug him and carry him all the way up that field below Crow Scar.'

'Mrs Butterworth could have done it,' Kathy chipped

in. They all giggled. Mrs Butterworth was the butcher's wife, an enormous red-faced woman who towered above her meek hunched husband.

'Don't be silly,' Anne said, allowing herself a smile. 'Why should she do it? Besides, the effort would probably give her a heart attack.'

'Jimmy Collins told me the police have been talking to Penny Cartwright and the major,' Kathy said. 'He said the old man didn't give them much time.'

'How would Jimmy Collins know?' Anne asked.

'He was in the shop downstairs. "Where there's a will, there's a way," my mother always says. I think Penny did it. I think her and Mr Steadman were having a torrid love affair and when she wanted him to leave his wife and marry her he wouldn't do it so she killed him.'

'Don't be so stupid,' Anne said. 'If it was really like that she'd have killed Mrs Steadman, not him.'

That silenced Kathy, but Hazel picked up the thread. 'Well if that wasn't why,' she said, 'there could have been plenty of other reasons. Everybody knows she went away for ages and took drugs and was pro . . . prom . . .'

'Promiscuous?' suggested Anne.

'Yes, promiscuous, clever clogs – that's what I said. Maybe she had his baby or he knew something about her past. They've known each other a long time, you know.'

The others were silent, taking it all in. 'You might be right about the last bit,' Anne allowed, 'but she wouldn't kill him just because she had his baby, would she? I think it was Jack Barker.'

'Why would he do it?' Kathy asked.

'Maybe he was just doing research for his next book,' Hazel joked.

'And maybe he's in love with Penny Cartwright and

wanted to get Mr Steadman out of the way so he could have her all to himself,' Anne said. 'And there's another thing: I heard the police gave Teddy Hackett a nasty time the other day.'

'He certainly looked a little pale when I saw him,' Hazel added.

'My dad heard them arguing a couple of weeks ago – Hackett and Mr Steadman,' Anne said.

'But they can't think he did it,' Hazel reasoned, 'or they'd have arrested him in custody by now. I bet he's got a skintight alibi.'

'It's "watertight", you fool.' Anne laughed. 'And he can't be "arrested in custody", only "in custody".'

'All right, Miss Know-it-all. So what?'

'I wonder who she was,' Kathy said. 'Teddy Hackett's alibi.'

And they all laughed. To them, Hackett, with his droopy moustache, receding hairline, gold medallions and beer belly hanging over his fancy belt buckle, was a figure of ridicule, the male equivalent of mutton dressed as lamb.

'What do you think, Sally?' Anne asked. 'You're very quiet today.'

'I've got a few ideas of my own,' Sally replied slowly and quietly. 'But I've got to check them out.'

And with that she walked out, leaving them all gaping again, not knowing whether to believe her or not.

8

ONE

By seven thirty, the lounge bar of the Dog and Gun was almost full. It was a long narrow room with only one vaguely demarcated aisle down the centre. The audience was clustered around small tables, and a white-jacketed waiter had been employed so that people wouldn't have to move about to get drinks. He moved awkwardly among the crowd, a tray of black and amber drinks tottering menacingly at shoulder height. The jukebox had been unplugged for the evening, and piped folk music played softly enough to make conversation easy. Dim wall lights gave the room a dark orange glow, and at the bar the brass rail, polished hand pumps and coloured bottles by the mirrors gleamed. At the far end of the room was a low wooden platform, too makeshift to be dignified with the name of a stage, and on it stood a couple of microphones on stands, two large speakers, three stools and an amplifier with its red light on.

Banks and Sandra sat with Harriet and David about halfway down the room on the right-hand side. Harriet, pixieish in looks, animated and intelligent in character, drove a mobile library around the more remote dales villages. Her husband David was an assistant bank manager in Eastvale and, if truth be told, Banks found him a bit of a bore.

David had clearly said something that required more than a mere nod in response, but Banks had been watching a fresh-faced young camper, probably under eighteen, who was already displaying the effects of too much alcohol in his desire to show off to his girlfriend.

'Pardon?' Banks said, cupping his hand to his ear.

'I said, I suppose you know all about computers yourself, being on the force,' David repeated. 'I'm afraid I've been boring you.'

'Not at all,' lied Banks. He tamped down the tobacco in his pipe and lit it in defiance of Sandra's sharply aimed frown. 'No, not at all. But yes, I know a little bit about computer languages.' That old-fashioned phrase, 'on the force', made him smile. It was an odd way of looking at his job, he thought. On what force? The forces of law and order, no doubt. 'May the force be with you.' The force of good against evil? It was a stiff dry phrase that hardly did the job justice.

While telling David what little he did know about the subject, Banks noticed Penny Cartwright come in with Jack Barker. The two of them made their way to the front, where chairs had been saved for them. Shortly afterwards, a nervous spotty young man took the stage, tapped the microphones, said 'testing' in each one three or four times, then welcomed everyone to folk night at the Dog and Gun. One by one, conversations died down until all that could be heard was the barman ringing up sales and the steady humming of the amplifier. The microphone shrieked when the young man got too close, and he backed off quickly, pulling a face. Banks couldn't catch the names of all the scheduled performers, but he gathered that Penny was set to sing two forty-minute sets, the first starting at eight thirty and the second at about ten fifteen.

After more notices and introductions, a duo clambered on to the stage. The boy had only a guitar, but the girl spread several ancient and obscure stringed instruments on the floor around her. First they launched into a Bob Dylan song, and what they lacked in talent, Banks thought, they made up for in enthusiasm. After the applause, the young man made jokes about the notes he had missed and apologized for the rawness of his technique. It worked: after that the audience wanted him to succeed and most people were willing to overlook the rough edges.

The girl said nothing but concentrated on tuning what looked to Banks like a mandolin. She played extremely well on the next number, a medley of old English dances. On the whole, the audience was respectful and attentive, but there were occasional, unavoidable interruptions as the waiter passed by and more drinks were ordered. Someone told the inebriated young camper to shut up, too.

Banks and David seemed to have settled into buying rounds, the two men drinking pints of bitter and the women lager and lime. Banks had to watch his intake because he didn't want to appear even slightly intoxicated in the village where he was conducting a murder investigation. Two pints in an hour and a half wasn't at all bad, he told himself, but it was only just after eight o'clock. He was aware that he tended to speed up towards closing time.

The first intermission came and people started making their ways to the toilets and the bar. As he walked down the narrow aisle, Jack Barker noticed Banks's party and came over.

'Good evening,' he said, extending his hand. 'What a

surprise to find you here. I'd no idea you were a folkie.'
There was just enough of a twinkle in his eye to make
the irony apparent. 'Mind if I join you for a moment?'
He grabbed a nearby chair and pulled it up before Banks
could object. 'Is it just Miss Cartwright you've come to
hear?'

'Actually, it's Ms Cartwright,' Banks corrected him.
'And yes, I've heard she's very good.' His tone was
brusque; he wished Barker would go away.

'You're in for a real treat, Chief Inspector, a real treat.
People come from miles away to hear Penny Cartwright,
you know. She's got a solid reputation in these parts,
especially since she gave up fame and fortune to return to
her roots. People appreciate that.'

From what Banks had heard, appreciation wasn't quite
the word for the gossip that had surrounded Penny's
return to her roots, but he kept quiet. Barker obviously
wanted to show off, and, short of being rude, there was
no way to stop him. Sandra returned from the Ladies and
looked at Barker curiously. There was no escape, Banks
realized, cursing himself; he would have to introduce
them.

Barker favoured the women with what Banks suspected was a well-practised Clark Gable smile.

'Delighted,' he said theatrically, taking Sandra's hand.
'I never imagined a policeman's wife could be so charming and so beautiful.' Banks was irritated; David simply
looked on, a vacant grin on his face.

It was not only Barker's charm and social finesse that
annoyed Banks. It was all very well socializing in the
community, but to be seen with his wife openly frater-
nizing with a suspect jarred against his deepest instincts
as a detective. It made him feel conspicuous, for one

thing, and that was a feeling he disliked. Gristhorpe's advice – get in there and let them talk to you – was all very well, but a line had to be drawn. He was off duty, and the whole thing was just too pally for his taste. He was sucking on his dead pipe, glowering and contributing monosyllables only when necessary.

'How do you manage to fit in here?' Sandra asked after Barker had told her his occupation. 'Aren't writers usually regarded with a good deal of suspicion?'

Barker nodded. 'True. They didn't like me being here at first,' he replied. 'Not one bit. You're right – people don't trust writers in small communities, and they've good reason not to. Some communities have had bad experiences with chaps who live among them, fit in, then go and write devastating critiques, hardly even bothering to disguise names and identities. It's like the way some Indians see photographers – people who steal their souls. Quite right too, in my opinion. The kind of writers they have in mind are unscrupulous. They give us all a bad name.'

'But don't you think writers have to be a little ruthless?' Harriet asked. 'Especially if they're to tell the truth.'

'Perhaps. But the ones I'm talking about accept your hospitality, then strip you naked on the page. Some writers even worm their way into people's confidence and set up situations, manipulate events just to see how their "characters" will react. I knew one chap, for example, who used to throw regular parties. This was in London. Real lavish dos they were, no expense spared – champers, single malt Scotch, beluga caviar, quail – more than anyone could hope to devour in an evening. When everyone got sozzled and started arguing, crying or pawing other people's partners, there he was, sober as a judge, sitting in a corner making mental notes. It took people a long time to figure out what was going on – after all, they were having a good time – but sure enough, they'd appear, thinly disguised, in stories published in magazines, and their friends and colleagues would recognize them. A couple of marriages broke up, reputations were destroyed. All in the name of "art". After a while, attendance dropped dramatically.'

'What happened to him?' Harriet asked, sitting on the edge of her chair.

Barker shrugged. 'Moved on, I suppose. I've no idea where he is now. Pastures new. He still publishes regularly.'

'And is that what you do, Mr Barker?' Sandra asked. 'Move in on people and steal their souls.'

Barker laughed. 'Please, call me Jack,' he said, and Banks felt his upper lip begin to curl. 'No, that's not what I do at all. At first everyone was suspicious of me, but then they always are like that with incomers, as they call us. After a while, out of curiosity I suppose, someone read a couple of my books, then someone else, and their comments got around. As soon as everyone realized I wrote hard-boiled private-eye stories set in southern California in the thirties, they decided I wasn't a threat. Believe it or not, I even have a few fans here.'

'I know,' Harriet said. 'I've carried enough of your books around in the mobile library.'

Barker honoured her with a smile. 'As soon as they get to know you're harmless,' he went on, 'you're as close to being accepted as you'll ever be. It was the same with Harry.'

'What about Harry?' Banks asked, trying to sound casual but failing miserably. Sandra frowned at him for being a killjoy.

'All I meant,' Barker explained, 'was that Harry was a writer too, in his way, but nobody ever worried about him because he wrote about the Romans and old lead mines. I mean, only people like Penny and Michael Ramsden were interested. That stuff's as dry as dust to most people.' He looked back at the ladies and smiled again, clearly hoping to get off on another track.

'Do you know Ramsden well?' Banks asked, unmoved by Barker's discomfort and Sandra's piercing glances. Harriet and Sandra began to chat between themselves, and David looked on, lost.

'I've met him,' Barker replied curtly.

'What do you think of him?'

'Pleasant enough fellow,' he said, looking to the women for support in his levity. 'But you can hardly expect a writer to say nice things about an editor, can you? I spend two days working on a fine descriptive paragraph, and my editor wants it cut out because it slows the action.'

'Ramsden's not your publisher, though, is he?' Banks persisted.

'Good Lord, no. He only deals with academic stuff.'

'Did you know about Ramsden and Penny Cartwright?'

'That was years ago. What on earth are you getting at?'

'Just trying to sort out the tangle of relationships,' Banks answered, smiling. 'That's all.'

'Look, they're starting again,' Barker said, rising. 'Please excuse me.' He gave a brief bow to Harriet and Sandra, then made his way back to the front. It was almost eight thirty. As the lights dimmed, Banks saw him talking to Penny and glancing back over his shoulder. The last thing he noticed before it got too dim was Barker whispering in Penny's ear and Penny looking behind her and laughing.

As the master of ceremonies began his rambling and incoherent introduction, Sandra leaned over to Banks. 'You were a bit sharp with him, weren't you?' she said. 'Was it really necessary? You did promise we were having a social evening.'

Banks muttered a sullen apology and busied himself with his pipe. It wasn't a new situation, the job interfering with his personal life, but it never ceased to cause friction. Perhaps Sandra had expected the move to change all that. A new life. What rubbish, Banks thought. Different landscapes, same old people with the same old failings. He gestured to the waiter to bring another round. Bugger it, let someone else drive home. It was a social occasion, after all, he reminded himself ironically.

Penny Cartwright took the stage to much applause and several loud whistles from the back of the room. Banks was still furious with Barker for being so damn charming and witty, and with Sandra for encouraging him and with himself for spoiling it. He attacked the fresh pint of bitter with angry gusto and glared at his pipe as if it were at the root of all his troubles. It had gone out yet again and he was sick to death of tamping, emptying, cleaning, scraping and relighting it.

Penny began with an unaccompanied ballad called 'Still Growing'. It was a sad tale about an arranged marriage between a woman and a boy on the edge of manhood. The husband died young and the widow lamented, 'O once I had a sweetheart, but now I have none. / Death has put an end to his growing.' The story was simply and economically told, and Banks found himself entering into the music as he did with opera, his recent irritation wrapped up and put away in a dim corner of his mind. Her voice had both passion and control – it was that of a survivor singing about the lost and the less fortunate with honest sympathy. She was an alto, pitched lower than Banks had expected, husky on the low notes but pure and clear in the higher range.

Banks clapped loudly when she finished, and Sandra turned to him with raised eyebrows and a smile of appreciation. Other songs in the same traditional folk vein followed, and sometimes Penny accompanied herself on guitar while another young woman playing the flute or the fiddle joined her. Mixed in with the stories of demon lovers and forbidden affairs were light-hearted jigs and reels and sensational broadside ballads, like 'The Murder of Maria Marten'.

Despite his enjoyment of the music, Banks found his mind wandering back to Barker's reaction to the mention of Michael Ramsden. There had seemed to be a dislike beyond the general lack of love between writers and publishers. Ramsden had been a close friend of Steadman's and had known Penny Cartwright since childhood. Did they still see each other, despite what they said? Was Barker simply jealous? And if he was jealous of Ramsden, wasn't he also likely to have felt the same way about Steadman?

Banks looked at Penny and noticed Barker's finely chiselled handsome profile in silhouette. He was in love with her, of course. Ramsden had been right to suggest that possibility. And who could blame him? Her beauty was radiant; her talent was moving. But she and Ramsden had parted. Of course, it had happened years ago, before she had fully blossomed, and it could only have been puppy love. Still, such events endure in small communities. Perhaps to some of the more shrewish local gossips Penny would always be known as a wayward lass who lost that nice Michael Ramsden who had gone on and done so well for himself. And what did Ramsden really feel about their parting?

Banks laid his pipe to rest in the ashtray and Penny announced 'Like Musgrave and Lady Barnard', the last song of the set.

TWO

At about nine o'clock, Sally Lumb left the house on Hill Road. Because it was Friday, her mother was at bingo in Eastvale with Mrs Crawford, and her father was down in the public bar of the Bridge playing in a local darts match. They wouldn't be back till about eleven o'clock, which gave her plenty of time. There would be no awkward questions to answer.

Despite the gathering clouds, it was a warm evening: a bit too hot and sticky, if anything. Sally knew from experience that such signs meant a storm was on its way. She walked down the hill and turned left, by the Bridge, on to High Street. It was a quiet time in Helmthorpe; most people were either in the pubs or sat glued to the idiot box in their living rooms. There'd be nothing much stirring until closing time unless a party of campers got too rowdy at the Hare and Hounds disco and Big Cyril had to chuck them out.

She walked on down the street and paused outside the Dog and Gun. The front door was open and she could hear singing from inside. Penny Cartwright, by the sound of it. Sally had heard her before but hadn't known she was singing in the village that evening. She looked at her watch. Plenty of time. The words of the song drifted out on the humid air:

'A grave, a grave,' Lord Barnard cried,
   'To put these lovers in;
But bury my lady on the top
   For she was of noble kin.'

With the familiar tune in her mind, Sally walked on, pausing for a moment to listen to the broad beck flowing under the bridge at the eastern end of High Street. She quickened her pace and, leaving the road, struck out up the long wild southern slope of the dale, past where she and Kevin had seen Penny the other day. She had an appointment to keep, a warning to give. Everything would be sorted out soon.

THREE

During the intermission, Penny Cartwright walked by Banks on her way out of the pub and flashed him a cool smile of acknowledgment. Barker, following closely behind her, nodded and bowed to Harriet and Sandra.

'She's so talented and beautiful,' Sandra said after they'd gone. 'Surely she can't be one of your suspects?'

Banks just told her that Penny had been a friend of the victim, and Sandra left it at that. The four chatted about the music, which they had all enjoyed, ordered more drinks, suffered through a mercifully short set of contemporary 'protest' folk music, and awaited Penny's second set. She came back at ten fifteen and walked straight to the stage.

This time there was a new, slightly distant quality in her performance. She was still involved in what she did, but it didn't have the same emotional cutting edge. Banks listened to the ballads and was struck by the parallel that he was dealing with exactly the same kinds of feelings and events that the old songs were forged from. And he wondered how the ballad of Harry Steadman would end. Nobody would be 'hung high', of course, not these days. But who would the killer turn out to be? What was his motive, and what would be Banks's own part in the song? All of a sudden, it seemed as if he was in another century, and that this beautiful young woman in the spotlight, life's disappointments and cruelties showing just enough in her voice to intensify her beauty, was singing a tragic ballad about the murder of Harry Steadman.

The sharp change to a brisk singalong tune snapped him out of his reverie, and he finished off his drink, noting that he immediately felt impatient for another. He was drunk, or at least tipsy, and it wasn't far off closing time. If Barker was in love with the girl, and if there had been anything between her and Steadman . . . If Ramsden still . . . If Mrs Steadman knew . . . If Steadman and his wife hadn't been quite as close as everyone made out . . . The random thoughts curled like pipe smoke and evaporated in the air.

When the set ended to loud and prolonged applause, Banks caught the passing waiter and ordered another pint for himself and a half for David. Sandra looked at him with a hint of reprimand in her eyes, but he just shrugged and grinned foolishly. He had never had a problem with alcohol, but he knew he could sometimes be quite adolescent in his consumption of numerous pints. He could tell that Sandra was worried he might make an idiot of himself, but he knew he could handle his drink. He hadn't had all that much, anyway. There might even be room for another one if he had time.

FOUR

There was going to be a storm, Sally was sure of it. She sat on the low packhorse bridge dangling her legs over the warm stone as she watched the sun go down. When it had disappeared behind the hills, leaving a halo of dark red-gold, it seemed to shine upwards from the depths of the earth and pick out the relief of the heavy grey clouds that massed high above. Insects buzzed on the still, humid air.

It was an isolated spot, ideal for such business, barely even suitable for cars. During her walk, Sally had enjoyed the peace and the strange tremors of excitement that the anticipation of a storm seemed to lay on the landscape. The colours were richer, the wild flowers and rough grass more vibrant, and the clouds' shadows seemed palpable masses on the distant valley side.

But now she was nervous, and she didn't know why. It was the coming storm, she told herself, the electricity in the air, the isolation, the gathering darkness. Soon the wind would shake the rough moorland grass and rain would lash the dale. It was the perfect place for a secret meeting; she understood that. If they were seen together, word might get back to the chief inspector and awkward questions would be asked. She wanted to handle this herself, perhaps save a life and catch a killer. Nonetheless, she knew deep down that her shivers were not entirely due to the weather.

Idly, she cast a loose stone from the bridge into the shallow slow-moving beck. After the rain, she thought, it would be swift, sparkling and ringing with fresh water cascading down the valley side and right under Helm-thorpe High Street.

She looked at her watch. Twenty to ten. Tired of waiting, she wished it was all over. The aftermath of sunset was quickly vanishing as the clouds thickened overhead. A curlew called plaintively in the distance. The place began to feel like a wilderness in a gothic romance. It was creepy, even though she'd been there often enough. A flock of rooks spun across the sky like oily rags. Sally became aware of a new sound throbbing through the silence. A car. She pricked up her ears, cast another stone in the beck and stood to face the track. Yes, she could see the headlights as they dipped and flashed on the winding road. It wouldn't be long now.

FIVE

The storm finally broke at about five a.m. Sharp cracks of thunder woke Banks from a vaguely unpleasant dream. He had a dry mouth and a thick head. So much for control. But at least he hadn't made a fool of himself; that he remembered.

Careful not to disturb Sandra, he walked over to the window and looked out on the back garden just in time to see a jagged bolt of lightning streak from north to south across the sky. The first few drops of rain, fat and heavy, came slowly. They burst at intervals on the windowpane and smacked against the slates of the sloping tool shed roof; then they came more quickly and slapped against the leaves of the trees that lined the back alley beyond the garden gate. Soon the rain was coursing down the window and over the slates into the gutter before it gurgled down the drainpipe.

Banks made his way to the bathroom, took two Panadol

tablets and went back to bed. Sandra hadn't woken and the children remained silent. He remembered when Tracy had been afraid of storms and had always run to her parents' bed, where she nestled between them and felt safe. But now she knew what caused the electrical activity – knew more about it than Banks did – and the fear had gone. Brian had never really cared either way, except that an evening thunderstorm meant the television had to be unplugged sometimes in the middle of his favourite programme. It was something Banks's father had always done, and Banks followed suit without really knowing why.

The steady rhythm of the rain and the sudden release from tension that the start of a storm brings helped Banks to drift uneasily off to sleep again. Only seconds later, it seemed, the alarm clock rang and it was time to get ready for work.

When Banks arrived at the station, he was surprised to find an unusual flurry of activity. Superintendent Gristhorpe was waiting for him.

'What's going on?' Banks asked, hanging his wet mackintosh in the cupboard.

'A young girl's been reported missing,' Gristhorpe told him, bushy eyebrows knitted together in a frown.

'From Eastvale?'

'Get yourself some coffee, lad. Then we'll talk about it.'

Banks took his mug to the small lunch room and poured himself a cup of fresh black coffee. Back in the office, he sat behind his desk and sipped the hot drink, waiting for Gristhorpe to begin. He knew there was never any point in hurrying the superintendent.

'Helmthorpe,' Gristhorpe said finally. 'Local bobby down there, Constable Weaver, got woken up by worried parents just after the storm broke. Seems their young lass hadn't come home, and they were worried. The mother said she sometimes stayed out late – she was at that age, sixteen or so – so they hadn't worried too much earlier. But when the storm woke them and she still wasn't back . . . Apparently she's not done anything like that before.'

'What's the girl's name?'

'Sally Lumb.' The words sounded flat and final in Gristhorpe's Yorkshire accent.

Banks rubbed his face and drank some more coffee. 'I was talking to her just the other day,' he said at last. 'In here. She came to see me.'

Gristhorpe nodded. 'I know. I saw the report. That's why I wanted to talk to you.'

'Attractive young girl,' Banks said, almost to himself. 'Looked older than she was. Sixteen. Interested in acting. She wanted to get away to the big city.' And all of a sudden he thought of Penny Cartwright, who had been to so many big cities only to return to Helmthorpe.

'We're covering that angle, Alan. You know as well as I do how most of these cases turn out. In all likelihood she's run off to Manchester or London. Her mother told Weaver there'd been a few rows at home lately. Seems the lass didn't get on too well with her father. She probably just took off somewhere.'

Banks nodded. 'Most likely.'

'But you don't believe it?'

'I didn't say that, sir.'

'No, but you sounded like it.'

'Shock, I suppose. There could have been an accident. She goes off with her boyfriend. You know, they find isolated places where they can kiss and cuddle. That area's full of old lead mines and gullies.'

'Aye, it's possible. For the moment we'll just have to

assume it's either that or she's run off. We've wired her description to all the big cities. I just hope to God we've not got a sex killer on our hands.' He paused and looked through the window, where the steady downpour had almost emptied Market Street and the square. Only a few shoppers soldiered on under umbrellas. 'Trouble is,' he went on, 'we can't organize search parties in this kind of weather. Too bloody dangerous by far up on the moors and valley sides.'

'What do *you* think's happened?' Banks asked.

'Me?' Gristhorpe shook his head. 'I don't know, Alan. Like I told you, I've been reading through that interview report again and I can't really see as she gave us any valuable information. She just helped us pinpoint the time the body was dumped, that's all. She didn't actually see anything.'

'You mean she wasn't a danger to anyone – to our killer?'

'Aye. Naturally you make connections when something like this happens. You'd be a poor copper if you didn't. But you can't let it get in the way. As it stands now, we've still got a murder to solve and we've got a missing girl to cope with, too.'

'But you do think there might be a connection?'

'I hope not. I bloody hope not. It's bad enough knowing there's someone who killed once out there, but a hell of a lot worse thinking they'd go as far as to kill a kid too.'

'We can't be sure she's dead yet, sir.'

Gristhorpe looked at Banks steadily for a few moments then turned back to the window. 'No,' he said. 'Was there anything else? Anything else to link her to the Steadman case?'

'Not that I know of. The only time I saw her was when

she came to tell me about hearing the car. I got the impression that she went away distinctly dischuffed with me for giving up the bright lights. We had Willy Fisher in at the time, too. He put up a bit of a struggle with two uniformed lads, and I think that unnerved her a bit.'

'What are you getting at, Alan?'

'I don't know, really. But maybe if she did figure anything out, she might not have come to me with it.'

'You can't blame yourself for that,' Gristhorpe said, rising wearily to leave. 'Let's hope she's run off somewhere. The link's got to be pursued, though. Were you thinking of going to Helmthorpe today?'

'No. It's so bloody miserable outside I thought I'd go over the paperwork again. Why?'

'The paperwork can wait. I'd feel easier if you did go.'

'Of course. What do you want me to do?'

'Have a word with the boyfriend, for a start. Find out if he saw her last night, or if not, why not. And Weaver tells me she hung around the coffee bar with three other girls. You might have a chat with them. Weaver will give you the names and details. Be as casual as you can. If she knew anything, or had any theories, she's far more likely to have told her friends than her parents. No need to trouble them.' Banks was relieved. Twice before he had had to spend time with the parents of missing children and he could think of no worse task.

'I'll take care of the rest,' Gristhorpe added. 'We'll be getting search parties organized as soon as this rain slackens off a bit.'

'Should I leave now?' Banks asked.

'No hurry. In fact, it might be better if you held off till mid-morning. I don't know a lot about teenage lasses, but I shouldn't imagine they'll be up and about right now. It might be best if you can find them in the coffee bar. It'll be a more comfortable environment for the kind of chat you want, and you'll get them all together.'

Banks nodded. 'You'll keep me up to date, sir?'

'Yes, of course. Just check in with Weaver. I'll send Sergeant Hatchley on later, too. He's busy getting the girl's description around the country right now.'

'Just a small point,' Banks said, 'but it might be a good idea if you had someone get in touch with theatre companies, drama schools, that kind of place. If she has run off, the odds are she's headed for the stage.'

'Aye,' Gristhorpe said, 'I'll do that.' Then, looking tired and worried, he left the office.

Outside, it was still pouring bucketfuls on to Market Street and looked as if it would never stop. Banks stared down at the shifting pattern of umbrellas as pedestrians dodged one another crossing the square on the way to work. He scratched his chin and found a rough patch the electric razor had missed. Gristhorpe was right; they had to think in terms of a connection with the Steadman business. It had to be pursued quickly, as well, and the irony was that they had to hope they were wrong.

Banks looked over Sally Lumb's interview transcript and tried to visualize her as she had sat before him. Was there something she hadn't told him? As he read the printed words he had written up from his notes, he tried to picture her face, remembering pauses, changes in expression. No. If there was anything else, it must have occurred to her after the interview, and she might then have gone to the wrong person with her information or ideas. Banks tried to stop himself imagining her battered body stuffed down a disused mineshaft, but the images were hard to dismiss. Sally may have been eager to move away to the big city but she had struck him as a sensible girl, even calculating – the kind who would make a clean and open move when the right time came. According to her mother, nothing dramatic had happened at home to make her run away. Rows were common enough surely, and, if anything, the parents seemed too liberal. Banks remembered the curfews (broken, many of them) of his own adolescence as he tried to coax his pipe alight. The blasted thing remained as reluctant as ever. In a sudden flash of anger and frustration, he threw it across the room and the stem snapped in two.

SIX

As Banks approached Helmthorpe later that Saturday morning, the coloured tents across the river strained at their ropes in the wind and rain like the sails of hidden boats, and the dark water danced wildly with ripples. In such weather, the houses themselves looked like dull outcrops of the stone they were built from, and the valley sides were shrouded in haze. A few locals and unfortunate holidaymakers tramped the streets.

Banks pulled into the small parking space next to the police station, and the first person he saw inside was PC Weaver. The constable looked pale, and there were dark smudges under his eyes.

'We can't even organize a search,' he said, pointing out of the window. 'Our men would get bogged down on the moors, and the visibility's hopeless.'

'I know,' Banks said. 'Any luck?'

Weaver shook his head. 'Her parents last saw her just before they went out for the evening at about seven thirty.

Before that, her friends saw her in the coffee bar earlier in the afternoon. We've not had time to ask much yet, sir. I've still got some lads out there. There'll likely be more information coming in before long.'

Banks nodded. 'And she didn't say to anyone where she was going?'

'No, sir. Her mother thought she might have met her boyfriend somewhere.'

'Did she?'

'He says not, sir,' Weaver pointed toward a bedraggled young man in a clinging wet T-shirt and soggy jeans, hair plastered down by the rain. 'That's him there, sir. He's pretty upset, and I see no reason not to believe him.'

'Have you questioned him?'

'Just talked to him, really, sir. Not questioned him proper. I mean, I thought I'd leave that . . .'

'That's fine, Constable,' Banks said, smiling his approval. 'You did right.'

He walked over to Kevin, who was staring fixedly at a 'Crime Doesn't Pay' poster and chewing his fingernails. Banks introduced himself and sat down on the bench.

'How long have you known Sally?' he asked.

Kevin rubbed his eyes. 'Years, I suppose. We only started going out together this summer.'

'How do you feel about Swainsdale?'

'What?'

'How do you feel about living in the dales, your home? Sally doesn't like it much, does she? Wasn't she always talking about going away?'

'Oh aye, she talked,' Kevin said scornfully. 'She's full of big talk is Sally. Got a lot of grand ideas.'

'Don't you think she might have run off to London or somewhere, then?'

Kevin shook his head. 'No. I can't see her leaving like that. That's why I'm worried. She'd've told me.'

'Perhaps she's running from you, too.'

'Don't be daft. We've just started going together. We're in love.' He bent forward and put his head in his hands. 'I love her. We're going to get married, start a little farm . . . I know Sally, and she just wouldn't run off without telling me. She wouldn't.'

Banks held himself back from agreeing. Whatever Kevin believed, there was still hope. He couldn't picture Sally Lumb settling down to domestic rural life in the dales, though. Kevin had a lot to learn about women and about dreams, but he seemed a decent and honest enough boy on the surface. Banks was inclined to agree with Weaver and see no harm in him, but he had to press on with the questioning.

'Did you talk to Sally yesterday?' he asked.

Kevin shook his head.

'You didn't see her at all yesterday evening?'

'No. I was playing cricket with some mates over in Aykbridge.'

'Did Sally know about that? Didn't she expect to see you?'

'Aye, she knew. You can't see each other every night, can you?' he burst out. 'You'd soon get sick of each other, then, wouldn't you? You've got to do other things some-times, don't you?'

He was blaming himself, and Banks helped him fight back the guilt. He wanted to ask him about the night he and Sally had heard the car; he wanted to know if she had said anything more about it, or if either of them had noticed something they hadn't mentioned. But if he did that, he realized, he would be putting ideas into Kevin's mind, making him think that Sally's disappearance was somehow related to Steadman's murder. He would have to do that eventually, but it could wait. If there was anything, Kevin would probably blurt it out himself in his attempt to help find Sally.

It was almost noon. If the girls were going to meet up as usual in the coffee bar, they'd probably be there by now, Weaver told him. Banks dashed out to the car. In good weather, he would have walked the short distance, but after only a moment's exposure to the heavy rain, droplets were running down his neck from his sodden collar.

The three girls sat in silence, toying with straws angled in their Coke cans. Banks told them who he was and pulled up a chair to the stained and cracked Formica table. The video games and pinball machine were silent.

'Do you think Sally's the kind of girl to run away without telling anyone?' he asked first.

They all shook their heads slowly. The plain-looking girl with thick glasses, who had introduced herself as Anne Downes, answered, 'She's full of ideas, is Sally. But that's all they are. She's nowhere to run to. She doesn't know anyone outside Swainsdale.'

'Was she doing well at school?'

'Well enough,' replied Kathy Chalmers, the one with the henna hair. 'She's clever. Not a swot, like. She could always get away without studying much and get good marks. She's bound to pass all her exams.'

'A sensible girl, you'd say?'

'As sensible as any of us teenagers,' Anne Downes answered, and the irony wasn't lost on Banks. 'It depends on your point of view.'

Kathy gave a short giggle and blushed. 'I'm sorry,' she

apologized, putting her hand over her mouth. 'But her parents might not have thought she was sensible. You know parents.'

Being one himself, Banks did. 'But she's not the kind of girl to . . .' He paused, searching for words to avoid the phrase 'get into trouble', with all its connotations. 'She doesn't cause trouble, make a nuisance of herself?'

Kathy shook her head. 'No. Not at all. She's well behaved enough. Gets on well with most of the teachers. She's just full of ideas, like Anne said. A big dreamer. She wouldn't do anything to hurt anybody.'

Banks wondered if the girls connected Sally's disappearance with the Steadman business; her visit to the Eastvale station was exactly the kind of thing she'd tell them about, and he wanted to know if she had made any remarks. Again, the problem was to avoid alerting and alarming them.

'I suppose you know she came to see me a few days ago?' he began casually. 'And I agree, she struck me as being exactly like you all say – bright, full of plans, well behaved. I didn't really get to hear much about any of her ideas, though.'

Kathy Chalmers blushed again. The other girl, Hazel Kirk, who had so far sat silently throughout the conversation, began to seem ill at ease. Again it was Anne Downes who answered with a forthrightness completely in harmony with her precocious intelligence.

'Take this murder business,' she began. 'I suppose that's what she went to see you about?'

Banks nodded.

'Well, she found it all rather glamorous, exciting, as if it was something she was watching on telly. I don't mean to say she wasn't sorry about poor Mr Steadman, we all were, it's just that she didn't see it from that point of view. To Sally it was an adventure. Do you know what I mean? It was all a bit of a game with her as the heroine.'

This was exactly what Banks wanted. He nodded in appreciation of Anne's observation. 'Did she talk about it much?' he asked.

'Only in a mysterious kind of way,' Anne answered.

'As if she knew something nobody else did?'

'Yes. Exactly like that. I think it made her feel important, that she'd noticed something and been to see you. She thought you were rather dishy at first.' Anne said this with a perfectly straight face, as if she didn't quite know what the word meant. 'Then she seemed disappointed with your response. I don't know what it was, she didn't say, but she got even more mysterious as the week went on.'

'Did she say anything specific?'

'Oh, she tried to convince us that she was hot on the trail,' Anne said, adjusting her glasses. 'That she had an idea who dunnit. But that's all. Just hints. She didn't do anything about it, as far as I know.'

Banks was dreading the moment, which surely couldn't be far off, when Anne would realize the significance of his line of questioning. But luckily it didn't come. He thanked the girls for their time and, as he left, noted again how distracted Hazel Kirk seemed to be. Instead of questioning her there and then, he decided to leave it for a while and see what developed.

9

ONE

It was time to concentrate on the Steadman case again. However disturbing her disappearance was, Banks thought, Sally Lumb might turn up in Birmingham or Bristol any moment. But Steadman was dead and his killer was still free.

He told Weaver where he was going and drove up the hill to Gratly, turning right after the small low bridge in the centre of the hamlet and pulling up outside Jack Barker's converted farmhouse by the side of the broad beck. The water was already running faster and louder over the series of terraced falls. In a day or two, when the rain percolated down from the moorlands and higher slopes, the stream would turn into a deafening torrent.

Banks realized as he rang the doorbell that he had not visited Barker at home before, and he wondered what the house would reveal of the man.

'Oh, it's you, Chief Inspector,' a puzzled-looking Barker said, after keeping Banks waiting at the door for an unusually long time. 'Come in. Excuse my surprise but I don't get very many visitors.'

Banks took off his wet mac and shoes in the hall and followed Barker inside. Although it wasn't cold, the rain had certainly put a damp chill in the stone, and Banks decided to keep his jacket on.

'Do you mind if we talk in the study?' Barker asked. 'It's warmer up there. I've just been working, and that's where the coffee pot is. You look as if you could do with some.'

'Good idea,' Banks replied, following his host through a sparsely furnished living room and up a very narrow flight of stone stairs into a cosy room that looked out on the fell sides at the back of the house. Two walls were lined with books, and by a third, where the door was, stood a filing cabinet and a small desk stacked with papers. Barker's work table, on which an electric typewriter hummed, stood directly by the window. Through the streaming rain, the sharply rising slope outside had the look of an Impressionist painting. At the centre of the room was a low coffee table. The red light of the automatic drip-filter machine was on, and the Pyrex pot was half full of rich dark coffee. By the table, there were two small but comfortable armchairs. The two men sat down with their coffee; both took black, no sugar.

'I'm sorry to disturb you at work,' Banks said, sipping the refreshing liquid.

'Think nothing of it. It's an occupational hazard.'

Banks raised an eyebrow.

'What I mean is,' Barker explained, 'that if you work at home, you're at home, aren't you? Fair game for any salesman and bill collector. Somehow, the old Protestant work ethic won't allow most people to accept that writing books in the comfort of one's own home is really work, if you see what I mean. I can't think why, mind you. It was common enough for weavers and loom operators to work at home before the Industrial Revolution. These days, work has to be something we hate, something we do in a noisy dirty factory or an antiseptic fluorescent office. No offence.'

But Banks could tell by the sparkle in his eyes that Barker was baiting him gently. 'None taken,' he replied. 'As a matter of fact, I'd be happier to spend a bit more time in my office and less of it tramping about the dales in this weather.'

Barker smiled and reached for a cigarette from the packet on the table. 'Anyway,' he said, 'I don't seem to get many visitors, except salesmen. I take the phone off the hook, too. Work was going well. I'd just got to a good part, and it's always been my practice to stop for a while when things get good. That way I feel excited about going back to work later.'

'That's an interesting work habit,' Banks remarked, trying to ignore the craving he felt when Barker lit his cigarette and inhaled deeply.

'Sorry,' Barker said, offering him a cigarette as if he had read his mind.

Banks shook his head. 'Trying to stop.'

'Of course. You're a pipe man, aren't you? Please feel free. Pipe smoke doesn't bother me at all.'

'It broke.'

After the two of them had laughed at the absurdity of the broken pipe, Banks gave in. 'Perhaps I will have a cigarette,' he said. As he reached for one, he noticed Barker tense up to face the inevitable questions. The cigarette tasted good. Every bit as good as he remembered. He didn't cough or feel dizzy. In fact, he felt no indication that he had ever given up cigarettes in the first place; it was like a reunion with a long lost friend.

'So, what can I do for you this time?' Barker asked, putting unnecessary emphasis on the last two words.

'I suppose you've heard about the girl from the village, Sally Lumb?' he asked.

'No. What about her?'

'You mean you don't know? I'd have thought in a community this size the news would spread fast. People certainly knew about Harold Steadman soon enough.'

'I haven't been out since I walked Penny home after the folk club last night.'

'The girl's missing,' Banks told him. 'She didn't go home last night.'

'Good Lord!' Barker said, looking towards the window. 'If she's wandered off and got lost in this weather . . . What do you think?'

'It's too early to know yet. She could have got lost, yes. But she grew up around here and she seemed like a sensible girl.'

'Run away?'

'Another possibility. We're checking on it.'

'But you don't think so?'

'We just don't know.'

'Have you got search parties out?'

'We can't in this weather.'

'But still . . . Something's got to be done.'

'We're doing all we can,' Banks assured him. 'Did you know her?'

Barker narrowed his eyes. 'I wouldn't say I really knew her, no. I've seen her around, of course, to say hello to. And she once came to me about a school project. Pretty girl.'

'Very,' Banks agreed.

'I don't suppose that's what you came to talk to me about though, is it?'

'No.' Banks stubbed out his cigarette. 'I wanted to ask you about Penny Cartwright.'

'What about her?'

'Are you in love with her?'

Barker laughed, but Banks could see the strain in his eyes. 'What a question. I don't know whether to tell you it's none of your business or applaud your insight.'

'You are, then?'

'I'll admit I'm rather smitten with Penny, yes. What red-blooded young bachelor wouldn't be? But I don't see what my feelings for her have to do with anything else.'

'Was she having an affair with Harold Steadman, do you think?'

Barker gazed at Banks for a few moments. 'Not that I know,' he answered slowly. 'But how would I know?'

'You knew the two of them quite well.'

'True. But a man's private life . . . and a woman's? If they wanted to conceal something like that from the world, it wouldn't have been very difficult, would it? Even here, it could be done. Look, if you want my answer to your question, you'll have to understand that it's just an opinion, like yours. Certainly neither of them confided in me, or anything like that. And I'd say no, they weren't having an affair. As you guessed, I am very fond of Penny and, given that, I'd naturally be interested in her relationships. As far as I can make out though, their friendship was based on mutual respect and admiration, not sexual desire.'

This was almost exactly what Banks had heard from Penny herself and from Emma Steadman. Indeed, the only person who seemed to think differently about Penny and Harold Steadman was the major, and he was very much a victim of his own obsessions. But what if he was right?

'You seemed rather sharp last night when I mentioned Michael Ramsden,' Banks said, changing tack. 'Do you have any particular reason to dislike him?'

'I don't dislike him. I hardly even knew him. He's been in the Bridge a few times with Harry, and he always seemed pleasant enough. I will admit that I found something a little sly about him, a bit off-putting, but that's a minor personal reaction; it's neither here nor there.'

'I suppose you knew about his relationship with Penny?'

'Yes, and I'm quite willing to confess to a touch of instinctive lover's jealousy. Come to that, I may have been envious of her relationship with Harry, too; it seemed so close and easy. But I've no claim on Penny's emotions, sad to say. And as far as Ramsden was concerned, that was years ago. They can't have been more than kids.'

'Where were you then?'

'What? On the night of the twelfth of February, nineteen sixty-three, between the hours of—'

'You know what I mean.'

'Ten years ago?'

'Yes.'

'I lived in London then, in a poky little bedsit in Notting Hill writing real novels that nobody wanted to buy. Penny wasn't around when I first came to Gratly – we didn't meet till she came back – but I did see her play once down south.'

'Why do you think Ramsden and Penny split up?'

'How should I know? It's not a question I've concerned myself with. Why does any young couple split up? I suppose they felt themselves moving in different directions. Christ, they were only kids.'

'That was when Michael lived at home with his parents, wasn't it? In the same house Steadman and his wife used to visit on holidays?'

'Yes,' Barker answered. 'Ten years ago. It was just before Ramsden went off to university. Penny was just discovering her talent then. Harry told me he used to teach her folk songs he'd collected.'

'And the kids just drifted apart?'

'Well, Michael went to university, and Penny went all over the place with the group. That kind of folk music was still popular then. It still is, actually. I mean, there's always a sizeable audience for it.'

'How was Penny discovered?'

'The usual way, as far as I know. An agent for a record company was scouting the provinces for new folk talent. He offered her a chance to make a demo and off she went. The rest is history, as they say.'

'Has she talked to you about the past much, the time she spent away?'

'Not a great deal, no.' Barker seemed interested in the conversation now, despite himself. He poured more coffee and Banks cadged another cigarette. 'I'm sure you know, Chief Inspector,' he went on, 'that we all have phases of our lives we're not particularly proud of. Often circumstances give us the opportunity to behave in a careless irresponsible way, and most of us take it. It pains me to admit that I was once a very young Teddy boy and I even ripped a few seats in the local fleapit.' He grinned. 'You won't arrest me, will you?'

'I think the statute of limitation has run out on seat-ripping,' Banks answered, smiling. 'It would be rather difficult to prove, too.'

'You make me feel old.' Banks sighed. 'But do you see what I mean? Penny was not only young and inexperienced, she was also, for the first time in her life, fairly well off, popular, in with the "in crowd". I don't doubt that she tried drugs and that sex was a fairly casual matter. "Make love, not war," as they used to say. But the important thing is that she grew up, left all that behind and pulled her life together. Plenty of people don't survive the modern music world, you know; Penny did. What I'd like to know is why on earth you seem so obsessed with the events of ten years ago.'

'I don't know,' Banks answered, scratching the scar at the side of his eye. 'Everybody speaks so highly of Steadman. He didn't seem to have an enemy in the world. Yet somebody murdered him. Don't you find that strange? He wasn't robbed, and his body was taken up to the hillside below Crow Scar. We don't know where he was killed. I suppose what I'm saying, Mr Barker, is that if the answer isn't in the present, which it doesn't seem to be, then it must be in the past, however unlikely that may seem to you.'

'And has this background information given you any clues?'

'None at all. Not yet. But there's one more thing that's been on my mind. Could Harold Steadman have been a homosexual?'

Barker almost choked on his coffee. 'That takes the biscuit,' he spluttered, wiping at the spilled liquid on his lap. 'Where on earth did you get a wild idea like that?'

Banks saw no reason to tell him that he had got the idea from Sergeant Hatchley, who had said in the Queen's Arms, in his usual manner, 'About this Steadman business, those weekend trips to Ramsden's place; do you think he was queer?'

Banks had admitted that it was an angle he had not considered; he had taken Steadman's dedication to work at face value and presumed that the overnight visits took place for the reasons Ramsden and Mrs Steadman had given him.

'Even assuming you're right,' Banks had said, 'it doesn't really help us much, does it? His wife can't have killed him out of disgust – she has an alibi. And Ramsden would hardly have killed his lover, even if he could have.'

'There's blackmail, though,' Hatchley had suggested. 'Steadman was a rich man.'

'Yes. It's a possibility. Who do you think was black-mailing him?'

'Could have been anyone he knew: Barker, the girl, Barnes, one of his old mates from Leeds.'

'We'll check it out, then,' Banks had said. 'Ask around about Ramsden, and I'll ask some more questions in Helmthorpe. I wouldn't hold out too much hope though. It doesn't feel right to me.'

How did you ask someone if a friend was homosexual, he wondered. Just come right out with it? How would they know? Penny would certainly assume Ramsden was straight if he had been ten years ago, and there was still a chance that she knew more about Steadman's sexual habits than she let on.

So now he sat in Barker's study waiting for him to get over the shock and attempt an answer. When it came, it was disappointing. Barker simply denied the possibility and would only admit, when pushed, that anything however outlandish was possible, but that didn't mean it was true.

'Look,' Barker said, leaning forward. 'I realize that I must be a suspect in this business. I've no alibi and I seem unable to convince you that I really had nothing against Harry – I'm not gay either, just for the record – but I assure you that I did not kill him, and I'm perfectly willing to help in any way I can. I just don't know how I can help, and, if you don't mind my saying so, some of the directions you're pursuing seem to me to be quite silly.'

'I can understand that,' Banks said, 'but it's for me to decide what's relevant and what isn't.'

'You pick up bits and pieces from everyone and put them together. Yes, I suppose that's true. None of us gets to touch any more than a small area of the elephant, do we? But you get to see the whole beast.'

Banks smiled at the analogy. 'Eventually, yes,' he said. 'I hope so. What are you working on, or don't you like to discuss work in progress?'

'I don't mind. As a matter of fact, you've just given me an idea. All that about putting the pieces together. I think I can use it. It's another in the Kenny Gibson series. Have you read any?'

Banks shook his head.

'Of course not,' Barker said. 'I ought to know by now that few real policemen read detective novels. Anyway, Kenny Gibson is a private eye in the Los Angeles area. Period stuff, the thirties. I get most of my background information from Raymond Chandler and the old *Black Mask* magazines, but don't tell anyone! This time he's working for a rich society woman whose husband has disappeared. The plot's taken care of; it's the characters and atmosphere that are really hard to do.'

'Sex and violence?'

'Enough to sell a few thousand copies.'

'Just out of interest,' Banks asked as he got up to leave, 'do you have it all planned out in advance – the plot, the solution?'

'Good Lord, no,' Barker answered, following him down the stairs. 'The plot takes care of itself as I go along. At least I hope it does. If it's going well, there are fewer and fewer options at each turn until it's perfectly clear who the criminal is. I'm never really sure where I'm going from one day to the next. It'd be boring any other way, don't you think?'

'Perhaps,' Banks answered, putting on his shoes and mac. 'In writing, yes. In fiction. But in real life, I'm not so sure. It'd be a damn sight easier if I knew who the criminal was without having to write the whole book and make all the mistakes along the way. Anyway, goodbye, and thanks for your time.'

'My pleasure,' said Barker.

And Banks ducked quickly through the rain to his car.

TWO

On High Street, Banks glimpsed Penny Cartwright nipping into the Bridge. Consulting his watch and his stomach, he decided it was well past lunch time, and he could do with a pie and a pint if the landlord had any food left.

Penny was at the bar shaking her umbrella when she glanced over her shoulder and saw Banks enter.

'Can't a lady indulge her alcoholic cravings without the police turning up?' she asked sharply.

'Of course,' Banks replied. 'As a matter of fact, I'd be honoured if you'd join me for a late lunch.'

Penny looked at him through narrowed eyes. 'Business or pleasure, Inspector?'

'Just a chat.'

'For "chat" read "interrogation", I'll bet. Go on then. I must be a fool. You're buying.'

They were lucky enough to get two steak and

mushroom pies and Penny asked for a double Scotch. Carrying the drinks, Banks followed her into the lounge.

'Why don't they do something with this place?' he asked, looking around and turning his nose up.

'Why should they? I wouldn't have taken you for one of these horse-brass and bedpan types.' Penny stood her umbrella by the fireplace and sat down, shaking her hair.

Banks laughed. 'I always thought they were bed-warmers. And no, I'm not, not at all. Give me spittoons and sawdust any day. I was simply thinking that the owner might see renovations as a way to do more business in the long run.'

'Oh, Inspector Banks! I can see you're not a true Yorkshireman yet. We don't care about a speck or two of dirt in these parts. It's the company and the ale that count, and this is one place the locals can count on for both.'

Banks grinned and accepted the criticism with a humble sigh.

'So what is it you want to know this time?' Penny asked, lighting a cigarette and leaning back in her chair.

'I enjoyed your performance last night. I liked the songs, and you've got a beautiful voice.'

Did she blush just a little? Banks couldn't be sure, the lighting in the room was so dim. But she faltered over accepting the compliment and was clearly embarrassed.

The pies arrived and they each took a few bites in silence before Banks opened the conversation again.

'I'm stuck. I'm not getting anywhere. And now there's a girl gone missing.'

Penny frowned. 'Yes. I've heard.'

'Do you know her? What do you think might have happened?'

'I know Sally a little, yes. She always wanted to know

about the big wide world out there. I think she was secretly a bit disappointed with me for leaving it behind and coming home. But she struck me as a sensible girl. I can't really picture her running off like that. And she was born and raised in these parts, like me. She knows the countryside around here like the back of her hand, so she wasn't likely to get lost either.'

'Which leaves?'

'I don't like to think about it. You hear of young girls going missing so often in the cities. But here . . .' Penny shuddered. 'I suppose it could mean we've got a maniac in our midst. What are the police doing, apart from buying me lunch?'

It was the second time Banks had been asked that, and he found it just as depressing to have so little to say in reply again. But Penny understood about the weather; she knew how dangerous it made Swainsdale, and she showed a surprising amount of sympathy for Banks's obvious frustration.

They sat in silence again and returned to their food. When they had finished, Banks put his knife and fork down and faced Penny.

'Tell me about your father,' he said.

'You sound like a bloody psychiatrist. What about him?'

'You must know better than anyone else what a hothead he is?'

'I probably gave him reason enough.'

'You mean the city, the wild life?'

She nodded. 'But honestly, you make it sound much worse than it was. What would you do in that position? Everything was new. I had money, people I thought were my friends. It was exciting then, people were trying new things just for the hell of it. My father didn't speak to me for a long time after I left. I couldn't explain; it was just too claustrophobic at home. But when I came back he was kind to me and helped me to get set up in the cottage. He takes it upon himself to act as my protector, I know. And yes, he has a temper. But he's harmless. You can't seriously suspect him of harming Harry, can you?'

Banks shook his head. 'Not any more, no. I think it was too well planned to be his kind of crime. I just wanted to know how you saw things. Tell me more about Michael Ramsden.'

Flustered, Penny reached for another cigarette. 'What about him?'

'You used to go out with him, didn't you? Can I have one of those?'

'Sure.' Penny gave him a Silk Cut. 'You know I used to go out with him. So what? It was years ago. Another lifetime.'

'Were you in love?'

'In love? Inspector, it's easy to be in love when you're sixteen, especially when everybody wants you to be. Michael was the bright boy of the village, and I was the talented lass. It was one match my father didn't oppose, and he's always held it against me that we didn't marry.'

'Did you think of marrying?'

'We were talking about getting engaged, like kids do. That's as far as it went. Look, I was young and innocent. Michael was just a boy. That's all there is to it.' Penny shifted in her seat and pushed her hair back over her shoulders.

'Was it a sexual relationship?'

'None of your bloody business.'

'Did he ditch you?'

'We just drifted apart.'

'Is that all?'

'It's all you're getting.' Penny stood up to leave, but Banks reached out and grabbed her arm. She stared at him angrily, and he let go as if he had received an electric shock. She rubbed the muscle.

'I'm sorry,' he said. 'Please sit down again. I haven't finished yet. Look, you might think I'm just prying into your personal life for the fun of it, but I'm not. I don't give a damn who you've slept with and who you haven't slept with, what drugs you've taken and what you haven't taken, unless it relates to Harold Steadman's murder. Is that clear? I don't even care how much hash you smoke now.'

Penny eyed Banks shrewdly. Finally she nodded.

'So why did you split up?' Banks asked.

'Buy me another drink and I'll tell you.'

'Same again?' Banks got up to go to the bar.

Penny nodded. 'I can't promise it'll be interesting, though,' she called after him.

'There was nothing mature about our relationship,' she said as Banks sat down with a pint and a double Scotch. 'Neither of us really knew anything different until something else came along.'

'Another man?'

'No. Not until later. Much later.'

'You mean university for Michael and a singing career for you?'

'Yes, partly. But it wasn't as simple as that.'

'What do you mean?'

Penny frowned as if she had just thought of something, or tried to grasp the shadow of a memory. 'I don't know. We just drifted apart, that's all there is to it. It was summer, ten years ago. Every bit as hot as this one. I told you it wasn't exciting.'

'But there must have been a reason.'

'Why do you want to know?'

'Because I think the answer to Steadman's death lies in the past, and I want to know as much about it as possible.'

'Why do you think that?'

'I'm asking the questions. Did he dump you because you wouldn't have sex with him?'

Penny blew out a stream of smoke. 'All right, so I wouldn't let him fuck me. Is that what you want to hear?' The word was clearly meant to shock Banks.

'You tell me.'

'Oh, this is bloody insufferable. Here.' She tossed him another cigarette. 'Maybe sex was part of it. He was certainly getting persistent. Perhaps I should have let him. I don't know . . . I'm sure I was ready. But then he seemed different. He got more withdrawn and distant. Things just felt strange. I was changing, too. I was singing in the village pubs and Michael was studying to go to university. Harry and Emma were up for quite a while and it was hot, very hot. Emma would hardly go outside because her skin burned so easily. Harry and I spent quite a bit of time at the Roman site near Fortford. It was just being excavated then. We went for walks as well, long walks in the sun.'

'Did Michael go with you?'

'Sometimes. But he wasn't very interested in that kind of thing then. He'd just discovered the joys of English Literature. It was all Shelley, Keats, Wordsworth and D. H. Lawrence for him. He spent most of the time with his nose stuck in a book of poems, whether he was with us or not. That's when he wasn't trying to stick his hands up my skirt.'

'Must have been Lawrence's influence.'

Penny's lips twitched in a brief smile. She put her hand to her forehead and swept back her hair. 'Maybe.'

'And Mrs Steadman?'

'As I said, she didn't like the sun. Sometimes she'd come if we went in the car and sit under a makeshift parasol by the side of the road while we had a picnic like characters from a Jane Austen novel. But she wasn't really interested in the Romans or folk traditions, either. Maybe it wasn't the best of marriages, I don't know. Lord knows, they didn't have much in common. But they put up with it, and I don't think they treated each other unkindly. Harry shouldn't have married, really. He was far too dedicated to his work. Mostly I just remember him and me tramping over the moors and naming wild flowers.'

Steadman must have been in his early thirties then, Banks calculated, and Penny was sixteen. That wasn't such an age difference to make attraction impossible. Quite the contrary: he was exactly the age a girl of sixteen might be attracted to, and Steadman had certainly been handsome, in a scholarly kind of way, right up to the end.

'Didn't you have a crush on Harry?' he asked. 'Surely it would have been perfectly natural?'

'Perhaps. But the main thing – the thing you don't seem able to understand – is that Harry really wasn't like that. He wasn't sexy, I suppose. More like an uncle. I know it must be hard for you to believe, but it's true.'

If I don't believe it, Banks thought, it's not for want of people trying to convince me. 'Don't you think Michael might have seen the relationship differently?' he suggested. 'A threat, perhaps. An older, more experienced man. Might that not have been why he seemed strange?'

'I can't say I ever thought of it that way,' Penny answered.

Banks wasn't sure whether he believed her or not; she lied and evaded issues so often he was becoming more and more convinced that she was an actress as well as a singer.

'It's possible though, isn't it?'

She nodded. 'I guess so. But he never said anything to me. You'd think he would have, wouldn't you?'

'You didn't argue? Michael never said anything about you going off with Harry? He didn't always insist on accompanying you?'

Penny shook her head at each question.

'He was very shy and awkward,' she said. 'It was very difficult for him to express himself emotionally. If he did think anything, he kept it to himself and suffered in silence.'

Banks sipped his pint of Theakston's, brooding on how best to put his next question. Penny offered him another Silk Cut.

'If I read you right, Inspector,' she said, 'you seem to be implying that Michael Ramsden might have killed Harry.'

'Am I?'

'Come on! Why all the questions about him being jealous?'

Banks said nothing.

'They became great friends, you know,' Penny went on. 'When Michael graduated and got interested in local history, he helped Harry a lot. He even persuaded his firm to publish Harry's books. It was more than just a publisher–author relationship.'

'That's what I was wondering,' Banks cut in, seizing

his opportunity. 'Is there any possibility of a homosexual relationship between them? I know it sounds odd, but think about it.'

Unlike Barker, Penny took the question seriously before concluding that she doubted it very much. 'This had better not be a trick,' she said. 'I hope you're not trying to trap me into admitting intimate knowledge of Harry's sexual preferences.'

Banks laughed. 'I'm not half as devious as you make out.'

Her eyes narrowed sharply. 'I'll bet. Anyway,' she went on, 'I really can't help you. You'd think you'd know all about a friend you've known for years, but it's just not so. Harry could have been gay, for all I know. Michael, on the other hand, seemed very much like a normal adolescent, but there's no reason why he couldn't have been bi. Who can tell these days?'

And she was right. Banks had known a sergeant on the Metropolitan force for six years – a married man with two children – before finding out at the inquest into his suicide that he had been homosexual.

'You still seem to be saying Michael did it,' she said. 'In fact, you're hounding all of us – his friends. Why? Why pick on us? What about his enemies? Couldn't it have been somebody just passing through who killed Harry?'

Banks shook his head. 'Contrary to popular belief,' he said, 'very few murders happen that way. I think the myth of the wandering vagrant killer was invented by the aristocracy to keep suspicion away from their own doorsteps. Most often people are killed by family or friends, and motives are usually money, sex, revenge or the need to cover up damaging facts. In Harold Steadman's case, we found no evidence of robbery and we've had no luck so far in digging up an enemy from his past. Believe me, Ms Cartwright, we dig deep. We've been checking the alibis of anyone outside his immediate circle who might have had even the remotest reason for killing him. Really, not many people walk around the country bashing others on the head for no reason. So far, statistics and evidence point to someone closer to home. According to his friends, though, he was too damn perfect to have an enemy, so where am I supposed to look? Obviously Mr Steadman was a far more complicated man than most people have admitted, and his network of relationships wasn't a simple one either. His murder wasn't a spur of the moment job, or at least the killer was frightened or cold-blooded enough to throw us off the scent by moving the body.'

'And you're not going to stop pestering us until you know who it is?'

'No.'

'Are you close?'

'I can't see it if I am, but detection doesn't work like that, anyway. It's not a matter of getting closer like a zoom lens, but of getting enough bits and pieces to transform chaos into a recognizable pattern.'

'And you never know when you have enough?'

'Yes. But you can't predict when that moment will come. It could be in the next ten seconds or the next ten years. You don't know what the pattern will look like when it's there, so you might not even recognize it at first. But, soon enough, you'll know you've got a design and not just a filing cabinet full of odds and sods.'

'What about money as a motive?' Penny asked. 'Harry was very well off.'

'He didn't leave a will, which was foolish of him.

Naturally, it all goes to Mrs Steadman. It would have been more convenient for us if he'd left it all to the National Trust and we could have pulled in the first nutty conservationist we could find, but life isn't as easy as fiction. Motive and opportunity just don't seem to go together in this case.'

'Well, that's your problem, isn't it?'

'Yes. Have I explained why I'm pestering you so much now?'

'Very clearly, thank you,' Penny said, giving him a mock bow.

'You don't see Michael much these days?'

'No, not often. Occasionally in the Bridge. He was always especially awkward with me after we split up, though. You're not suggesting that Michael is still in love with me, are you? Let me get this right. He thought Harry and I were having an affair all those years ago and backed off. But all the time he's been holding a grudge. He worked his way into Harry's confidence over the years just looking for an opportunity to do away with him, and finally took his revenge. Am I right?'

Banks laughed, but it sounded hollow. Perhaps Ramsden did have sufficient motive, but he would have been hard-pushed to make an opportunity. First of all, he could hardly come to Helmthorpe and hang around in the car park all evening waiting, even if he was certain Steadman would be going there. And if Steadman had gone to York, how did his car get back to Helmthorpe? Ramsden could hardly have driven two cars, and he would have needed his own to get home. There were certainly no buses at that time of night, and he would not have risked arranging for a taxi.

'It's ludicrous,' Penny said, as if she had been listening

in on Banks's thoughts. 'I see what you mean when you say you're stuck.' She finished her drink, put down the glass, and stood up to leave.

Banks stayed on, drinking rather gloomily and craving another cigarette. Then Hatchley walked in. The sergeant brought two pints over and wedged himself into the chair Penny had just left.

'Any developments?' Banks asked.

'Weaver's men have talked to someone who saw Sally Lumb in the public call box on Hill Road at four o'clock Friday afternoon,' Hatchley reported. 'And someone else thinks he saw her walking along Helmthorpe High Street at about nine o'clock.'

'What direction?'

'East.'

'She could have been going anywhere.'

'Except west,' Hatchley said. 'By the way, I've been in touch with a mate of mine in York. Keeps tabs on all the queers and perverts down there, and there's nothing on Ramsden at all. Not a dicky bird.'

'I didn't think there would be,' Banks said glumly. 'We're barking up the wrong tree, Sergeant.'

'That's as maybe, but who's going to lead us to the right 'un?'

Banks watched the rain stream down the dirty window-pane and sighed. 'Do you think the two are linked?' he asked. 'Steadman and the Lumb girl?'

Hatchley wiped his lips with the back of his hand and burped. 'Bit of a coincidence, isn't it? The girl has the only piece of real information we get about the dumping of Steadman's body, and she goes missing.'

'But she'd already told us what she knew.'

'Did the killer know that?' Hatchley asked.

'It doesn't matter, does it? He didn't even know any-body had heard him burying Steadman below Crow Scar, unless . . .'

'Unless the girl let him know.'

'Right. Either intentionally or otherwise. But that still assumes she knew more than she told us, that she knew who it was.'

'Not if it was unintentional,' Hatchley pointed out. 'A girl like that tells all her friends, maybe hints that she knows more than she does. This is a small place, remember. It's not like London. It's easy to be overheard here, and word travels quickly.'

'The coffee bar,' Banks muttered.

'Come again?'

'The coffee bar. The place she hung around with her friends. Come on, we'd better question those girls again. If they know what Sally knew, they could be in danger as well. I didn't want them to think that Sally had been killed, or that her disappearance had anything to do with Steadman, but there's no time for softly-softly any more.'

Hatchley gulped down the rest of his pint, then dragged himself to his feet and plodded along behind.

10

ONE

Anne Downes was both nervous and excited to find herself in the police station. Not that it was much of a place, but it was alive with important activity: people coming and going, phones ringing, the ancient telex machine clattering. The two other girls paid less attention to their surroundings and seemed more preoccupied with their internal sense of unease. Hazel was the worst, biting her nails and shifting position as if she had St Vitus's dance; Kathy pretended to lounge coolly, casually uninterested in the whole affair, but she was biting her lower lip so hard it turned red.

The policewoman had been friendly enough when she'd picked them up at the coffee bar and driven them the short distance to the station, and the small attractive chief inspector had smiled and said he wouldn't keep them long. But they all knew there was something going on.

Anne was the first to be called into the tiny interview room. Its walls were bare and the mere two chairs and a table made the place seem over-furnished. It was the kind of room that made you claustrophobic.

Banks sat opposite Anne, and a policewoman with a notebook in her hand stood in the corner by a narrow barred window.

'I'd just like to ask you a few questions, Anne,' Banks began.

She looked at him quizzically from behind the thick lenses and nodded.

'First of all, I suppose you know why I want to see you again?'

'Yes,' Anne replied. 'You think Sally's been murdered because of something she knew.'

Banks, taken aback by her directness, asked what her opinion was.

'I'd say it's possible, yes,' Anne answered, her young brow furrowed in thought. 'I've already told you that I don't believe she's run away or got lost, and that doesn't leave much more to choose from, does it, especially with this other business going on?'

She'd make a good detective, Banks thought – quick, perceptive, logical. 'Have you got any other ideas?' he asked.

'Maybe I was wrong,' Anne said, her voice beginning to shake.

'Wrong about what?'

'When I said Sally was all talk, all big ideas. Maybe she really did know something. Maybe she thought she'd make a name for herself by following it up.'

'Why should she do that?'

Anne adjusted her glasses and shook her head. The thick lenses magnified the tears forming in her eyes. 'I don't know,' she answered.

'Did she tell you anything at all that indicated she knew who the person was? Think about it. Anything.'

Anne thought, and the tears held off. 'No,' she said finally. 'She just hinted that she knew things, that she'd solved some kind of mystery. I mean, yes, she did sort of say that she knew who it was, but she didn't give us any names or anything. She said she had to make sure; she didn't want to cause any trouble.'

'Do Sally's parents have a telephone?'

'Yes. They've had one for ages. Why?'

'Can you think of any reason why Sally would use a public phone box on Friday afternoon?'

'No.'

'Not even if she wanted to call Kevin or some other boyfriend? I know that parents aren't always understanding.'

'There was only Kevin, and Sally's mum and dad knew about him. They weren't a hundred per cent keen, but he's a nice enough boy, so they didn't make a fuss about it.'

'Did Sally say where she was going on Friday evening?'

'No. I'd no idea she was going anywhere.'

'Thank you very much, Anne,' Banks said.

The policewoman showed her out and brought Kathy Chalmers in next. Kathy was upset by then, but there were no tears, and although she seemed to realize dimly what it was all about, she had nothing to add.

The last girl, Hazel Kirk, was another matter. She knew as well as the others what was going on, but she pretended ignorance. She said she couldn't even remember whether Sally had said anything about knowing who the killer was. The more Banks questioned her, the more fidgety and edgy she became. Finally she burst into tears and told Banks to leave her alone. He nodded to the policewoman, who moved forward to speak to her, and left the room.

Sergeant Hatchley was sitting on the edge of Weaver's desk looking over reports from provincial police and railway authorities. He glanced up as Banks approached. 'Any luck?'

Banks shook his head. 'The first one's the most intelligent, but even she couldn't tell us much. What she did say confirms our suspicions though. If Sally thought she knew who the killer was and arranged for a meeting, then we can be pretty sure what's happened to her. It must have been someone she knew, someone she wasn't afraid of. There's got to be a motive, dammit, and it's got to be right before our eyes.' He banged his fist on the desk, surprising Hatchley with the sudden violence. It reminded the sergeant that his boss came from a tough patch. He wasn't a plodder; he was used to action.

'Got a cigarette?' Banks asked.

'Thought you'd stopped and taken up pipe puffing,' Hatchley said, handing over his packet of Senior Service.

'Not any more. I never could stand the blasted thing.'

Hatchley smiled and gave him a light. 'Then I suggest, sir,' he said, 'that you start buying your own.'

The door of the interview room opened and a pacified Hazel Kirk came out to rejoin her waiting friends, who had all been whispering, wondering what was going on. The policewoman, looking concerned, stood in the doorway and beckoned Banks over.

'What is it?' he asked, closing the door behind him.

'The girl, sir,' the PC began. 'Why she was upset. It might mean something.'

'Well? Go on.'

'Sorry, sir. She got upset because Sally had told her she thought she knew who the killer was, and when she got home, Hazel told her parents.' She paused, and Banks drew on his cigarette waiting for her to continue. 'They just laughed and said Sally Lumb always did have an overactive imagination, but the girl's father had had a bit of a run-in with Steadman a few weeks ago, and Hazel thought . . .'

'Yes, I can imagine what she thought,' Banks said. For all his virtues, Steadman had certainly been a thorn in the side of some locals. 'What was it this time?' he asked. 'Arguments over land or charges of moral laxity?'

'Sir?'

'Sorry, it doesn't matter,' Banks said. 'Go on. What's the background?'

'She didn't say, sir. Wouldn't. I'm brought in from Wensleydale. Constable Weaver might know something.'

'Yes, of course. Thank you very much, Constable . . . ?'

'Smithies, sir.'

'Thank you very much, Constable Smithies. You did a good job calming her down and getting her to open up like that,' Banks said, then left her blushing in the interview room.

Weaver was on the phone when Banks reached the desk, but he cut the conversation short.

'The weather people from Reckston Moor, sir,' he explained. 'They say it'd be madness to send out search parties on the moors for at least twenty-four hours.'

'Bloody northern weather,' Banks cursed. Hatchley, eavesdropping, grinned and winked at Weaver, who ignored him.

'They don't expect the rain to let up for a while, and the land's boggy. Visibility is as bad as you can get up the valley sides. It's all moorland above there, sir, both ways, miles of it.'

'Yes, I know,' Banks said. 'And there's nothing we can do about it, is there? Just make sure everything's set to go the minute the situation improves. Have you arranged for helicopters?'

'Yes, sir. Superintendent Gristhorpe's handling it. But they can't go out in this weather.'

'No, of course not. Look, you know that girl who was in here a few minutes ago?'

Weaver nodded. 'Hazel Kirk. Yes.'

'Know anything about her father?'

'Robert Kirk. Family's been here for generations. Came from Scotland originally.'

'What does he do?'

'He works at Noble's in Eastvale. You know, the big shoe shop in that new shopping centre near the bus station.'

'I know it. Anything else.'

'He's very active in the local church, sir,' Weaver went on. 'One or two people think he's a bit of a religious nutter, if you know what I mean. Touch of the fire and brimstone. Strong Presbyterian streak – his ancestors brought it with them from Scotland, if you ask me. Anyway, he's always writing letters to the papers about too much sex on television. His latest fad is a campaign to ban rock videos and bring censorship into the music business. There's not much support for that round here though, sir. Nobody really cares one way or another.'

'What's your opinion of him?'

'Nutty but harmless.'

'Certain?'

Weaver nodded. 'Never been in trouble with us, sir. And he is very religious, like. Wouldn't harm a fly.'

'Religious people are often the most violent. Aren't the Iranians religious? Anyway, have a chat with him, would you, and ask him what he argued with Harold Steadman about.'

PETER ROBINSON

'There wasn't any argument, sir,' Weaver replied. 'Kirk
complained to the headmaster of Eastvale Comprehensive
about letting someone with such lax moral standards as
Harold Steadman mix with teenage girls.'

'What?'

'It's true, sir,' Weaver went on, grinning. 'He'd seen
Steadman with Penny Cartwright now and then, and to
Kirk she was nothing less than the whore of Babylon.
Remember, he was around when Penny left Helmthorpe
in the first place; all those rumours of incest, then the
Sodom and Gomorrah of the music business. Steadman
would sometimes give Hazel and the other girls a ride
home from school, and he'd take them on field trips and
invite them to his house. Kirk complained. Nobody took
him seriously, of course. I even overheard Steadman and
his mates having a good chuckle over the business in the
Bridge one night.'

'Why didn't you tell me this before?' Banks asked.
There was something in the icy quietness of his tone that
sent danger signals to Weaver.

'I— It didn't seem important, sir.'

'Didn't seem important?' Banks repeated. 'We're
investigating a murder, laddie. Do you realize that? Everything's important. Even if it's not important it's important
if it has anything to do with the victim and his circle. Do
you understand?'

'Yes, sir,' Weaver said shakily. 'Will that be all, sir?'

'Is that all?'

'Sir?'

'Is there anything else you ought to tell me?'

'No, sir. I don't think so, sir.'

'Then that's all. Come on, Sergeant Hatchley, let's get
back to civilization.'

'Bit rough on him, weren't you, sir?' said Hatchley as they turned up their collars and walked to their cars.

'It won't kill him.'

'Think there's owt in it, this Kirk business?'

'No. No more than there was in the major. Unless Kirk's a serious nutter, and Weaver assures me he isn't. Like nearly everything else in this case, there's just too much damn gossip. That's why it's hard to tell the lies from the truth. Kirk, Major Cartwright – nothing but gossip. Better run a check on his background though, just to make sure. I suppose he thinks Steadman was trying to corrupt his angelic young Hazel.'

'I wouldn't blame him,' Hatchley said. 'The jeans these kids wear nowadays . . . You'd need a bloody shoehorn to get into them.'

Banks laughed. 'Enough lewd thoughts about teen-agers, Sergeant.'

'Aye,' Hatchley said. 'It's a bloody good job we can't be arrested for what we think. Look, sir, there's a tobac-conist's. And it's open.'

TWO

It was late Sunday afternoon before the rain stopped completely, but the first search parties set out at mid-morning. By then it was only drizzling; the clouds had thinned, promising a fine day, and visibility was good. Plenty of locals had been willing to go out on Saturday, despite the weather conditions, but they had been warned against doing so.

The Sunday search was coordinated by Superintendent Gristhorpe, who had marked out areas on Ordnance

Survey maps and assigned these to each small party. He directed operations from the communications room in Eastvale Regional Headquarters, and as the reports came in, he shaded the ground that had been covered.

Meanwhile, enquiries continued in the major cities. In addition to their regular duties, police on car and foot patrols in Newcastle, Leeds, London, Liverpool, Manchester, Birmingham and other large cities were also keeping an eye out for the young blonde girl. Theatres, drama companies and acting schools were all checked carefully, and though numerous sightings were called in and followed up, they all proved to be false. Closer to home, Robert Kirk was investigated, questioned and let go. For one thing, he couldn't drive, and certainly nobody had carried Harold Steadman all the way from Helmthorpe to Crow Scar.

Sally's father, enraged with grief after receiving a letter from the Marion Boyars Academy of Theatre Arts saying they would be pleased to accept Sally as a student, had begun his search alone on Saturday in the rain. The weather so affected his rheumatism and his spirits that he was confined to bed by Dr Barnes the following day. Charles Lumb knew that Sally hadn't run away, despite their differences; anxiety and anger gave way to resignation. Even if the searchers did find her, what state would she be in after three or more nights out in the wilds?

On Sunday, the first area searched was the wide stretch of moorland to the north of Helmthorpe above Crow Scar. Gristhorpe, in making his decision, realized he might have been influenced by the fact that Steadman's body had been found on the northern slopes, but he reasoned that the area was, after all, the wildest spread of countryside – seven miles of rough high moors before the next dale – and had the greatest number of hiding places: old mines, steep quarries, potholes.

The only result of Sunday's effort was an accident in which a police constable drafted in from Askrigg fell down a twenty-foot bell pit. Fortunately, his fall was broken by accumulated water and mud, but it took over two hours of valuable time to rig up ropes and pull him out. Up on the moorland, two small parties got so bogged down in mud that they were unable to continue, and progress everywhere was slow.

By Monday, the sun was out to stay and conditions had improved. Gristhorpe, who had been up since five in the morning, sat red-eyed in the communications room logging check-in calls from search parties, and the map before him soon began to look like a chessboard. This was one task he refused to delegate.

At about three o'clock, the superintendent took Sergeant Rowe's advice and dropped by Banks's office to suggest a walk.

They walked into Market Street, which was crowded with tourists from the nearby cities who, seeing an end to the rain, had decided on an afternoon out. It was also market day, and the cobbled square in front of the church was thronged with colourful stalls selling everything from Marks and Spencer rejects to dinner sets and toilet-bowl brushes. There were stalls of second-hand paperbacks, yards of plain and patterned material – cotton, linen, muslin, rayon, denim, cheesecloth – spilling over almost to the ground, and stalls piled with crockery and cutlery. Skilled vendors drew crowds by shouting out the virtues of their wares as they juggled plates and saucers. The people milled around to listen, take photographs and, occasionally, to buy things. In the narrow twisting side streets around the central market square – old alleys where the sun never penetrated and you could shake hands across second-storey bay windows – the small souvenir and local delicacy shops with magnifying-glass windows did good business. Everything, from toffee and tea to spoons and fluffy toys, was labelled 'Yorkshire', no matter where it had actually been made.

Gristhorpe directed Banks to a small tea shop and the two of them settled down to tea and buns.

Gristhorpe ran his hand through his thick messy mop of grey hair and smiled weakly. 'Had to get out for a bit,' he said, spooning sugar into his mug. 'It gets so damn stuffy in that little room.'

'You look all-in,' Banks said, lighting a Benson and Hedges Special Mild. 'Perhaps you should go home and get some sleep.'

Gristhorpe grunted and waved away the smoke. 'Thought you'd given that filthy habit up,' he grumbled. 'Anyway, I suppose I am tired. I'm not as young as I used to be. But it's not just tiredness, Alan. Have you ever taken part in an operation like this before?'

'Not a search in open country, no. I've looked for missing teens in Soho, but nothing like this, in these conditions. Do you think there's any hope?'

Gristhorpe shook his head slowly. 'No. I think the girl's been killed. Stupid bloody kid. Why couldn't she have come to us?'

Banks had no answer. 'Have you been involved in this kind of search before?' he asked.

'More than twenty years ago now,' Gristhorpe said, adding an extra spoonful of sugar to his tea. 'And this makes it feel like only yesterday.'

'Who was it?'

'Young girl called Lesley Ann Downey. Only ten. And a lad called John Kilbride, twelve. You'll have heard about all that, though: Brady and Hindley, the Moors Murders?'

'You were in on that?'

'Manchester brought some of us in for the search. It's not that far away, you know. Still, that was different.'

'Sir?'

'Brady and Hindley were involved in Nazism, torture, fetishism – you name it. This time it's more calculated, if we're right. I don't know which is worse.'

'The result's the same.'

'Aye.' Gristhorpe gulped some tea and nibbled at his bun. 'Getting anywhere?'

Banks shook his head. 'Nothing new. Hackett's in the clear now. Barnes, too, by the looks of it. We're stuck.'

'It's always like that when the trail goes cold. You know that as well as I do, Alan. If the answer isn't staring you in the face within twenty-four hours, the whole thing goes stale. When you get stuck you just have to push a bit harder, that's all. Sometimes you get lucky.'

'I've been thinking about the time of Sally Lumb's disappearance,' Banks said, trying to waft his smoke away from Gristhorpe. 'She was last seen on Helmthorpe High Street walking east around nine o'clock on Friday evening.'

'Well?'

'I was in Helmthorpe at that time, in the Dog and Gun with Sandra and a couple of friends. We went to listen to Penny Cartwright sing. Jack Barker was there too.'

'So that lets them off the hook.'

'No, sir. That's just it. She finished her first set just after nine, then she and Barker disappeared from the pub for about an hour.'

'Right after Sally had been seen in the village?'

'Yes.'

'Better follow it up, then. What do you think?'

'I've talked to them both a couple of times. They're difficult, sharp. If I were easily swayed by sentiment, I'd say no, not a chance. Penny Cartwright seems sincere, and Barker's a clever bugger but likeable enough when you take the time to chat to him. He swears blind he'd nothing to do with Steadman's death. But I've met some damn good liars in my time. He's got no alibi and he might have been jealous about Steadman and the Cartwright woman.'

Gristhorpe ate the final few crumbs of his bun and suggested they carry on walking. They headed east and looped down by the river near the terraced gardens.

'The Swain's filling up,' Gristhorpe said. 'I hope we don't have a bloody flood to contend with, too.'

'Does that happen often?'

'Often enough. Usually at spring thaw after a particularly snowy winter. But if you get enough water channelled down from the dales, it might break the banks here.'

They turned up a dank waterside alley, where moss and lichen grew on the rough stone, skirted the base of Castle Hill and arrived back at the market square. Gristhorpe headed straight for the communications room and Banks accompanied him. There was nothing new.

THREE

Even Purcell's 'Hail Bright Cecilia' failed to cheer Banks up as he drove into Helmthorpe that evening. When he walked along High Street past the gift shop with its revolving racks of postcards and the small newsagent's with the evening papers outside fluttering in the light breeze, he could sense the mood of the village. Nothing was obvious; people went about their business as usual, shutting up shop for the day and coming home from work, but it felt like a place that had drawn in on itself. Even the air, despite the wind, seemed tight and grim. The small noises – footsteps, doors opening, distant telephones ringing – sounded eerie and isolated against the backdrop of the silent green valley sides and massive brow of Crow Scar, bright in the evening sun.

Push, Gristhorpe had said, so push he would. Push hard enough, in the right places, and something would give. Push those closest to Steadman – Penny, Ramsden, Emma, Barker – for if none of them had actually done it, Banks was sure that one of them knew who had. He would probably have to revisit Darnley and Talbot too. There was something one of them had said – a chance remark, a throwaway line – that Banks felt was important, but he couldn't remember what it was. It would return to him in time, he knew, but he couldn't afford to sit and wait; he had to push.

Would Sally Lumb have confronted any of them with her evidence? he asked himself as he took the short cut through the cemetery and turned right along the pathway to Gratly. It didn't seem likely; she wasn't a fool. But she had phoned someone, and had used a public call box for privacy. It must, then, have been someone she knew, someone she had no reason to fear.

The sheep on his right fled and stood facing the drystone wall, their backs to him; the ones on his left scampered down the grassy terraces to the stream and stood bleating under the willows. Funny creatures, Banks thought. If they're frightened, they simply run a short distance and turn their backs. It might be effective against people who wish them no harm, but he doubted if it would deter a hungry wolf.

Emma Steadman was watching television but turned the sound down after Banks followed her into the living room. The place was much barer now that most of the books and records were gone; it was more of an empty shell than a home.

Banks waited until Emma had made some tea, then sat opposite her at the low table.

'I've been meaning to ask you a few things for a while now,' he said. 'Mostly to do with the past.'

'The past?'

'Yes. Those wonderful summers you used to have up here when the Ramsden family ran the guest house.'

'What about them? You don't mind, do you?' she asked, picking up some knitting. 'It helps me relax, takes my mind off things. Sorry, go ahead.'

'Not at all. It's just that the impression I got was of your husband running around the dales with Penny Cartwright while Michael Ramsden buried his head in his books.'

Emma smiled but said nothing.

'And you never thought anything of it.'

'Perhaps if you'd known my husband, Chief Inspector, you wouldn't think anything of it, either.'

'But something's missing.'

'What?'

'You. What were you doing?'

Emma sighed and put her knitting down on her lap. 'Contrary to what you seem to believe, I'm not simply a passive housewife. I did have, and still do have, interests of my own. Back in Leeds I was involved in amateur dramatics for a while. On holidays in Gratly I used to knit and read. I even tried my hand at writing a few short stories – unsuccessfully, I'm afraid – but I can't prove it; I threw them away. I also went for walks.'

'Alone?'

'Yes, alone. Is that so strange?'

Banks shrugged.

'What you seem to forget is that we were only up here for a month or so at a time. During that period I spent a lot more time with my husband than you think. I did accompany them sometimes, especially if they went by car. But I'm very susceptible to the sun, so I never ventured far on sunny days unless I could find some shade. I still fail to see why you find all this so fascinating.'

'Sometimes present events have their roots in the past. Did you enjoy your visits?'

'They made a nice break. Leeds isn't the cleanest city in the world, I enjoyed the fresh air, the landscape.'

'One more thing. I've been given to believe that your husband was universally liked. Even Teddy Hackett, who had good reason to disagree with him, thought of him as a friend. Since I've been looking into his death though, I've found at least two people who didn't feel the same way – Major Cartwright and Robert Kirk. We might regard them as cranks, but I'm beginning to wonder if there's anyone else. Someone I don't know about. You were a close group all those years ago, and your husband was still close to Michael Ramsden and Penny Cartwright when he died. Was there anybody else around? Anybody who might have held a grudge?'

Emma Steadman pursed her lips and shook her head slowly.

'Think about it.'

'I am. Of course there were other people around, but I can't imagine any of them had a reason to harm Harold.'

'The point is, Mrs Steadman, that somebody did. And if none of you can help me find out who it was, I don't know who can. Is there any reason why he was killed at this particular time rather than, say, a year ago, or five years ago?'

'I've no idea.'

'You must know something about his affairs. Was he planning to do anything with his money? Write a will, leave it to the National Trust or something? Was there any other land he was after, anyone else's toes he was treading on?'

'No. No to all those questions. And I think I would have known, yes.'

'Well, that doesn't leave much, does it?'

'You think one of us did it, don't you?'

Banks kept silent.

'Do you think I did it? For his money?'

'You couldn't have, could you?'

'Maybe you think Mrs Stanton was lying to give me an alibi?'

'No.'

'Then why keep bothering me? I only buried my husband a few days ago.'

As Banks could think of no answer to that question, he sighed and got up to leave. Before Emma closed the door on him, he turned and spoke again: 'Just consider what I said, will you? Try to remember any enemies your husband might have made, however insignificant they might have seemed at the time. Think about it. I'll be back.'

Penny Cartwright was listening to music, and when

she grudgingly let Banks in, flashing him a 'you again' look, she didn't bother to turn it down.

'I won't keep you,' Banks said, sitting on a hard-backed chair by the window and lighting a cigarette. 'It's just about the other night.'

'What night? There's been a lot lately,' Penny said, pouring herself a drink.

'Friday night.'

'What about it?'

'You were singing at the Dog and Gun, remember?'

Penny scowled at him. 'Of course I remember. You were there too. What is this?'

'Just refreshing your memory. Between sets you went off with Jack Barker. You were gone for about an hour. Where were you?'

'What's that got to do with anything?'

'Look, it's about time you got this right. I ask the questions; you answer. Understand?'

'Oh, poor Inspector Banks,' Penny cooed, 'have I been undermining your authority?' Her eyes challenged him. 'What was the question again?'

'Friday night, between sets. Where were you?'

'We went for a walk.'

'Where?'

'Oh, hither and thither.'

'Can you be more specific?'

'Not really. I go for a lot of walks. There's a lot of places to walk around Helmthorpe. That's why so many tourists come here in summer.'

'Stop the games and tell me where you went.'

'Or else?'

After a thirty-second staring match, Penny looked away and reached for a cigarette.

'All right,' she said. 'We came here.'

'What for?'

'What do you think?'

'Sex?'

'That's not the kind of question a lady answers. And it's nothing to do with your investigation.'

Banks leaned forward and spoke quietly. 'Would it interest you to know that I've got a damned good idea why you came here? And I've got some colleagues back in Eastvale who'd be more than happy to come out here and prove it for me. Help me and you help yourself.'

'I'm not admitting anything.'

'Where were you at four o'clock on Friday afternoon?'

'I was here practising. Why?'

'Anybody with you?'

'No. There usually isn't when I practise.'

'Did you receive any telephone calls?'

Penny looked confused. 'Telephone calls? No. What are you getting at?'

'And you refuse to tell me what you did during the interval on Friday evening?'

'Wait a minute. Sally. Sally Lumb. She disappeared on Friday, didn't she? Christ, you bastard!' She glared at Banks. Angry tears made her eyes glitter. 'Are you implying that I had something to do with that?'

'What did you do?'

'If you already know, why do you want me to tell you?'

'I need to hear it from you.'

Penny sagged in her chair and looked away. 'All right. So we came back here and smoked a couple of joints. Big deal. Is that what you wanted to hear? What are you going to do now, bring in the dogs and tear the place apart?'

Banks stood up to leave. 'I'm not going to do anything.

I remember the difference between the last set and the first, how you seemed more remote, detached. If it's any consolation to you,' he said, opening the door, 'I believe you, and I'm glad I was right.'

But Penny didn't move or say anything to make his exit easier.

FOUR

Later, as Penny lay in bed that night unable to sleep, the images came again, just as they had been coming ever since Harold Steadman's death: those summers so long ago – innocent, idyllic. Or so they had seemed.

It was a time she had had neither reason nor inclination to think about over the past ten years – the kind of period, like an idealized childhood, that one looks back on when one gets older and life loses its edge. Life had been too busy, too exciting, and when she finally had crashed, she had been as far in her mind from idyllic summers as ever a person could be. It had seemed, then, that her earlier life had been lived by somebody else. Next she had come back to Helmthorpe, where they were all together again. Now Harold was dead and that wretched detective was probing, asking questions, churning up memories, like tides stir sand.

So she re-examined it. She reran the walks to Wensleydale along the Pennine Way and the drives to Richmond or the Lake District in Harold's old Morris 1100 like old movies, and she spotted things she had never noticed at the time – little things, vague and unclear, but certainly disturbing. And the more she thought about old times, the less she liked what she was thinking.

She turned over again and tried to cast the images from her mind. They were like dreams, she told herself. She had taken the truth, in all its purity, and warped it in her imagination. That must be what had happened. The problem was that now these dreams seemed so real. She couldn't shake them, and she wouldn't rest until she knew what was fantasy and what was reality. How could the past, something that had really happened, become so altered, so unclear? And as she finally drifted towards sleep, she began to wonder what she should do about it.

11

ONE

The numerous becks that ran down the slopes of Swainsdale to the river were flowing copiously, bringing rainwater from the higher land. A fine mist, like baby's hair, rose from the valley sides as the sun warmed the waterlogged earth. The colours were newly rinsed, too; fresh vibrant greens sloped up from the road, and bright skullcaps of purple heather, softened by the thin veil of mist, fringed the peaks.

Penny, walking with Jack Barker along High Street, was the first to notice a small crowd gathered on the bridge, under which a combination of becks, grown almost to the strength of a river themselves, cascaded from the southern heights down to the Swain.

A woman in a sleeveless yellow dress was pointing up the valley side, and the others followed her gaze, leaning over the low stone parapet. Penny and Barker soon reached the spot and stopped to see what the excitement was. They had an uninterrupted view up the dale side along the beck's course, on to which backed several gardens full of bright flowers. Some distance away they could see what looked like a child's rag doll tumbling recklessly down the swollen stream. It was hypnotic, Penny thought, to watch the thing turn cartwheels and flail, snag on the rocks and break free as the water pushed and dragged it.

Then the woman in the yellow dress put her hand over her mouth and gasped. The others, including Penny, whose long-distance eyesight had never been good, leaned further over and screwed up their eyes to peer more closely. It was only after the shock wave had rippled through the crowd that Penny realized what was happening. It was not a rag doll that came head over heels down the stream, but a body. Tufts of clothing still clung to the torn flesh. It looked raw, like a side of beef in a butcher's window; patches of skin had been ripped clean off, hair torn away from the scalp, and splintered bones stuck through at elbows and shins.

There was no face to recognize, but Penny knew, as did all the other locals on the bridge, that it was the body of Sally Lumb come back to the village where she was born.

Penny wrenched her eyes away while Barker and the others still stared in disbelief. Somebody mentioned an ambulance, somebody else the police, and the group split up in chaos.

Penny and Barker walked in a daze until they got to the Hare and Hounds, then they went inside and ordered double Scotches.

'Seen a ghost?' the barman asked.

'Something like that,' Barker said, and gave a garbled version of what had happened. Soon, customers went streaming out to look, leaving drinks on tables, cardigans and handbags on chairs.

The barman gave them each another double Scotch on the house and rushed off to see himself. The pub was empty; anybody could have walked in and robbed the place blind, but nobody did. Penny downed the fiery whisky; she was aware of her hand gripping Barker's so tight that the nails must have dug into his flesh.

TWO

'It's a bugger, Alan,' Gristhorpe said, rubbing his eyes, which had lost much of their childlike innocence through lack of sleep. He looked tired, pale and hurt, as if the whole affair, done right on his doorstep, was a personal affront. 'A bugger . . .'

They were in the Queen's Arms opposite the station, and it was almost afternoon closing time. Only a few dedicated drinkers and tourists in need of a late sandwich and shandy sat scattered around the lounge.

'We've got nothing so far,' the superintendent went on, sniffing as Banks lit a cigarette. 'The body was so bloody waterlogged and badly battered Glendenning couldn't give us any idea of what killed her. For all he can say, she might have fallen in and hit her head, or just drowned. A full autopsy's going to take time, and even then they can't promise owt.'

'What's Glendenning doing now?'

'You know him, Alan – couldn't wait to get at it. Stomach contents, organs, tissue samples. God knows, they've got to keep looking. It could even be poison.'

'What do you think?' Banks asked, sipping his pint of Theakston's bitter.

Gristhorpe shook his head. 'I don't know. They've got their jobs to do. Does it matter what killed her at this point? If we're right, and it's what we think it is, there was probably just a blow to the head, like Steadman. Glendenning might not even be able to verify that.'

'I just wish we knew a bit more about why it happened,' Banks said. 'Certainly I think there's a connection to the Steadman case – has to be – I just don't know what it is. The girl knew something and instead of coming to me she confronted the killer. I suppose she wasn't sure and simply wanted to find out for herself. Add it all up and we've still got nothing. So she knew something. What? She phoned someone. Who? Why? They met. Where?'

'We might be able to answer that last one soon,' Gristhorpe said. 'I've got men following the becks all the way up the hillside looking for physical evidence. There'll be some kind of grisly map of her progress.'

THREE

'That's scotched work for today,' Jack Barker punned weakly as he accepted his third refill from Penny. It was over two hours since they had seen the wreckage of Sally Lumb tumble down the valley side. Penny had stopped after her second drink, but Barker was still at it.

'Maybe you shouldn't,' Penny warned him.

'It's already too late. Thanks for your concern, though.'

When Penny looked down at Barker, she felt the stirring of something like love. Whatever it was, the feeling disoriented her and she was angry with herself for not knowing what to do. Though it had felt good at first when they had come back to the cottage and he had held her, she hated the feelings of weakness that came with it. She knew that her feelings for him were not platonic, but instead of reaching out, she drew in and strengthened her shell.

Barker seemed to sense something of her chaotic emotions, she thought, when he reached out again for her hand, which she allowed him to hold lightly.

'I suppose I always did have a weak stomach,' he said.

'Pathetic really, isn't it? Here I am writing about blood and guts for a living and as soon as I see . . .' His words trailed off and he started to shake. He put his glass on the table, spilling some Scotch as he did so. Then Penny sat beside him and held him. It seemed ages to her before either of them moved, and each would have said the other broke away first.

'You should get some sleep, Jack,' Penny said softly.

'What the hell's going on, Penny?' he asked. 'What's happening to this place?'

'I don't know,' Penny answered, stroking his hair. 'At least, I . . .'

'What?'

'Nothing,' she said. 'Or maybe nothing. I don't know. But it's got to stop.'

FOUR

'Under a packhorse bridge,' Banks said. 'That's what the super told me. On the south slope.'

'What does that mean?' Sandra asked. They were having an early evening drink in the Queen's Arms. Sandra had just finished shopping, and Banks had suggested that, as they had seen so little of one another the past few days, they meet for a chat. Brian and Tracy were old enough to manage on their own for an hour or two.

'It means he was wrong about where to look first, and he's kicking himself for that.'

'But he couldn't have known,' Sandra said. 'It made perfect sense to look on the north side first.'

'That's what everyone says, but you know what he's like.'

'Yes. Just like you. Stubborn. Takes it all on himself.'

'He'll get over it,' Banks said. 'Anyway, they found clothes fibres on the stones under this bridge. She must have been hidden there and covered with stones. Then when the heavy rains came, some of the stones were washed aside and she was carried down the valley. They've not found any traces above the bridge, and it looked like an ideal place – isolated but accessible by car, just.'

'Does it help, finding the body?'

'Not really. Not the state it's in. And too much time has gone by. We'll ask around of course – anybody heading that way, or back – but we can't expect too much. Whoever we're dealing with is smart, and he's not likely to make silly mistakes.'

'This probably had to be done in a hurry, though,' Sandra reminded him. 'There wouldn't have been much time for planning.'

'Still, it's not going to be easy.'

'Is it ever?'

Banks shrugged and lit a cigarette.

'By the way,' Sandra said. 'I haven't had a chance to say so before now, but I'm glad you got rid of that bloody pipe.'

'It didn't suit me.'

'No.'

'Too *Country Life*?'

Sandra laughed. 'Yes, I'd say so. You'd not fool many, though. Least of all yourself.'

'There's not many would say they're glad to see a person smoke, either,' Banks said, holding out the pack while Sandra, an occasional smoker, helped herself. 'But I do intend to cut down and stick to these mild things.'

'Promises!'

'The girl, you know,' Banks said after a brief pause, 'was a virgin as far as forensic could make out. Hadn't been shot, stabbed, poisoned or sexually assaulted. Virgin.'

'I wonder if that's a good thing,' Sandra asked.

'What? That she hadn't been assaulted?'

'No. That she died a virgin.'

'It won't make any difference to her now, poor beggar,' said Banks. 'And I doubt it's the kind of thing they inscribe on tombstones. But at least we can be sure she wasn't tormented or tortured. She probably died very quickly, without even knowing what was happening.'

'Are you going to get the killer soon, Alan?' Sandra asked, swirling the smooth fragments of ice in the bottom of her glass. 'And don't treat me like a reporter. Be honest.'

'I'd like to say yes, but we've got so damn little to go on. We can trace the girl's movements until about nine o'clock Friday evening, and that's it.'

'While we were at the folk club?'

'Yes.'

Sandra shivered. 'We were so close.'

'Does that make a difference?'

'It's just a funny feeling, that's all. What about the writer and the singer?'

'She could be protecting him, or they could be working together. It's hard to know what to believe when things are clouded by so much gossip. The others all go back so far, too. Lord knows what complex webs of feelings they've set up between one another over the years. It seems to me that in a place like Helmthorpe emotions go deeper and last longer than in a big city.'

'Nonsense. Think about all those feuds and gang rivalries in London.'

'That's business, in a way. I mean the ordinary things between people.'

'Who had the best motive?' Sandra asked.

'The one with the least opportunity.' Banks smiled at the irony. 'That's if you call a lot of money a good motive. There could also be all kinds of jealousies involved. That's why I can't leave Barker and Penny Cartwright out of it altogether.'

'The wife inherits?'

'Yes.'

'She came in for some bridge work yesterday.'

'What did you think of her?'

'I didn't see much of her, really. Only when she came to the window to confirm her appointment. She seemed quite an attractive woman.'

'She didn't look much to me.'

'That's typical of a man,' Sandra said. 'All you can see is the surface.'

'But you must admit she's let herself go.'

'It looks like it, yes,' Sandra said slowly. 'But I don't think so. It's all there. She's fine under all those awful clothes. Her bone structure's good, too. Of course, if you'd known her before or not seen her for a long time, she'd definitely look as if she'd gone downhill, I suppose.'

'A pretty young thing.'

'Pardon?'

'Oh, nothing,' Banks said. 'Just remembering something. Go on.'

'All I'm saying is the potential's there for her to be an attractive woman. She can't be much older than me.'

'Late thirties.'

'Well, then. She must only look plain because she wants to, because it doesn't matter to her. Not all women are obsessed with their looks, you know. Perhaps there are other things more important to her.'

'Perhaps. What you're saying,' Banks went on slowly, 'is that with the right hairstyle, good clothes and a little make-up . . .'

'She could be quite a stunner, yes.'

FIVE

Penny was at the stove roasting spices for a curry when Barker made his way down the narrow stairs.

'So, the sleeper awakes,' she greeted him.

'What time is it?'

'Seven o'clock.'

'At night?'

'Yes. It's still the same day. Hungry? I shouldn't think so, with a hangover like you must have. Anyway, I'm making a curry. Take it or leave it.'

'Your generosity and grace overwhelm me,' Barker said. 'As a matter of fact, I don't feel too bad. I've just got a hell of a headache.'

'Aspirin's in the bathroom cabinet.'

'What happened?' Barker asked.

'You mean you don't remember?'

'Not after the third drink. Or was it the fourth?' He rubbed his eyes with his knuckles.

'You really don't remember?' Penny repeated, sounding shocked. 'Well, that's a fine compliment, isn't it?'

'You mean . . . ?'

Penny laughed. 'Don't be a fool, Jack. I'm only kidding. You got tired and I helped you upstairs to sleep it off. That's all.'

'All?'

'Yes. You don't think I'd fall into bed with you the way you were earlier, do you?'

'I'll get some aspirin,' Jack said, and made his painful way back upstairs to the bathroom.

'We'll let that simmer for a while,' Penny said when he came back, 'and have a sit-down. Drink?'

'My God, no!' Barker groaned. 'But on the other hand, hair of the dog and all that. Not whisky, though.'

'Beer do?'

'Yes.'

'Sam Smith's?'

'Fine.'

'Good. It's all I've got. Chilled too.'

Penny got the beer and Barker sat on the sofa drinking out of the bottle.

'What you said, Penny,' he began, 'about not, you know, sleeping with me in a state like that . . .'

'I doubt you'd have been able to get it up, would you?' she mocked, a mischievous smile crinkling the corners of her mouth.

'I might be a bit slow,' Barker replied, 'but are you implying that if I'd been sober . . . I mean, you might actually . . . you know?'

Penny put her finger to his lips and stopped him. 'That's for me to know and you to find out,' she said.

'Dammit, Penny,' he said, 'you can't just ignore me half the time and then tease me the rest. It's not fair. I'm upset enough as it is about the girl floating down and all that.'

'I'm sorry, Jack. It just doesn't come out right. I stop one game and start another, don't I?'

'That's how it seems. Why don't you give me a straight answer?'

'What's the question?'

'I've already asked you.'

'Oh, that. I'm glad you were drunk, Jack, because no, I don't think I would have. Is that straight enough?'

'It seems to be,' Barker said, disappointment clear in his tone.

Penny went on quickly, 'It's not as simple as you think. What I mean is, I'm glad I wasn't forced into making a decision there and then. I'm weak, I might have said yes and regretted it. It would have been so easy then, so natural to make love after being confronted with death. But I wouldn't have been able to get Sally out of my mind, that awful torn body . . .'

'I understand that. But why would you regret it?'

Penny shrugged. 'Lots of reasons. So much has happened. It's too quick, too soon. It would be easy to jump into bed with you. You're an attractive man. But I want more than that, Jack. I don't just want to be like one of the bimbos you sleep with when you're down in London publicizing your books.'

'I don't, and you never could be.'

'Whatever. I've had enough disappointments in my life. I want some stability. I know it sounds conventional and corny, but I want to settle down, and I think I might be better off doing it by myself. I'm not one of these women who depends on a man.'

'It's just as well; I'm hardly dependable.' Barker lit a cigarette and coughed. 'Look,' he said. 'I don't care whether this is the right place and time or what it is, but

I love you, Penny. That's what I'm trying to get at. Not whether you'll sleep with me or not. There, I've said it. Maybe I've made a fool of myself.'

Penny looked at him carefully for a long time, then she said, 'I don't know if I can handle being in love.'

'Try it,' Barker said, leaning forward and stroking her hair. 'You never know, you might like it.'

Penny looked away. Barker moved closer and took her in his arms. She tensed, but didn't break the embrace.

Finally, she disengaged herself and looked at him seriously. 'Don't expect too much of me,' she said. 'I'm used to fending for myself and I like it.'

'You and I,' Jack said, 'we've been living alone so long it's frightening to think about change. So let's just take it easy, slowly.'

A bell rang in the kitchen.

'That's telling me the curry's ready.' Penny got up.

Barker followed her into the kitchen and leaned in the narrow doorway as she stirred the pungent sauce. 'Do you know,' he said, 'it took that bloody policeman, as you call him, to make me realize that I was jealous of you and Harry. I wondered, why the hell should you give so much of yourself to him and so little to me?'

'That's not fair, Jack.' Penny's face darkened as she turned to him. 'Don't talk like that. You sound just like Banks.'

'I'm sorry,' Barker apologized. 'I didn't mean anything by it.'

'Forget it.'

'The past won't go away, Penny,' Barker said. 'There's a lot of things need explaining.'

'Like what?' Penny asked suspiciously, taking the pot off the ring.

'You know more about it than I do.'

'More about what?'

'Everything that's happened. Come on, Penny, don't tell me you haven't got any ideas. You know more about this business than you're letting on.'

'Why should you think that?'

'I don't really know,' Barker answered. 'It's just that you've been awfully mysterious and touchy about it these past few days.'

Penny turned back to the curry in silence.

'Well?' Barker asked.

'Well what?'

'Do you?'

'Do I what?'

'Oh come on. You know what I mean. Do you know something I don't?'

'How do I know what you know?'

'I don't know anything. Do you?'

'Of course not,' Penny said, putting the curry into dishes. 'It's your imagination, Jack. You writers! Don't you think if I knew something I'd tell you?'

'As a matter of fact, I don't. Sally Lumb didn't tell anyone either. Or she told the wrong person.'

'And you think it was me?'

'Don't be ridiculous.'

'Go on, you might as well say it,' Penny shouted, brandishing the spoon like a club. 'Just like Banks. Go on!'

'I don't know what you're talking about.'

'Friday evening, when she disappeared.'

'But we were in the Dog and Gun.'

'Not all the time.'

'So? You came home for a rest and I went for a walk. So what?'

'You don't know?'

'Know what?'

'Banks hasn't been to pester you?'

'About what?'

'That's when Sally was last seen. While we were away. Somebody saw her in High Street about nine o'clock.'

'So Banks thinks . . . ?'

Penny shrugged. 'He asked me. You?'

'No. I've not seen him for a few days.'

'You will. He's getting very pushy.'

'I suppose he must be desperate. Surely you don't think I was implying you had anything to do with it?'

'Well, weren't you?'

'I'd hardly declare my undying love to someone I thought was a murderess, would I?'

Penny smiled.

'And what about you?' he went on. 'Do you believe me?'

'About what?'

'That I just went for a walk.'

'Well, yes. Of course I do. I don't even remember how all this started.'

'I was simply asking you if you knew anything you hadn't told me. That's all.'

'And I thought I'd answered that,' Penny said, her dark eyes narrowing. 'I've been no more mysterious about it than you have.'

'Oh come off it, Penny. You can't get out of it that easily. You've been around here much longer than I have. You're bound to know more about what goes on than I do.'

'You seem to be treating me like a criminal, Jack. Is this your idea of love? If this is what it comes down to, just how bloody jealous were you?'

'Forget it.' Barker sighed. 'Just forget I opened my mouth.'

'I'd like to, Jack. I really would.'

They eyed each other warily, then Penny broke off to carry the bowls through to the dining table. She pushed one towards Barker, who sat down to eat.

'You've put me in a right mood for a romantic candle-light dinner, you have,' she complained. 'I'm not even hungry now.'

'Try some,' Barker said, offering her a spoonful. 'It's very good.'

'I've lost my appetite.' Penny reached for a cigarette, then changed her mind and picked up her jacket. 'I'm going out.'

'But you can't,' Barker protested. 'We've got a lot to talk about. What about the candles? You've made dinner.'

'Eat it yourself,' Penny told him, opening the door. 'Eat the bloody candles too, for all I care.'

Barker half rose from the table. 'But where are you going?'

'To see a man about a dog,' she said, and slammed the door behind her.

SIX

Though the sun still lingered low on the horizon, it was dark on Market Street in the shadow of the buildings on the western side, and the cobbled square was deserted. Banks hadn't even bothered to turn on his office light after returning to go over his notes. Sandra had gone home to assure Brian and Tracy that they weren't becoming latchkey children. The door was closed and the dark room was full of smoke. Occasionally he heard footsteps in the corridor outside, but nobody seemed to know he was there.

As was his habit when a case felt near to its end, he sat by the window smoking and rearranged the details in his mind four or five times. After about an hour things still looked the same. The pattern, the picture, was complete, and however unbelievable it was, it had to be right. Eliminate the impossible and whatever is left, however improbable, must be the truth. Or so Sherlock Holmes had said.

It was time for action.

Banks played no music as he drove towards the purplish-red sunset west along Swainsdale; his mind was far too active to take in anything more. Finally he swung up the hill to Gratly, turned sharp left after the bridge and pulled up outside the Steadman house. There were no lights on. Banks cursed and walked down the path to Mrs Stanton's.

'Oh, hello Inspector,' she greeted him. 'I didn't expect to see you again. Please come in.'

'Thank you very much,' Banks said, 'but I don't think I will. I'm a bit pushed for time. If you could just answer a couple of quick questions?'

Mrs Stanton frowned and nodded.

'First of all, have you any idea where Mrs Steadman is?'

'No, I haven't. I think I heard her car about an hour or so ago, but I've no idea where she was going.'

'Did you see her?'

'No, I wasn't looking. Even if I was it wouldn't matter, though. They've got a door from the kitchen goes straight into the garage. Money,' she said. 'They've even got those automatic doors. Just press a button.'

'Which direction did she drive off in?'

'Well, she didn't come past here.'

'So she went east?'

'Aye.'

'Do you remember that Saturday you spent watching television with her?' Mrs Stanton nodded slowly. 'Do you know if she went out again after she got home?'

Mrs Stanton shook her head. 'I certainly didn't hear her, and I was up for more than an hour pottering around.'

'Last Friday night, did she go out at all?'

'Couldn't tell you, Inspector. That was my bingo night.'

'Your husband?'

'Pub. As usual.'

'This was a regular Friday night arrangement?'

'Ha! For him it's a reg'lar every night arrangement.'

'And you?'

'Aye, I go to bingo every Friday. So does half of Swainsdale.'

'Mrs Steadman?'

'Never. Not her. Not that she's a snob, mind. What pleases some folks leaves others cold. Each to his own is what I say.'

'Thank you very much, Mrs Stanton,' Banks said, leaving her mystified as he got back into the Cortina and set off toward Helmthorpe.

He parked illegally in High Street by the church, right at the bottom of Penny's street. There was a light on in her front room. Banks walked quickly up the path and knocked.

He was surprised when Jack Barker answered the door.

'Come in, Chief Inspector,' Barker said. 'Penny's not

here, I'm afraid. Or have you come to ask me where I was on Friday evening?'

Banks ignored the taunt; he had no time for games. 'Has she said anything odd lately about the Steadman business?' he asked.

Puzzled, Barker shook his head. 'No. Why?'

'Because I got the impression she was holding something back. Something she might not have been sure about herself. I was hoping I could persuade her to tell me what it was.'

Barker lit a cigarette. 'As a matter of fact,' he said, 'Penny has been a bit strange the few times I've seen her lately. Secretive and touchy. She hasn't said anything, though.'

Banks sat down and began tapping the frayed arm of the chair. 'You two,' he said, looking around the room. 'Are you . . . er . . . ?'

'Playing house? Not really. No such luck. I was here for dinner. We just had a bit of a row about the very thing you just mentioned, actually. She left and I'm waiting for her to come back.'

'Oh?'

'I suggested she knew more than she was letting on, and she accused me of treating her like a criminal, just like you did.'

'That's what she thinks?'

'Well, you have been giving her a rough time; you can't deny it.'

Banks looked at his watch. 'Is she coming back soon?'

'I've no idea.'

'No idea? Where is she?'

'I told you,' Barker said. 'We had a row and she stormed out.'

'Where to?'

'I don't know.'

'Did she say anything?'

'She said she was going to see a man about a dog.'

'A lot of help that is.'

'Just what I thought.'

'And you'd been on at her about knowing something?'

'Yes.'

'Did she take the car?'

'Yes.'

'Right.' Banks got to his feet. 'Come on.'

Without thinking, Barker jumped up and obeyed the command. Banks only gave him time to blow out the candles and lock the door.

'Look, what's going on?' Barker asked as they shot into the darkening dale. 'You're driving like a bloody lunatic. Is something wrong? Is Penny in danger?'

'Why should she be?'

'For Christ's sake, I don't know. But you're behaving damned oddly, if you ask me. What the hell's happening?'

Banks didn't reply. He focused all his concentration on driving, and the silence intensified as darkness grew. On the northern outskirts of Eastvale, he turned on to the York Road.

'Where are we going?' Barker asked a few minutes later.

'Almost there,' Banks replied. 'And I want you to do exactly as I say. Remember that. I've only brought you with me because I know you're fond of Penny and you happened to be in her house. I'd no time to waste, and you might be some use, but do as I say.' He broke off to overtake a lorry.

Barker gripped the dashboard. 'So you've not brought me along for the pleasure of my company?'

'Give me a break.'

'Seriously, Chief Inspector, is she in danger?'

'I don't know. I don't know what we're going to find. Don't worry, though, it won't be long now,' he said, and the tyres squealed as he turned sharp left. About a quarter of a mile along the bumpy minor road, Banks pulled into a driveway and Barker pointed and said, 'That's her car. That's Penny's car.'

A face peered through a chink in the curtains as they jumped out of the Cortina and hurried towards the door.

'No time for pleasantries,' Banks said after trying the handle to no avail. He stood back and gave a hard kick, which splintered the wood around the lock and sent the door flying open. With Barker close behind, he rushed into the living room and quickly took in the strange tableau.

There were three people. Michael Ramsden stood facing Banks, white-faced and slack-jawed. Penny lay inert on the couch. And a woman stood with her back to them all.

In a split second, it came to life. Barker gasped and ran over to Penny, and Ramsden started to shake.

'My God,' he groaned, 'I knew this would happen. I knew it.'

'Shut up!' the woman said, and turned to face Banks.

She wore a clinging red dress that accentuated her curves; her hair was drawn back into a tight V on her forehead and carefully applied blusher highlighted the cheekbones of her heart-shaped face. But the most striking thing about her was her eyes. Before, Banks had only seen them watery and distorted through thick lenses, but now she was wearing contacts they were the chilly green of moss on stones, and the power that shone through them was hard and piercing. It was Emma Steadman, transformed almost beyond recognition.

Ramsden collapsed into an armchair, head in hands, whimpering, while Emma continued to glare at Banks.

'You bastard,' she said, and spat at him. 'You ruined it all.' Then she lapsed into a silence he never heard her break.

12

ONE

But Ramsden talked as willingly as a sinner in the confessional, and what he said over the first two hours following his arrest gave the police enough evidence to charge both of them. Banks was astonished at Ramsden's compulsion to unburden himself, and realized only then what terrible pressure the man must have been under, what inner control he must have exerted.

As for Penny, she said she had been doing a great deal of thinking over the last few days. Steadman's death, Banks's questions and Sally's disappearance had all forced her to look more deeply into a past she had ignored for so long, and especially into the events of a summer ten years ago.

At first she remembered nothing. She hadn't lied; everything had seemed innocent to her. But then, she said, the more she found herself dwelling on the memory, the more little things seemed to take on greater significance than they had done at the time. Glances exchanged between Emma Steadman and Michael Ramsden – had they really happened or were they just her imagination? Ramsden's insistent overtures, then his increasing lack of interest – again, had it really happened that way? Was there, perhaps, a simple explanation? All these things had inflamed her curiosity.

Finally, after the argument with Jack Barker, she knew it wouldn't all just go away. She had to do something or her doubts about the past would poison any chance of a future. So she went to visit Ramsden to find out if there was any truth in her suspicions.

Yes, she knew what had happened to Sally Lumb and she also knew the police linked the girl's death to Steadman's, but she honestly didn't believe she had anything to fear from Michael Ramsden. After all, they'd known each other off and on since childhood.

She questioned Ramsden and, finding his responses nervous and evasive, pushed even harder. They drank tea and ate biscuits, and Ramsden tried to convince her that there was nothing in her fears. Eventually she found difficulty focusing; the room darkened and she felt as if she were looking at it through the wrong end of a telescope. Then Penny fell asleep. When she awoke she was in Barker's arms and it was all over.

Banks told her that Ramsden had sworn he wouldn't have hurt her. True, he had drugged her with some prescription Nembutal and driven to the public telephone on the main road to send for Emma, but only because he was confused and didn't know what to do. When Emma had insisted that they would have to kill Penny because she knew too much, Ramsden claimed that he had tried to stand up to her. She had called him weak and said she would do what was necessary if he wasn't man enough. She said it would be easy to arrange an accident. According to Ramsden, they were still arguing when Banks and Barker arrived.

Penny listened to all this at about one o'clock in the morning over a pot of fresh coffee in Banks's smoky office. All she could say when he had finished was, 'I was right, wasn't I? He wouldn't have hurt me.'

Banks shook his head. 'He would,' he insisted, 'if Emma Steadman told him to.'

TWO

It was a couple of days before all the loose ends were tied up. Hatchley made notes and wrote up the statements, complaining all the while about DC Richmond sunning himself in Surrey, and Gristhorpe went over the details. Emma Steadman said nothing; she didn't even bother to deny Ramsden's accusations. To Banks, she was a woman who had risked everything and lost. There was no room for regret or recrimination now it was all over.

Later in the week, Banks took Sandra over to Helmthorpe, where they heard Penny sing at a special memorial concert for Sally Lumb. Afterwards, as it was a warm night and the show ended early, they went with Penny and Jack Barker for a drink in the beer garden of the Dog and Gun. Crow Scar gathered the failing light and gleamed as the hills around it fell into shadow. It looked like a pale curtain hanging in the sky.

Sandra and the others pressed Banks for an explanation of the Steadman business, and though he felt very uncomfortable in the role they forced on him, he did feel he owed Barker and Penny something; nor had he had much time to talk to Sandra since the arrests, and she had helped him arrive at the correct pattern.

'When did it start?' Sandra asked first.

'About ten years back,' Banks told her. 'That makes Penny here sixteen, Michael Ramsden eighteen, Steadman about thirty-three and his wife just twenty-eight. Harold Steadman had a promising career as a university lecturer.

If he wasn't exactly rich, he was certainly comfortably off, and he did have the inheritance to look forward to. Emma too, must have been quite pleased with life in those days, but I imagine she quickly got bored. She was beginning to fade into the background like so many faculty wives.

'When I talked to Talbot and Darnley, two of Steadman's colleagues at Leeds University, one of them remembered Emma as a "pretty young thing" at first, then she just seemed to disappear into the woodwork. I dare say she'd have liked to go abroad for her holidays more often, but no, Steadman had discovered Helmthorpe – Gratly rather – and that satisfied all his requirements for a busman's holiday, so that was that. For Emma, life seemed to be passing by too quickly and too dully, and she felt too young to give it all up.

'That summer was beautiful, just like this one.' Banks paused to look around at the other drinkers with their jackets and cardigans hung on the backs of chairs. 'How often can you do this in England?' he asked, sipping chilled lager. 'Especially in Yorkshire. Anyway, Penny and Michael were the pride of the village – two bright kids with their whole lives ahead of them. Michael was a lean serious romantic young fellow, and if he imagined he was losing Penny to an older wiser man, then he still had a steady diet of Keats and Shelley to keep him nicely melancholy. Penny here simply enjoyed Steadman's company, as she's told me often enough. They had a lot in common, and there were no amorous inclinations on either side. Or if there were, they were well repressed.'

He glanced at Penny, who looked down into her beer.

'So,' Banks went on after a deep breath, 'one sunny day Penny's out with Steadman looking at the Roman excavations in Fortford say, and Michael's languishing in the garden reading "Ode to a Nightingale" or something. His parents are out shopping in Leeds or York and won't be back till it's time to prepare the evening meal. Emma Steadman is moping around the place staying out of the sun, and probably feeling bored and neglected. I'm making this up, by the way. Ramsden didn't give me a blow by blow account. Anyway, Emma seduces young Michael. Not so difficult when you consider his age and his obsession with sex. Surely it's every schoolboy's fantasy – the experienced older woman. To Emma, he must have seemed like a younger more vital version of her husband. Perhaps he wrote poetry for her. He was certainly gawky and shy, and she gave him his first sexual experience.

'Most people probably thought of Emma Steadman as a married woman going quickly to seed, but Michael made her feel wanted, and then she began to see definite advantages in not being thought particularly attractive. That way, nobody would think of her as the type to be having an affair.'

Banks stopped to drink some more lager, pleased to see that he hadn't lost his audience. 'The affair went on over the years,' he continued. 'There were gaps and breaks, of course, but Ramsden told us they often got together in London when Emma went down for a weekend's "shopping", or when she went to "Norwich" to "visit her family". I don't think her husband paid her a great deal of attention, he was far too busy poring over ruins.

'Anyway, Emma developed a powerful hold over Michael. As his first lover, she had a natural advantage. She taught him all he knew. And he was still shy in company and found it hard to meet girls his own age. But why bother? Emma was there and she gave him all he needed, far more than the inexperienced girls of his own age group could have given him. And, in turn, he made her feel young, sexy and powerful. They fed off each other, I suppose.

'Over the years, Emma developed two distinct personalities. Now I'm not suggesting for a moment that she's mentally ill – there's nothing at all clinically wrong with her – all her actions were deliberate, willed, calculated. But she had one face for the world and another for Ramsden. If you think about it, it wasn't that difficult for her to change her appearance. She only had to do it to please Ramsden, and he was strongly under her influence anyway. Visiting him in London would have been no problem, of course. But even after she moved to Gratly and he moved to York, it was simple enough. She could easily do herself up a bit in the car on the way to see him – a little make-up, a hairbrush. She could even change her clothes after she arrived, if she wanted. With Harold gone, it was even easier. Her neighbour told me there's a door from the kitchen right into the garage, and it's a lonely road over the moors to Ramsden's place. But it wasn't just looks, it was attitude, too. With Ramsden she felt her sexual power, something that was more or less turned off the rest of the time.

'As time went by, everything she expected to happen, happened. Steadman threw himself more and more into his work, and she found herself, except for Ramsden, increasingly isolated. Why did she stay with her husband? I'm only guessing here, but I can think of two good reasons. First of all security, and secondly the promise of the inheritance, the possibility that things might improve when they became rich. And what happens? The money comes through all right, but nothing changes. In fact, things get worse. And here I can sympathize with her, to some extent. She's a woman with dreams – travel, excitement, wealth, a social life – but all that happens is her husband buys the Ramsden house and she ends up even more bored and cut off while he spends the money on historical research. A dedicated man. Even though I can't condone what she did to him, I can understand why she was driven to it. Steadman wasn't exactly sensitive to her needs, emotional or material. He was selfish and mean. There they were, rich as bloody Croesus, and he spends his time drinking in the Bridge and his money on his work. I'm sure Emma Steadman would have preferred the country club. In fact she was little more than a prisoner, and the only person her husband was really close to was Penny again.'

'That's not quite true,' Penny said. 'He was close to Michael. He liked him.'

'Yes,' Banks agreed. 'But that was much more of a working relationship. Michael was of use to him. I think they were colleagues, or partners, rather than friends. Don't forget, Michael killed him.'

'She made him.'

'Yes, but he did it.'

A waiter came out and they ordered another round.

'Go on,' Penny urged him after the drinks arrived.

'Michael Ramsden is ambitious but he's weak. He's not good with people. He shared Steadman's interests, yes, but he wasn't obsessed – a word that offended one of Steadman's colleagues, but apt, I think. Also, Ramsden resented Harold Steadman, and this really had nothing to do with you, Penny, even if he did feel jealous all those years ago. No, he resented Steadman in the way many of us come to detest people we first set up as examples, models, call them what you will. He hated always playing second fiddle – the publisher, the assistant – never the creative one, the leader, although he was busy working on a novel himself. Emma must have played on this, I think, dwelling on her husband's bad points when she was with Ramsden, playing on Michael's growing resentment towards his mentor. Soon he began to recognize Steadman's meanness and his lack of consideration for anybody with interests other than his own. I think too that he was always, deep down, irritated at the way Harold could communicate so easily with Penny, how fond they were of one another. Anyway, this animosity grew and grew over the years, fuelled by sexual desire for Emma, and finally there came a chance to get rich, to take it all.

'Emma Steadman used Ramsden, manipulated him without a doubt. But that doesn't absolve him from blame. Slowly, she introduced the idea of murder to him, helped him over his initial resistance and nervousness. She did this partly by playing on his existing feelings about her husband, and partly through sex. Denial, satisfaction. More denial, greater satisfaction than he'd ever had before. That's what he told me, anyway. He's not a fool; he knew what was happening and he went along with it. Together, they killed Harold Steadman.

'Naturally, as Emma stood to inherit, she'd be the first suspect so she had to be sure of an airtight alibi, which she had. Also, Ramsden seemed to have neither motive nor opportunity, no matter how I went at him, until the connection with Emma finally came into focus. There were also a number of other possibilities I had to pursue.'

Both Barker and Penny looked at him reprovingly as he said this.

'Yes,' he went on, acknowledging them. 'You two.

Hackett, for a while. Barnes. Even the major and Robert Kirk, fleetingly. Believe me, I blame myself for not arriving at the answer before Sally Lumb had to die, too, but I couldn't see the truth for the gossip, or the past for the present.'

'Why did Sally have to die?' Barker asked. 'Surely she couldn't have been a threat? What could she have known?'

'Sally was older than her years in many ways,' Banks replied. 'She misread the situation. But I'll get back to her a bit later. On the Saturday that Steadman was killed, Ramsden drove close to Gratly. He parked his car in one of those derelict old barns on the minor road just east of the Steadman house, the one Emma always used to get to York. Remember, Ramsden had been brought up in Gratly; he knew every twist and dip in the dale.'

'But how did he get back?' Penny asked. 'It's an impossibly long walk, and the only bus to Eastvale goes early in the morning.'

'Easy,' Banks answered. 'He wouldn't have taken the bus anyway; too many people might have noticed him. Emma Steadman drove him back. She picked him up on the road at a prearranged time – a fairly isolated spot so there'd be no chance of their being seen. Then she dropped him off at the end of his lane and went shopping in York. We've checked on that now, and her neighbour remembers it because Emma brought back some material she'd asked for. There was nothing unusual in all that. Emma Steadman often spent afternoons shopping in York. After all, she was a lady of leisure. They just had to be careful not to be seen. And even if they had been, Ramsden looked enough like Steadman from a distance through a car window, so nobody would have thought twice about seeing them.'

'What about that night?' Penny asked. 'After Harry had the row with my father?'

'That's another thing hindsight tells me I should have known,' Banks answered. 'There was only one place Steadman would have gone after the argument, and that's exactly where he intended to go in the first place, to Ramsden's. Remember he was a dedicated man, and you, Penny, were the only person he allowed to make emotional inroads into his valuable time. So he did exactly what he intended; he drove to York. And Ramsden killed him.

'It was all planned in advance, perhaps even rehearsed. Ramsden already had plastic sheeting on the floor because he was painting his living room. He hit Steadman from behind with a hammer, wrapped his body in the sheet, bundled it in the boot of Steadman's own car, drove it up near Crow Scar and buried it. He couldn't bury him in the plastic because that might have given too much away, but he told us where he buried it and we've dug it up.'

Penny put her head in her hands and Barker put his arms around her.

'I'm sorry, Penny,' Banks said. 'I know it sounds brutal, but it was.'

Penny nodded and took a sip of her drink, then reached for a cigarette. 'I know,' she said. 'It's not your fault. I'm sorry to be such a crybaby. It's just the shock. Please go on.'

'It was well after midnight and the village was deserted. He put Steadman's car back in the car park, cut through the graveyard and over the beck, then drove his own car home to York. All he had to worry about was getting stopped on the way, but the road he chose made that most unlikely. As I said, the whole thing was carefully planned to throw all suspicion away from Ramsden and Emma Steadman, who had the best motive. It even helped them that Steadman's car was a beige Sierra. They're quite common around here. I looked in the car park myself yesterday and saw three of them. And there are others that look much the same, especially in dim light – Allegros, for example. Of course there were minor risks, but there was a hell of a lot at stake. It was worth it.'

'What about Sally then?' Sandra asked. 'How does she fit into it?'

'She wasn't part of the plan at all,' Banks said. 'She was just one of the innocent bystanders whose memory got jogged too much for her own good. Like Penny here.'

'There but for the grace of God,' Penny muttered.

'Too true,' Banks agreed. 'Whatever you believe, Emma would have convinced Ramsden it was necessary to get rid of you. She'd probably have had to do it herself, but he wouldn't have stopped her. He was too far gone.'

'You said he seemed almost glad when you arrived,' Penny said.

'Yes, in a way. It was the end; he was free. I really think he was relieved. Anyway, according to Ramsden, Sally said she saw him and Emma together in Leeds. They were very careful; they'd never think of going out in York or Eastvale, but Leeds seemed safe enough. None of Steadman's old colleagues would have recognized Emma, and she knew the kind of places they went to, the places to avoid. Sally was there with her boyfriend. I've talked to him again and he said they did go to Leeds once when he borrowed a friend's car, and Sally pulled him out of a pub, Whitelock's, pretty sharpish when she spotted someone she knew. But she didn't realize who it was at the time.

She was more concerned with Ramsden not seeing her than about who he was with. I suspect she and Kevin went to quite a few pubs. Sally certainly looked old enough to pass for eighteen, but she was under age, so she couldn't afford to get caught.

'Now, most people would have just thought that Michael Ramsden had got himself a good-looking girl-friend, and I'm sure that's what Sally believed until events in Helmthorpe made her start re-examining little things like that. She was perceptive and imaginative. But it wasn't until I'd managed to link Emma and Ramsden that I knew how Sally fitted in at all. One thing I noticed when I saw her was that she seemed very skilled with make-up for a girl of her age, and she was interested in acting, the theatre. She had seen Ramsden in Leeds with an attractive woman, forgotten about it, then seen the image again when her mind was on the Steadman business – maybe at the funeral, when she had plenty of time to examine what everyone was wearing and how they looked. I was there too, and I noticed how she seemed to be scrutinizing us all, though it didn't mean anything to me at the time. However it happened, she remembered, and she became convinced it was Emma, carefully made up, she had seen with Ramsden. So Sally phoned her.

'That was where she went wrong. Emma Steadman told Ramsden later that Sally had gone on about *Wuthering Heights* on the phone, and about how she thought Ramsden had killed Harold Steadman so he could marry Emma just to get his hands on the house and money. Sally was convinced that Ramsden would murder Emma too, after he had married her. She seemed to think the Ramsdens had gone down in the world and that Michael must resent Steadman tremendously for buying the house from his family and taking over. She suggested a secret meeting to discuss things and see if they could find a way to deal with the situation. She thought that, together, they could solve the case and make the police look silly. Emma was terrified of anything that could link her with Ramsden, so she killed the girl.'

'Emma killed Sally Lumb?' Penny repeated numbly.

'Yes. Up by the packhorse bridge on Friday night. She hid the body under the bridge – the water was low then – and piled stones on it.'

'But why on earth did Sally meet her like that?' Barker asked. 'She must have known it might be dangerous.'

'Not at all. As far as Sally was concerned, she was simply warning Emma, saving her life. Besides, even if she did have second thoughts, ask Penny. She was about to do much the same thing, and she never seriously considered that Ramsden would harm her.'

'But that was different,' Penny argued. 'I'd known Michael all my life. I knew he wouldn't hurt me, even if what I thought was true.'

'Somebody would have hurt you,' Banks replied. 'You wouldn't find much comfort in being right about Ramsden while Emma was killing you. It wouldn't matter then, would it?'

'Only to the police, I suppose.'

'You're wrong about that,' Banks said, leaning forward and looking straight into her eyes. 'It matters to everyone except the corpse. Murder is the one crime that can't be put right. It upsets the balance. The dead can't be restored like stolen property; death doesn't heal like physical or emotional scars left by assault or rape. It's final. The end. Sally Lumb made a mistake and she died for it.'

'She was reading the wrong book,' Barker said. 'And

misreading it, at that. She should have been reading *Madame Bovary*. That's about a woman who considers murdering her husband.'

Banks hadn't read *Madame Bovary* but made a mental note to do so as soon as possible. When the waiter reappeared, Banks and Penny were the only ones to order more drinks.

Banks lit another cigarette. 'Ramsden got really scared after Emma killed Sally,' he said. 'But life went on and no thunderbolts from heaven struck him down. Then Penny started to figure things out. You know the rest.'

Penny shivered and draped her shawl over her shoulders.

'Emma Steadman was far more powerful than any of us had imagined,' Banks said. 'She also had a solid alibi for her husband's murder. There was no way she could have done that, and though I flirted with the idea that she might have paid someone, it didn't seem likely. Sergeant Hatchley was right – she wouldn't have known how to contact a hired killer. Besides, if she had, it would have meant someone else to fear, someone who knew about her and what she'd done. Ramsden was ideal; Emma could control him, and he stood to gain too. Sally knew that Mrs Steadman couldn't have carried the body up Tavistock's field – another reason not to fear her – but she didn't know that Ramsden seemed to have a perfect alibi. I certainly didn't tell her, and I don't think anyone else did.

'I was thinking about all the wrong combinations,' he said to Penny. 'You and Steadman, you and Ramsden, you and Barker here. For a while I even wondered whether Ramsden and Steadman were homosexually involved. Like everyone else, I was taken in by Emma

Steadman's outer drabness. I just couldn't picture her as a woman of passion and power. I didn't even try. But she had the most dangerous combination of all, a passionate and calculating nature.'

'What did make you think of her?' asked Barker. 'I'd never have got it in a million years.'

'That's because you only write books,' Banks joked, 'while I do the real work.'

'Touché. But really? I'm curious.'

'Tell me, didn't you ever notice anything odd about Emma Steadman?'

Barker thought for a while. 'No,' he answered. 'I can't say I did. I didn't really see a lot of her. When I did I always felt a bit uneasy.'

'Why?'

'I don't know. There are some women just make you feel like that.'

'You didn't tell me that when I asked you about her.'

'Never really thought of it till you mentioned it just now,' Barker said. 'Besides, what difference would it have made?'

'None, I suppose,' Banks admitted. 'It's just that I felt uneasy with her too. Claustrophobic even. It was a kind of gut reaction, and I ought to know better than that.'

'But what did it mean?' Barker asked.

'This is all hindsight,' Banks said, 'so it did me no good until it was too late, but I think I was responding to her sexual power unconsciously and I was put off by her appearance. I couldn't accept being attracted to her so I felt dislike, revulsion. It might sound silly, but I couldn't see beneath the surface. Still, that was the last thing I realized. First of all there was something Darnley had said in Leeds that I couldn't for the life of me remember. It was just the kind of casual, throwaway remark anyone might overlook.'

'What was it?' Penny asked.

'He said that Emma had been a pretty little thing at first in Leeds. Of course, that meant nothing at the time. Then Sally disappeared. I thought she must be connected in some way to the Steadman business but I couldn't figure out how. I knew about her theatrical interests, but there was no way of getting from that to seeing Michael Ramsden as Steadman's killer. Besides, I was still too busy looking in every direction but the right one. I was blinded by Emma's alibi, too.

'Finally, Sandra said she'd seen Emma and noticed that she still looked pretty good. That was when the bits and pieces seemed to fit together: a pretty young thing, Sally's skill at make-up – which is just altering appearances when you get right down to it – and Emma Steadman as the outline, still, of an attractive woman. And she did tell me she'd been involved in amateur dramatics. When I thought about what others had told me about Emma, I realized that nobody had ever mentioned her being attractive. Penny wouldn't of course – like her husband, I don't think you ever really noticed Emma – and Jack here hadn't known her that far back. Ramsden never said that she was attractive either, and that, finally, seemed odd. Then I got to thinking about Ramsden alone with her at the house that summer, about how he suddenly seemed to drift away from Penny. I'd always seen him as a kind of pale loiterer, but it took me a long time to see Emma Steadman as a *belle dame*. My view of the past was wrong, just like Teddy Hackett said Steadman's was, and everyone else seemed to look back on that summer through rose-tinted glasses. If truth be told, it was a period

of desire, greed, deception, adultery – hardly an idyll at
all. Even Sally got it wrong.

'When I asked my questions, I never had Ramsden and
Emma in mind, but it was easy enough to review what I'd
learned in the light of a new perspective. Once I'd got that
far, it seemed possible. Two people working together
could have handled the Steadman killing, while both
seeming to have solid alibis. Sally could have posed a
threat to Emma if she had seen her transformed from the
drab housewife into the sexy siren with Michael
Ramsden. All I had to do then was go and push even
harder. At least I knew I was going in the right direction.
But events turned out differently.'

'You were certainly fixed in your ideas about me and
Harry,' Penny said.

'Yes,' Banks agreed. 'Maybe Ramsden and Emma was
a combination I shouldn't have overlooked. But it's easy
to say that now it's over. Whenever I thought of that
summer I knew there was something missing, so I
assumed that people had been lying to me, hiding
something. They hadn't. As far as you knew, it had all
happened the way you told me. Almost all, anyway.'

'Don't blame yourself,' Sandra said to him, winking at
Penny. 'After all, you're only a man.'

'I'll drink to that,' Penny said, raising her glass and
nudging Jack Barker.

While Banks joined in the toast and the chit-chat that
followed, he thought deep guilty thoughts about Sally
Lumb, who had seen beneath the surface only to find yet
another romantic illusion. Above them, as all traces of the
sun disappeared, Crow Scar began to gleam like bone in
the light of the rising moon.

extracts reading groups
competitions books new
discounts extracts extracts
competitions extracts
books new discounts
events books
new the reading groups
interviews
events extracts
discounts
new books events
events new events
discounts extracts discounts
www.panmacmillan.com
extracts events reading groups
competitions books extracts new
reading groups
books